CW00539227

# THE
# Couple
## ON THE
# Train

BOOKS BY CLAIRE COOPER

*The Elevator*

WRITING AS C. J. COOPER
*The Book Club*
*Lie to Me*

# THE Couple ON THE Train

## CLAIRE COOPER

bookouture

Published by Bookouture in 2024

An imprint of Storyfire Ltd.
Carmelite House
50 Victoria Embankment
London EC4Y 0DZ

www.bookouture.com

Copyright © Claire Cooper, 2024

Claire Cooper has asserted her right to be
identified as the author of this work.

All rights reserved. No part of this publication may be reproduced, stored in
any retrieval system, or transmitted, in any form or by any means, electronic,
mechanical, photocopying, recording or otherwise, without the prior written
permission of the publishers.

ISBN: 978-1-83525-840-8
eBook ISBN: 978-1-83525-839-2

This book is a work of fiction. Names, characters, businesses, organizations,
places and events other than those clearly in the public domain, are either the
product of the author's imagination or are used fictitiously. Any resemblance
to actual persons, living or dead, events or locales is entirely coincidental.

*For Mum, always.*

# ONE

There are times I am deeply grateful I live at the end of the line. This is one of them.

I watch from my seat next to the window as more hot and sticky commuters shuffle down the carriage, wedging themselves in the aisle. The woman sitting diagonally opposite me looks up angrily as a rucksack almost swipes her in the face, but its owner is oblivious, staring glassily into the middle distance. He's wearing the same expression as almost everyone here – the look of a man who's been dragged from sleep before he was ready, who's girding his loins for a day doing stuff he'd rather not be. It was the same look I was wearing until a few months ago. But not anymore.

I have my phone in my hand, and I can't help myself. I tap at the screen and bring up the article once more, though I know it by heart. *Wheel of Fortune* runs the title, and I even love the silly pun. The subtitle mentions Millie, of course, not me, but that's okay. If it hadn't been for her Instagram post, none of this would ever have happened. I study the photo yet again, five of us grouped around the obligatory potter's wheel. I'm in the middle, thanks to Millie, wearing an outfit I spent days choosing to look as if it had just been thrown on. For once, I was pleased with my hair, pulled up in its usual bun, a few dark tendrils escaping at the sides. Not groomed, but arty – I look the part. I scroll down to the second photo, the one of the pot Millie showed in her post. *Laura Fraser's History*, it's captioned, and I love it all over again, the swirling shades of grey and midnight blue glaze, the dead and dying flowers trailing down its side. I called it *History*, but I'm hoping this pot will create my future.

I look up in case anyone is nosing at what I'm reading – but they're all staring downwards, concentrating on their phones. No one's interested in what I'm doing. No one knows who I am – not yet, anyway.

'So you're a big deal now, right?' That's what Guy said when Sam showed him the article. His face could have curdled milk, but I didn't rise to it. 'Well, while I'm still paying your bills, you can get your arse behind that desk on time.'

The memory has my eyes flicking to the clock on my phone. I should be okay this morning: it's a lot easier to get out of bed when it feels like the end might be in sight.

The pressure at my side eases as the woman on my right stands up, and the energy in the carriage rises a notch. We're pulling into a station, and I tuck my feet in dutifully as the person opposite gets up too. The train comes to a stop and the doors open, bodies disgorging onto the platform. Everyone else in my group of four seats is leaving, and for a brief, glorious moment, I feel myself exhale. But then the seat depresses as a man sits next to me, his left knee already encroaching on my space, and a couple take the spots opposite, the woman nudging my foot with hers as she folds herself into place.

She lays her bag on her lap, and I see that it's rather beautiful. Black fabric, covered in felt flowers in an array of colours. I steal a glance to see how the rest of her measures up: she's staring out of the window, so I'm safe to look, even though we're moving again now, and there's nothing but darkness beyond the glass. She's wearing a black coat, wool by the looks of it, expensive, buttoned up to the collar. Her hair is blonde, glossy, cut into a bob that slopes sharply upwards from her chin. She's wearing make-up, and at first glance she looks about my age. But then I look closer and see the lines etched into the delicate skin around her eyes.

She's angled her body away from the man next to her, but his arm is looped through hers, so they're definitely together. There's something in the way she's staring out of the window that gives the strong impression she's trying to ignore him. Perhaps they've had a row. She's pissed off with him; he's trying to pretend she isn't.

I slide my gaze to him. He's staring straight ahead, the hood of his jacket pulled up. He has dark hair and a beard that's thick but neatly trimmed, and he's wearing sunglasses, although it's the middle of winter. I smile to myself, assuming he thinks he's Too Cool for School. But then something makes me look more closely, and the smile fades.

There's a tension in his shoulders and his lower jaw is working back and forth. If it weren't for the noise of the train, I think I'd hear him grinding his teeth. His right knee jiggles up and down then stops. A second later, his left takes over. Is he nervous? Angry? The beard and those dark glasses make it impossible to read his expression. And then I realise the glasses make it impossible to see what he's looking at too. He could be watching me, about to call me out for staring.

Hastily, I look down at my phone, try to concentrate on the article. But the hands of the woman opposite me are at the edge of my vision. They're clasped together on top of her bag, her knuckles white. I can't help myself, and I look up again to see her still gazing into the blackness beyond the train window.

She's biting her lip, her nostrils flaring as if she's struggling to keep her breathing under control.

Should I ask if she's okay? But that's stupid. I don't know her. She's just sitting on a train, minding her own business. And no one's talking, not at this time in the morning. Everyone would hear me. They'd think I was nuts.

I look around the carriage, trying to appear casual. No one else has noticed anything. The guy next to me has turned to face the aisle, giving up his manspreading now there's a taller man opposite him. He has headphones in, is scrolling through something on his phone.

Am I imagining things?

The train judders, slows. We're coming to the next station. The man opposite turns away from the woman, but his grip on her arm doesn't loosen and I see her wince as the movement tugs at her shoulder. I catch her eye and what I see there confuses me. An appeal. She wants something from me. Is it help?

I open my mouth to speak, but the man is pulling her to her feet. He's halfway down the aisle already, and she almost stumbles to keep up. I half rise from my seat, and she turns and looks at me over her shoulder, something desperate in her expression. Her eyes cut to the seat she's just left, then back to me, but before I can say something, do something, another passenger is standing between us. I try to peer over his shoulder, but the crowd at the door is already too thick. The doors slide open, and I catch a glimpse of the back of a hooded head moving towards them. But she's too short for me to see, already lost in the crowd. The doors are beeping the warning that they're about to close, and I stand there, frozen.

The doors shut with a thwump, and I sink back down.

What am I doing? Should I be following them? Calling the police? I scan the platform, but the pair of them have gone, swallowed up in the sea of people.

The train is moving. The seats around me remain empty. I breathe deeply once, twice. Across the aisle, a woman is reading a novel. A teenager standing at the door gazes at his phone. A dapper older gent in a trilby stares into the middle distance. Everyone is calm.

And then I realise: I am doing it again. Imagining danger where there is none. It's a long time since that was the way I lived – *hypervigilant* was how the counsellor described it to my mum. 'It's natural,' she'd reassured her. 'A common response after trauma.' But even now it raises its head occasionally. Reminds me that I can't ever leave the past behind.

I shake my head at myself. At least I didn't make a scene. I lean against the window, close my eyes for a moment. My breathing steadies. I'm safe. The woman who was sitting opposite me is safe. Nothing bad has happened here.

When I open my eyes, my gaze falls on the seat opposite. There is something there, a small corner of white tucked into the edge next to the window. And I remember the woman staring at me, her eyes flicking to the seat, then back to me.

I feel something flip over in my stomach – but I remind myself this is what I do. Rationalising my fantasies helps manage my reaction to them, but they're still there. Still lurking just below the surface, waiting for evidence that my worst imaginings were right all along.

This is just a piece of paper. Someone's shopping list, probably. A bit of junk mail. Nothing to worry about.

I lean forward and pick it up to prove to myself I'm being silly. It's been folded several times, the creases pressed tight. I open it up, already reading as I smooth out the paper.

And then the world falls away as the words connect with my brain.

*Help me.*

# TWO

The train has stopped at the next station, and before I know what I'm doing, I'm pushing to the door, jumping onto the platform. I need to tell someone what's happened. The police. I need to tell the police.

I make for the escalators, aiming for the left-hand side so I can run up. I move quickly, panting as I near the top, but I don't slow down. Another few steps, another escalator. There's a young girl standing on the left, chatting to her friends. I don't have time to be polite and I push past her. She stumbles into one of them, and I hear their collective outrage sputtering behind me.

There's a kiosk for station staff at the top, but no one in it. No sign of anyone in authority. I place my card on a ticket reader and I'm through the barriers, scanning the space beyond for a uniform, a fluorescent tabard. There's no one. I pull out my phone, but there's no reception down here, so I climb another set of stairs, heading into wintry sunshine.

999. I should dial 999.

My fingers hover over the keypad, but I pause. Is this really an emergency? What am I going to tell them? I bite my lip.

Every second I delay is a second that woman could be in danger. Speed matters, I know that all too well. And I remember the way she looked at me. That silent appeal. She needs my help. I can't let her down.

I tap out the numbers.

'Which service do you require?'

It takes me a second to find my voice. 'Police,' I say.

———

Guy swivels his chair round as I walk through the office door, one ankle resting on his knee. His trouser leg has ridden up, and I see a band of red sock below an inch of hairy flesh.

'Look what the cat dragged in,' he sneers, loud enough for everyone to hear.

'I left a message—'

'So you did. Super-Laura to the rescue.' He looks around the room, as if expecting everyone to collapse in mirth at his attempted witticism. They're all trying to ignore him – all except Sam, who gives me a sympathetic grimace.

'So what was it again? A damsel in distress?' Guy raises an eyebrow in what he probably imagines is a sardonic fashion. It makes him look even more like a gargoyle than usual. 'On the train, have I got that right?'

I swallow. 'She looked as if she was in trouble.'

'And you had to be the one to help.'

'No one else—'

'Despite the fact that you were supposed to have your arse on that chair' – he consults his watch ostentatiously – 'one hour and forty-three minutes ago.'

'I couldn't just—'

'Get in on time? No, of course not. That would be asking too much, wouldn't it?'

'Come on, Guy.' It's Sam, bless him. 'She couldn't ignore some woman being manhandled.'

'Manhandled, was it?' Guy leers as if he's on the verge of saying something crass. I wait, hoping that this time he'll cross the line, give me something to take to HR. But he's too savvy for that – especially with a roomful of witnesses.

'So what did the coppers say?'

'They're investigating. They'll be in touch.' It sounds just as convincing as it did when the officer on the phone said it.

'Oho! Not rushing out the blues and twos, then?' He grins nastily. 'You want to watch yourself, Laura. They don't take kindly to time wasters.'

I consider several replies and reject them. I know there's no point, and with any luck, I'll be out of here soon. There's nothing to be gained by getting into a row. Perhaps I'm growing as a person.

Guy waits for the retort and I see his face fall a fraction when it doesn't come. 'Well, now you're here, perhaps you'd be so kind as to get on with some actual work?' He swivels back to his computer, and I stare at him for a moment, noticing the flecks of dandruff dotting the back of his jacket. He truly is revolting.

'Are you okay?'

Sam leans across from the adjacent desk as I take off my coat and slide into my chair.

'Fine, thanks.' I smile, but I don't want to talk. My head is full of the woman on the train, the way she looked at me as she moved – no, as she was pulled – to the door. The police took a description, but I know she and that man would have been long gone by the time an officer got to the station. And a blonde woman in a black coat, a man with a beard and a hooded jacket – it's not exactly distinctive.

'Did you have to go to the police station?'

I shake my head. 'They asked me questions over the

phone.' The 999 operator had put me through to an officer, and I told him what I'd seen, what station they'd got off at. They'd have CCTV there, it occurs to me now. Even if they didn't get there in time to catch them, they'll be able to look at the video, perhaps identify who it was. That would be a start, at least.

Sam is still studying me, concern mingled with something else in those deep brown eyes. He's been considering asking me out again, I can tell. He's a nice guy, but it isn't going to happen.

I fire up my computer and keep my eyes fixed on the screen. 'I'd better get on,' I say, and he nods and turns away.


It's mid-afternoon and the man on the phone is huffing that he's been charged for a discount club membership he didn't want. We get the same calls a dozen times a day, one of the joys of working in mail order customer services. I'm supposed to persuade him to change his mind, but life's too short. I refund the payment and get him off the line just as my mobile starts to ring.

'Laura Fraser?' There's an authority to the woman's voice that instantly puts me on high alert. 'My name is DC Nadia Hollis.'

'Have you found her?' I blurt out. 'Is she okay?'

'I'm afraid we haven't been able to locate anyone fitting the description you gave.'

It's what I was worried about. 'They must have already left the station. I phoned as soon as I read the note, but it must have been too late.'

'I'd like to take a fuller statement from you. Are you able to come in?'

She gives me the address of the police station, and I confirm I'll be there as soon as I can. I look at Guy's desk as I speak, relieved that he's not there to hear me. He's gone out to a meeting, and I notice that he's taken all his stuff. I'm betting he's planning to go straight home; I hope I'm right.

'You need to head off,' Sam says, a statement not a question. 'What do you want me to tell him if he comes back?'

I consider for a moment, but there's no reason I can give Guy that will make him happy I've left early. I decide that honesty is the best policy.

'Tell him the police have asked me to come to the station,' I reply. And then, because a little polish never hurts, 'They said it was urgent.'

I pack up my stuff and head for the door, a few heads turning to watch me. As I make my way to the exit, I realise – I shouldn't have needed to invent that addition. It *is* urgent. A woman was being taken somewhere against her will. She asked for my help.

So why did DC Hollis sound as if she had all the time in the world?

# THREE

DC Hollis holds the door open and ushers me inside. 'Sorry it's not the nicest,' she says. 'We had a burst pipe last week and the interview rooms are out of action.'

I step into a box with a small table and two wooden chairs on either side. They look like the kind of thing that would have gone with a Victorian school desk. There's padding around the top of the walls. Soundproofing, I assume. She sees me looking. 'So no one can hear you scream,' she says, smiling.

I smile back, even though this is the Met, and it isn't funny.

There's a tape recorder on the table, and with a jolt, I realise I'm in the custody suite. But I don't have time to dwell on that, because DC Hollis is directing me to a chair, asking if I'd like a glass of water. I decline. I don't want to be here any longer than I need to be.

'So, Laura,' she says. 'Is it okay if I call you that?'

I nod, trying to size her up. She has short blonde hair in a pixie cut, a suit that nips in at the waist. She looks a whole lot sharper than the detectives back in Gramwell. I hope the impression is more than skin deep.

I nod at the tape recorder. 'Are you going to record this?'

'Oh, that. No, no need for it today.'

I'm relieved. The idea of my words being taken down – used against me, isn't that what they say? – I don't like it. But then I wonder again, does it mean they aren't taking this seriously?

DC Hollis places a flat brown folder on the table and opens it. There's some paper with printed text inside. 'Thanks for coming in. I have your account of what happened this morning. You were on your way to work, is that right?'

'That's right.' My mouth has gone dry, I realise. It's being in this room. It's designed to make you feel guilty.

'Could you take me through what happened, in your own words?'

She studies me as I speak, and I concentrate, trying to describe accurately what I saw. She doesn't respond when I tell her the man opposite me was holding the woman's arm to stop her getting away. 'He turned away from her at one point,' I say, wanting to explain, worried that she thinks I'm imagining things. 'But he kept holding onto her the whole time. I saw him pull at her shoulder when he moved.'

'But she didn't say anything to him?'

I shake my head.

'And she didn't say anything to you, either? Didn't give any indication that she was there under duress?'

'She didn't speak, no. She couldn't, could she, if she was frightened of him? But she looked at me, and I could tell. It was just something about her expression. It was like she was asking me for help.'

'Okay—'

'I know how that sounds. I'm not explaining it properly. But I swear, she wanted me to do something.'

'That's okay, Laura.' I'm relieved that she doesn't sound as if she's humouring me. 'It was your instinct that she needed help. Instincts are important.'

'And then there was the note,' I remind her.

She nods. 'Yes, of course. Do you have it with you?'

I reach for my purse, where the scrap of paper is tucked behind my credit card for safe keeping. I hand it over and watch her open it. She stares at it for longer than it can possibly take to read two words. I wonder what she's seeing that I've missed.

'Did you see her leave this?'

'No, but she must have. She wanted me to find it.'

'Why do you say that?'

'He was pulling her to the door and she looked back at me. Then she stared at the seat, like she wanted me to follow what she was looking at.'

'But she didn't say anything?'

'No. He was right next to her, he'd have heard. And there wasn't time, anyway. They'd gone before I understood what she was doing.'

'Can you describe her for me?'

I've already done that. She must have the words in front of her, in that folder of hers. Is she testing me? Wondering if my story will change if she makes me repeat it?

I try to remember everything I said before. I describe the woman's hair, her coat. She was tall, attractive – but there was nothing about her that would make her stand out from a crowd of commuters. Nothing except that bag.

When I finish, I say, 'There's CCTV at the station where she got off, right? You could review it. I could help, point them out to you.'

She ignores that. 'Did she look unwell? Unkempt?'

'No, she looked normal. Quite smart, actually. As if she was going to work.'

As soon as I say it, I wish I hadn't. It's the truth – but sometimes the truth doesn't get you the right results.

She asks more questions, gets me to describe the man again.

But I know I've undermined my own case, and I can't help feeling she's just going through the motions.

'Okay,' she says finally, 'let's leave it there for now.'

I stare at her. 'So what happens next?'

'I've requested the CCTV. We'll review it.'

I nod, grateful that she's taking me seriously. 'Today, right? Because she's with that guy right now. He could be doing anything to her.'

DC Hollis closes the folder and clasps her hands over it. And there's something in the way she does it – I know even before she opens her mouth again that I'm not going to like what comes next.

'I understand that you're concerned, Laura,' she says. 'But my problem is, we don't know a crime has taken place.'

'But the note—'

'I understand why you're worried. But we have no way of knowing that the woman you saw was the person who wrote it. And if she really was asking for help, wouldn't she have included some more useful information? A name, even?'

'Perhaps she didn't have time—'

'And it would be a strange thing to do, wouldn't it? For someone to use the Tube to take a woman somewhere by force?' I start to interrupt her again, and she holds up a hand. 'That's not to say it couldn't happen, and I'm not dismissing what you've said. You've done the right thing bringing this to us. I promise you, I'll review the CCTV. If there's anything to find, we'll find it.'

She pushes the note back across the table to me.

'But isn't this evidence?' I protest.

She suppresses a sigh. 'We don't have any reports of a missing person answering your description, Laura. If that changes, this becomes a priority. Until then...' She tails off. Then, 'Like I said, I'll review the CCTV.'

She's getting to her feet, and I have no choice but to follow her. I'm still tucking the note back into my purse as she ushers me into the corridor.

She takes me to the gate we came through. I'm flustered – she's saying goodbye, and I still can't decide whether I've been fobbed off or if this is as good as it gets. Is it possible there's an innocent explanation for what I saw? If no one has been reported missing, I suppose there's only so much she can do.

'Will you let me know if you find her?' I ask. 'I mean, if you see her on the CCTV?'

She's turning away, her attention already on the next thing on her to-do list. 'If we need anything more from you, I'll be in touch.'

And before I can reply, she's gone.

*

I've spent weeks watching her. Learning her routines, noting where she'll be and when. Timing is important. A minute too late and the opportunity could be lost. Everything must be planned to the last moment, no room for error.

And I admit I take pleasure in it, watching her go about her day, knowing she has no idea I'm there. I find myself noticing new things about her: her height, that hair, the way she carries herself. She looks well – far better than she deserves.

I worried at first that planning might feel different to doing. That seeing her in the flesh might make me reconsider. But it's had the opposite effect. It's reminded me why this has to be done. Why she can't be allowed to carry on as if nothing happened. I've even let myself think about the way it all ends.

How good it's going to feel when she finally gets what's coming to her.

# FOUR

My eyes flit around the carriage, but it's too full to see more than a handful of the people in it. Bodies cased in heavy coats are packed in, most having managed to wriggle into a position where they can see their phones. No one is talking – it's too early in the morning, and besides, everyone seems to be travelling alone.

I'm in my usual seat, but this time there are two women sitting opposite. One is leaning against the window, eyes closed and mouth open. The other is tapping at her phone, looking bored. There's a guy on my right again, but he's blond and heavily built. There's no sign of the couple I saw two days ago.

I've heard nothing more from the police. I have DC Hollis's phone number, and a few times I've got as far as selecting it from my contacts. But I know there's no point. She as good as told me not to bother her.

I rang my mum last night. I don't know why I expected it to help. She and Dad are in one of their loved-up phases, it seems. They were about to go out, dinner and dancing, apparently. I tried telling her about the woman on the train, but she was hardly listening. 'You're doing it again, Laura,' she said. 'I can only say the same thing so many times.'

I felt the familiar surge of frustration. 'But she looked right at me, Mum. And how do you explain that note?'

'It could be anything! You didn't see her write it, did you?'

'No, but—'

'Well, then. It probably had nothing to do with her. It could have been some kid asking for help with their homework, for all you know.'

'She looked at me. She wanted me to find it.' I'm trying to sound confident, but I hear the whine in my voice. Is it any wonder I get on her nerves?

'Or someone asking for help making dinner. Someone who'd stuffed it into their pocket and it just fell out.'

'You didn't see her face. She wanted me to help her.'

A sigh. 'You need to stop this, Laura. How long will it take for you to get it into your head that what happened wasn't your fault?'

I didn't say anything to that, and then she was telling me she had to go, they were going to be late.

I wish I could believe her, believe DC Hollis, that there's nothing to worry about. But I remember the look in that woman's eyes as she was pulled down the train carriage. I *know* she was in trouble. I know she needs my help.

I keep my eyes peeled throughout the journey, scanning the platform every time we pull into a station. But there's nothing.

---

At work, I keep my head down, wanting to get through the day as quickly as possible so I can head home and resume my search. Guy makes a couple of sarcastic remarks, but by his standards, I get off lightly.

I'm out of there the moment the clock on my computer

clicks to 17:00, almost through the door by the time I've finished replying to Sam's 'See you tomorrow'.

My heart rate rises as I enter the station. I check every face, every coat, every bag. But there's no sign of them. Why would there be? I know in my bones that man was forcing her to go with him. So why would the two of them show up at another train station?

A voice in the back of my head replays DC Hollis's words. *It would be strange, wouldn't it? To use the Tube to take a woman somewhere by force.* It's true. But it's what was happening, all the same. I know fear when I see it, and I saw it in her eyes. Yet no one believes me. No one's in a hurry to do anything, even though that man could be hurting her right now.

Back at my flat, I make coffee to help me focus, and open my laptop. I search for images of the station where the man and woman got off. There are a surprising number of them – the main entrance, the ticket hall upstairs, trains coming onto platforms that look much emptier and cleaner than they are in real life. I don't know what I'm looking for. Something to spark a memory, perhaps. Something to give me some clue to what I should do next.

A calendar notification interrupts my search, and my heart leaps as I see the reminder:

Prepare for meeting with Oliver Frampton.

I'd set it to appear a week before our appointment at a smart Shoreditch bar, with a reminder every twenty-four hours after that. Not that I'd need it, I thought then; there was no chance of me forgetting Oliver. And yet the events of the last couple of days have almost succeeded in driving him from my head.

For a moment I'm tempted to stop what I'm doing. Close down Google and work through the photos of my pots, selecting the best ones, the ones that will help him imagine one of them – maybe even more than one – lit up on a beautiful white plinth in his beautiful white gallery. I can almost picture an orange dot on the label beneath – *sold*. My mouse is already moving to close the search window before I stop myself.

That can't be my priority right now. There's plenty of time to sort out my portfolio. This time, I'm putting someone else first. And I'll be able to concentrate better when I know that woman is safe.

I take my bag from the floor next to me and reach for my purse. The scrap of paper is already looking dog-eared. I've folded and unfolded it too many times, trying to imagine what lies behind those two little words.

*Help me.*

I close my eyes and I can almost hear her voice. *Help me, Laura.* But that was another place, another time. And if it's too late to change what happened that day, it's not too late for the woman on the train. It can't be. I won't let it.

I look down at the paper, running my fingers over the words. The pen has been pressed hard enough to leave indentations. It *was* the woman on the train who wrote this. And she wrote it in a hurry, taking advantage of some brief moment when she wasn't observed, praying for the opportunity to pass it to someone who'd act on it. I'm not going to let her down.

I peer closer and see something I hadn't noticed before: faint grey print beneath the biro. I hold it to the light so I can see it better, but the text is so pale it's barely visible. I grab my phone and snap it, enlarge the photo.

Two columns: on the left, the letters YA FIC. Some kind of code perhaps? On the right numbers, 6.99. The .99 means it's a price, surely. This must be a receipt, the printer on its last drops of ink. The biro is covering part of the text at the top, and the image isn't clear enough to make it out. I snap another photo, taking my time to make sure it's perfectly in focus. I zoom in and now I can read it: *Gray's Books* and a phone number, the code indicating it's in London.

I go back to Google, tapping the name and city into the search box. It gives me an address, a phone number the same as the one on the receipt. There's a photograph too: a smart-looking shop with gold lettering above plate glass windows, books arranged in a display with pumpkins and a broom, presumably for Halloween. It's the kind of place I can imagine the woman on the train going. Maybe someone there will remember her.

*Closed*, Google informs me in red font. *Opens 10 a.m.* I check tomorrow's opening hours: I'll have to leave work early if I'm going to get there before it shuts. That won't go down well with Guy, but it's too bad. If the police won't do anything, I have to. And this is my only lead.

In the morning, I debate phoning in sick. We don't get sick pay, though, and I can't afford it. So instead I go for the opposite approach and get in early.

Guy breezes in half an hour later, doing an exaggerated double take when he sees me already at my desk. 'You're not due in until nine,' he says suspiciously, and I know what's behind the tone: they don't pay overtime either.

'I wanted to catch up.' I make the effort to sound concilia-tory. 'And I was hoping to leave a bit early. I have a doctor's appointment this afternoon.'

'Oh yeah?' He raises a disbelieving eyebrow, but I'm prepared.

'I've been getting really heavy periods—'

His expression changes instantly to one of horror. I some-times regret not being old enough for the menopause to have credibly kicked in. With Guy, it would be the gift that kept on giving. Well, until he sacked me, anyway.

He's waving his fingers at me, a gesture I interpret as meaning he's heard enough. 'I'll get on then, shall I?' I say sweetly, but he's already turning away, pretending to examine the papers on his desk.

When Sam arrives, he looks surprised to see me. 'I do get in early sometimes, you know,' I huff. He makes a few attempts to engage me in chat, asking me about my evening, telling me about some drama he's been binge-watching on TV. I try to respond politely – Sam's only been here a few months, and I get the impression he doesn't have many friends – but it's clear he's already forgotten about the woman on the train. For me, she's all I can think about: where she is, what might be happening to her.

The hours drag, and it's not quite four o'clock when I decide I can't take it anymore.

'You're off?' Sam looks at me curiously.

'Doctor's appointment.' I nod in Guy's direction. 'It's all right. Time off for good behaviour.'

He looks sceptical, but I don't feel like repeating the lie. I wave on my way out, and he watches me go, a faint frown etching lines across his brow.

The bookshop is in a leafy corner of south London, and I'm one of a handful of people to disembark at what the internet assures me is the nearest station. It's a short walk to the high street and it's nice enough, but not somewhere you'd make an effort to go to. If the woman on the train really did come here, I'm betting she lives or works nearby.

I find the bookshop on a side street, sandwiched between a picture framer's and a chi chi grocery store, the kind of place where you can buy pickled artichoke hearts, but heaven forbid you want a bag of spuds. I push open the door and an old-fashioned bell tinkles merrily as I step over the threshold.

The minute I'm inside, I'm assailed by memories. It's something in the air or the light, the smell of paper, the soft carpet underfoot. Motes of dust glitter in a sunbeam. It makes me catch my breath and I stop in my tracks, taking it all in.

The shop is bigger than it looked from outside, shelves in the middle as well as stretching along the outer walls. The cash desk is nowhere to be seen.

I should search someone out, but instead I find myself gravitating to a bookcase. I scan the titles, run my finger along the spines. The years fall away and it's like being sixteen again, a hazy after-school trip, a Saturday morning browsing. How many hours did I spend there, waiting for him to saunter over, to ask me what I thought of his last recommendation, to suggest another? I remember his voice, his hands as he'd reach out and pluck something from the shelf.

I turn away and head further into the shop. There are no dark nooks and crannies here – everything is well lit, clean. Bookcases at one end seem at first to mark the end of the shop, but there's a sign with an arrow saying *Pay here* that points to the left, and a corridor of books leads through a doorway into another area. The till is in a corner, a woman in her early twenties sitting behind it, paperback in hand.

She looks up as I approach, smiles. 'Can I help?'

I clear my throat. 'Hi. Yes, I hope so.' I pause, realising too late that I haven't thought through what I'm going to say. 'This is probably going to sound a bit weird.'

She puts the book on the desk upside down. She doesn't use a bookmark and it's going to crack the spine. Will would never have done something like that.

'I'm trying to find someone – a lady who asked for my help. I don't have her contact details, but I think she came here. I was hoping someone might remember her.'

The woman's face has grown wary. 'You don't have her contact details?' she says, and I can imagine what she's thinking. She probably has me down as some kind of stalker.

'I met her on a train,' I say hurriedly. 'There wasn't much time to talk, but she passed me a note. It was written on a receipt – one of your receipts.'

I pull out the piece of paper and hand it over. She takes it automatically, and I see the alarm in her eyes as she reads the words.

'What is this?' she says. 'Have you been to the police?'

I nod. 'They said they couldn't do anything.'

'But if she was asking for help—'

'I know. That's why I can't let her down. This receipt is all I have. It's dated three weeks ago. Do you remember her?'

She holds the scrap of paper at an angle, trying to make out the details.

'The twenty-sixth. That was a Thursday,' she muses. 'I wouldn't have been here then. Give me a minute.'

She stands and heads through a door behind her marked *Private*. She's taken the receipt, and I feel a spark of panic. What if she has something to do with this? That receipt is the only evidence I have.

I tap my foot, turn on the spot, searching for some kind of clue in the surroundings. The books back here are non-fiction, large volumes on art history and museum collections. The shelves almost touch the ceiling – anyone wanting something from the top would need a ladder. I follow them upwards and my gaze catches on a metal box with a glassy eye: a CCTV camera trained on the desk.

The door opens and the shop assistant is back, accompanied by an older woman with grey hair and glasses on a chain around her neck. The manager, perhaps. She looks irritated, as if I've disturbed her from something important.

'This is yours?' she says, holding out the receipt.

I take it from her, relieved to have it back, and repeat my story. I tell it just the way I told it before, including the bit about being passed the note; I don't have time to waste on them second-guessing if the woman on the train really wrote it. I wish now I'd taken the same approach with DC Hollis.

The older woman taps an arm of her glasses against her lips. 'This is all very concerning,' she says, and I feel a sudden, inappropriate urge to laugh. *You've got that right, lady.*

'I just want to get in touch with her. Make sure everything is okay.'

'It was a Thursday,' the younger woman says, and I'm grateful to her. She wants to help. 'Would you have been in then, Tabitha?'

The woman called Tabitha studies me. 'I do remember the customer, as it happens,' she says slowly.

'That's great!' Relief floods through me. 'Do you have a name? An address?'

Her face is closed. 'We can't give out information about customers.'

'But she needs help!' I hear the edge of panic in my voice and catch myself; something tells me this woman won't respond to an impassioned plea. I start again, trying to speak slowly, deliberately, the way she does. 'This could be very serious,' I say. 'I think she might be in real danger.'

She looks at me shrewdly. 'But the police don't believe that.'

I consider ignoring the challenge in her words, but somehow I know that won't work either. And she's right, after all. No one believes anything is wrong. No one believes the woman on the train was being taken somewhere against her will. No one but me.

I meet her eyes. 'No,' I say simply. 'But they're wrong.'

We stare at each other, and I wait for the moment she tells me to leave. But then she's ushering the other woman out of the way, tapping the keyboard on the desk.

'Describe her,' she orders.

I repeat what I told the police, relaying the woman's hair colour and cut, her coat, the bag she was carrying.

Tabitha looks up at that and nods. 'I remember her.'

At last we're getting somewhere. 'She bought something here,' I prompt. 'There was a code on the receipt—'

'YA FIC, yes. Young adult fiction. It was for a nephew, she said. She wanted another one in the series, but we didn't have it in stock. She ordered it.'

My heart leaps in my chest. 'Then you have her contact details?'

She shakes her head. 'Just a name. Marina.'

'No surname?' But Marina is an unusual enough name. If she lives near here, that might be enough for the police to track her down.

Tabitha is looking at the computer screen. 'No, I'm afraid not. And before you ask, she didn't leave a phone number either. She said her phone was being fixed, so there was no point. She said she'd be back in a week to pick up the book.'

My mind is whirring. She must be local to the shop, must be in the area regularly. 'Did she? Come back, I mean.'

Tabitha looks uneasy. 'No. But it was only a couple of weeks ago.'

'People do that sometimes,' the younger woman chimes in. 'Order something then decide they don't want it. Or they buy it on Amazon instead.'

Tabitha glares at her as if she's said a dirty word. 'I really don't think there's any more we can tell you.'

I feel her shutting down, but I can't leave it like this. There's a pile of cardboard bookmarks on the desk, freebies advertising a local author's latest release. I grab one of them. 'Do you have a pen? I'm going to leave my number. Please call me if she comes back.'

Tabitha looks dubious, but she hands me a pen. 'I'm sure everything's fine,' she says. But she doesn't sound convinced.

I scribble on the bookmark, adding my email address for good measure. I hand it back to Tabitha, who frowns but takes it anyway. Then I turn to go, making my way back through the corridors of books. So many stories here, so much make-believe. But this is real. I can't just turn a page and forget what I've seen. I can't ignore a woman who's begged me for help.

*Marina.* I have a name at least. But as the bell tinkles on the shop door and I step out into the cold winter's air, I have to acknowledge the truth: I'm no closer to finding her than I was when I came here.

# FIVE

I am running, the ground soft underfoot, branches whipping at my face. The voice carries on the frigid air: *Help me.* It is desperate. She needs me.

I slip, a dart of pain, right myself, keep running. My leg throbs, but I ignore it. The light is dimming. The trees hold out their arms to the inky sky.

*Help me.*

Her voice is fading. I turn, but every path looks the same. And suddenly I know: I'm too late.

I wake drenched in sweat, my heart thudding in my chest. For a moment I lie there, her voice echoing as if she were in the room with me.

I reach for the glass of water I keep on the bedside table, sip it while my heartbeat slows. I've had the same dream for the last three nights, ever since my visit to the bookshop. I close my eyes, but I already know it's pointless. My nerves are stretched too tight for sleep.

I get out of bed and pull out the portfolio case I keep underneath it. I may as well do something useful.

I work through the photographs slowly, the ones I've spent the weekend selecting for my meeting with Oliver Frampton. They're the best of what I have, and yesterday, I thought they were good enough. But the cold dawn light shows me I was wrong. Millie's endorsement of my work may have been enough for her 2.3 million TikTok followers, enough to bring me to Oliver's attention – but if I'm going to show him I'm more than a one hit social media wonder, I need something better than this.

I take each picture in turn, scribbling notes to myself on the back about how to improve them. I need better lighting, better angles. A couple of my favourite pots aren't photographed at all. I need to get to the studio, spend a couple of hours bringing my portfolio up to scratch.

All this has been like a dream: Millie's friend arriving early at the community centre for a Zumba class, wandering to the art room. She'd been looking for a gift for Millie's birthday, she said, and even then I felt the thrill of proximity to stardom. It was an impossible task, she told me, finding something for the influencer who was sent whatever she wanted – and didn't want – free of charge. But a piece of art – she'd picked up the pots, feeling the weight of them, remarking on the colours. I was pleased when she bought one, even though, strictly speaking, I wasn't supposed to sell anything at the community centre. I thought that was the end of it, just a story to tell my mum, but then Millie, wonderful Millie, loved the vase. Better yet, she raved about it in a thirty-second video. And suddenly, everything was different.

There was a broadsheet piece about the 'new wave of British ceramicists'. I remember the interview, the journalist asking about my inspiration. 'Your work deals with themes of death and decay,' she said, head tipped to one side, as if waiting for nuggets of pure gold to drop from my lips. 'What role do you think your childhood trauma plays in your designs?'

I'd expected her to raise it – any journo worth their salt would have done their research, and it wouldn't have been hard to find the story. But it threw me all the same. My first instinct was to try to deflect the question, but you need to give people something if you're going to keep their attention. So I talked about my art being a way to deal with the past, to move beyond it. *There's a redemptive quality to Fraser's work*, the journalist wrote, *the promise that even our darkest moments offer the hope of renewal.*

I'd started to believe maybe that was true, but now I see how naïve that was. A sudden flurry of interest in my art isn't going to make everything that happened worthwhile. I need to prove that I've learned from it. That if I can't put right the mistakes I made then, I can at least stop myself from making them a second time.

That's why I have to find Marina. I have to help her.

I replace the photographs in the case and slide it back under the bed.


It feels like seconds later that the alarm pulls me from my sleep. I'm so tired I feel sick, but I drag myself from beneath the duvet and stumble to the shower. The water cascades over my head and splashes onto the floor of the bathtub with a noise my half-numb brain interprets as footsteps running through puddles.

*Help me.*

I shake off the water and dry myself hurriedly. Back in my bedroom, I dress, then retrieve the portfolio case and my good camera. I'll head to the studio after work, take some better photos for the meeting with Oliver.

On the Tube I scan the faces around me, but it's the same as always. No sign of Marina or the man she was with. I'm starting to fear that my memory of them is fading; that if I saw her without her flowery bag, or him without his sunglasses, I'd have no chance of recognising them. I need a stroke of luck, some chance encounter to put me on their trail again. But if I can't trust my memories, even that slim possibility won't be enough.

There's a young man sitting opposite me, listening to music without headphones. The tinny beats scratch at the inside of my skull, and I look daggers at him. He ignores me.

I try to focus on Marina. Marina, who must live or work somewhere in south-west London. Marina, who buys books for her nephew, who ordered one but didn't collect it. Somewhere in that ragbag of facts, there must be a clue, something to bring me closer to her. I remember the bookstore, the bright lighting and plush carpets, so different from the one in Gramwell. The records kept on the store's computer system, not in a notebook with a cardboard cover. The CCTV cameras that might have been enough to deter a couple of teenagers from flirting in a darkened corner...

*CCTV.* Of course.

That camera was positioned directly over the cash desk. Marina would have stood there to pay, to place her order. There will be images of her, something I can take to the police. And if they still won't act, at least I'll have something to bolster my treacherous memory, something to reassure myself that she's real, that what I saw really happened.

The portfolio case is tucked behind my knees, and I reach down and touch it to reassure myself that what I'm about to do won't be a disaster. There are still three days before the meeting with Oliver Frampton. It won't hurt to leave the photos until tomorrow.

The bell tinkles its greeting as I step into the bookshop. I check my watch – I've left work early again, risking another row with Guy, but it's still less than half an hour until it closes. I suspect my request won't be welcome.

I make my way straight to the cash desk, passing a group of chairs that have been laid out in a circle since my last visit. I'm pleased to see Tabitha is behind the till this time. She's clearly the one in charge, the person I'm going to have to convince.

She looks up and her face falls a fraction at the sight of me. I am the proverbial bad penny. 'Hello again,' she says, not smiling.

I point to the camera above her head. 'This is working, right? I need to see the footage from the day Marina came here.'

Her lips tighten. 'I can't do that. There are rules. GDPR.'

It's what I expected her to say. 'But you'd share it with the police?'

She nods. 'If they asked.'

'But they're not going to do that, because they don't believe anything's wrong.'

'I can't help that.'

'You're the manager, right?'

She stiffens. 'The deputy manager, actually.'

I consider trying to go over her head, but if that doesn't work, I'll have burnt my bridges. I don't want to risk that when there's still a chance she'll give me what I need.

'Look,' I say, 'I don't want to get anyone in trouble. I just want to check it was really Marina I saw before I go back to the police. They might take it seriously if I could give them a name. If I could tell them she expected to come back here but never did.'

I see Tabitha weighing up what I've said and plough on. 'You said you'd share the footage with them if they asked. They told me they'd check the cameras in the station too. If it's the same person, they'd have to listen.'

I don't wait for her to poke holes in my imperfect logic. 'Please. Just let me have a quick look at the CCTV. If Marina is the woman on the train, I'll go back to the police, hand this all over to them.'

Behind me, I hear the bell tinkle again. Women's voices, two or three of them by the sound of it. I look at Tabitha questioningly.

'I really don't have time for this,' she says; then, over my shoulder: 'I'll be with you in a moment, ladies.'

'Please,' I repeat, 'I'll be quick.'

The bell sounds again, more voices. I can see Tabitha is torn. She wants to follow the rules, but the allure of getting me out of her shop is strong.

A burst of laughter from the front of the store seems to make up her mind. 'Through here,' she says, pushing open the door marked *Private.* I dart around the cash desk and follow her into a small corridor, piles of books lining the floor on either side. Tabitha disappears through a doorway on the left, and I trail behind, finding myself in a small, neat office. There's just enough space for a desk with a computer, a pen pot, and an in- and out-tray of the kind I didn't think people really used anymore.

Tabitha skirts around the desk and, still standing, starts tapping the keyboard.

'What was the date?'

I remind her and she clicks away at the mouse. 'Five fifteen,' I add. If Marina works office hours, it occurs to me, she must work somewhere nearby. It's not easy to get anywhere in London in fifteen minutes.

Tabitha mutters under her breath. Then, 'Right, this is the file for the twenty-sixth. Use the bar at the bottom to scroll through the film. I'll be back in two minutes.'

She grabs a couple of bottles of mineral water from the top of a filing cabinet and bustles out. I take her place behind the desk and examine the video. It's better quality than I expected, colour not black and white. I feel my pulse in my throat as I guide the mouse along the scroll bar. There's the cash desk, Tabitha seated behind it, her fingers moving over the keyboard.

There's a time stamp on the right-hand side of the picture and I watch the digits change as I manoeuvre the mouse: 14:23, 16:18, 17:12.

*There.*

I click and the scene comes to life. A woman is approaching the cash desk. She's blonde and wears a black coat. Marina? I can't be sure.

The woman is placing a book on the counter. I bite my lip, willing her to look round. But she's focused on Tabitha, on whatever they're talking about.

And then she shifts position, adjusts something on her shoulder. It's the strap of a handbag. I peer closer, straining to see it better. She's removing it, placing it on the counter. My breath catches in my throat: multicoloured flowers on black fabric. It's the same bag she had on the train. *Marina.*

On the screen, Tabitha is turning away, reaching for something on the shelf behind the desk. The other woman turns too, then looks up – directly at the camera. I freeze, my memory sharpening, as if someone has turned a dial and brought it into focus. It's the woman I saw on the train. There's no doubt about it.

Thank God. I haven't been on a wild-goose chase. She was really here. She ordered that book, but she hasn't been back to collect it. Now DC Hollis will have to listen to me.

I pause the video and look for some way to print out the image – but there's no printer icon, and I can't see a menu. I could ask Tabitha when she gets back, but I can already hear her reply: *GDPR.*

I hear the door in the corridor open and quicky fumble for my phone. Tabitha will be back at any moment: this is my only chance. I snap a photo of the screen. I click the mouse again to unfreeze the footage and change the phone setting to video. I glance up at the door – it's starting to open. I need just a few seconds more.

Tabitha enters, a pile of books in her hands. I stab at my phone to stop recording and thrust it into my pocket.

'Well?' She strides into the room and places the books on the desk. 'Did you find anything?'

I nod. 'It's definitely her.'

She stares at me. 'You understand you can't have a copy, don't you?'

I hold her gaze – did she see what I was doing? 'Yes. But you won't delete it? Not until the police have been in touch?'

'It wipes automatically after a month.' She holds up a hand as I start to remonstrate. 'I'll find a way to save a copy. I can't keep it forever, though. There are—'

'Rules, yes I know.' I realise I've sounded sarcastic, so smile to take the edge off. 'Thanks for letting me see it.'

She takes a book from the top of the pile and holds it out to me. 'Here.'

I read the title: *Create Your Destiny: The Caves of Agoroth*. There's a picture, three teenagers running, the mouth of a rocky cavern yawning open behind them.

'It's the book Marina ordered,' Tabitha says. 'I thought you might want to see it.'

'Thank you,' I say, feeling bad now about snapping at her. But I can tell by the look on her face that I'm still not making her Christmas card list.

'It's £6.99,' she says tersely. 'You can pay on your way out.'

---

I've been in the shop no more than twenty minutes, but when I step outside, the temperature has dropped and the light faded. I pull the collar of my coat closer. It's not late, but the street is empty, and my footsteps ring out on the pavement. The back of my neck prickles, and I find myself turning and looking over my shoulder. There's no sign of another soul.

I turn back, telling myself I'm being ridiculous. But the street is lined with doorways, dark hollows that could swallow someone in seconds. What if the man who took Marina lives near here too? What if he followed her that day she went to the bookshop?

I pick up my pace and slide my hand into my pocket, reach for my keys, thread them between my fingers.

*Could I do it?* I wonder. If it came to it, if it were a fight for my life, could I really use those keys as a weapon? Would I have it in me to jab them into someone's eyes, the way the self-defence manuals say to do? Into their throat?

I glance over my shoulder again. Still nothing. But I feel it, all the same. A presence. A consciousness in the dusk.

I want to break into a run, but instead I straighten my shoulders, raise my head, lengthen my stride. *Look confident*, I tell myself. *Like someone who isn't an easy target.*

I can hear my breathing in my ears. I tighten my fingers around the keys. Not far now. Up ahead, the glow of traffic lights marks the junction with the main road. There'll be people there, people who'll hear me if I scream.

If I glance back again, I'll look nervous. I do it anyway. The road behind is dark, darker than it should be in London. Shadows stretch long fingers along the pavement.

*Eyes or throat?*

A jolt as my toe catches a crack in the paving. I pitch forward, trying to right myself but falling heavily onto my knees.

For a moment, panic floods my senses. Then I'm up and running, needles of pain piercing my ankle.

*Someone's behind me.*

And suddenly the rumble of traffic intensifies, and the darkness recedes, and I'm rounding the corner onto a street with people and shops. I spin around. A mother is pushing a buggy, her phone to her ear. Another woman is being tugged along by a dog with curly fur. A man in low slung jeans waves to someone across the road.

No one seems to be paying any attention to me.

The keys are digging into my skin and I uncurl my fingers. I breathe deep once, twice, and turn more slowly, making sure I haven't missed anyone.

And now the panic is draining away, replaced by the familiar embarrassment. Did anyone see me tearing down the street? Thank God I didn't fly into anyone as I turned that corner, that all I have to show for my paranoia is a sprained ankle. I'm not in any danger – why would I be? No one knows I'm here. No one except Tabitha and her colleague knows I'm looking for Marina. And even if they did, what would it matter? I've been to the police, and they didn't care.

On the left, just ahead, golden light spills from the entrance to the train station. I put my keys in my pocket, cupping my hand around them as I walk.

There was no one there. But if there had been—

*Eyes or throat?* Could I really hurt someone like that?

I enter the station and reach for my debit card.

*Eyes or throat?* Could I do it?

Who am I kidding?

I know exactly what I'm capable of.

*

*I move silently, watch from the shadows. She turns, scans the street behind her, pretends she's not worried. She has learned the mantra of women walking alone: never show weakness. And though I am invisible, I see the split second of hesitation before she turns away, the way her hand slips into her pocket.*

*She knows I'm here. She can feel me.*

*She's afraid.*

*Electricity dances across my skin, snaps along my veins. I wait for my moment, then follow. Slip into the lamplight, fade back to the gloom. I am a creature of darkness. A thing of teeth and claws.*

*I've never felt so alive.*

# SIX

First thing the next day, I leave a message for DC Hollis. I tell the woman who answers the phone that it's important. 'I'm sure it is,' she says, in a tone that means *I'm sure it isn't.*

I half-expect not to hear anything more, and I spend the morning considering how long I should leave it before pitching up at the station. Guy is in one of his most aggravating moods. 'All the mugs are dirty,' he complains loudly to no one in particular. 'Do you think you lazy gits could do your own washing up once in a while?'

I suppress the retort that rises to my lips. Guy knows full well that when it comes to dirty crockery in the staff kitchen, he's the prime culprit. But despite my best efforts to ignore him, he somehow catches my eye.

'You think you're too good for washing up, Laura?'

I keep my eyes fastened on my computer screen. If I don't engage, perhaps he'll leave me alone.

'Or maybe you think our cups aren't worth cleaning?'

I type something senseless in the hope he'll give up.

'They're not up to your standards, is that it? Think we should get you to make us some fancy-shmancy new ones?'

He smirks around the room. A couple of people snigger. I know they're probably just relieved he's not picking on them, but it gets to me, all the same.

'Think we should *commission* something? Like your pal Millie?'

'You couldn't afford it,' I mutter. As soon as the words are out, I know it was a mistake.

'What was that?'

'Nothing.'

'I'm pretty sure I heard you say something.' He strides over to my desk. 'So let's have it again, shall we? Nice and loud, so everyone can hear.'

He leans on my desk, his face close to mine. I smell sweat and the sour undertone of alcohol.

I've had enough of this. I'm sick and tired of him thinking he can talk to me however he wants. I draw myself upright, stare him straight in the eye. 'I *said—*'

'Caller for you, Laura.'

Sam scoots his swivel chair over to my desk.

'She says you were speaking to her earlier.' He shrugs apologetically at Guy. 'She'll only talk to you.'

For a moment, I consider ignoring him. Telling Guy where to stick his job and walking out of there. But I have to pay the rent.

I stare at Guy for a long second, and then I press the button next to the red light on my phone.

'Hello, Laura speaking. How can I help?'

Guy turns and saunters back to his desk. There's no reply on the phone, and when I look over at Sam, he gives a minute shake of the head. He's dialled the helpline from his mobile, I realise. Given me an out before I could say something I'd regret.

I play along for a bit, pretending to be engrossed in a conversation about returns. It beats having to deal with real-life customers. Guy is already bored. He's wandered over to one of the new starters, a pretty girl in her early twenties. I watch him lean down, invading her personal space. It makes me feel sick, but at least he's forgotten about me for now.

I put down the phone, and immediately a notification from the work messaging system appears on my screen. It's Sam. I click on the chat icon.

Don't let him get to you.

I type back a thank you. He's probably saved my job, after all. Another message pings back straight away:

A few of us are going out for drinks after work. Fancy coming?

I'm mildly surprised, but it's good he's finally making friends. For a moment, I consider joining them. If we went as a group, it might be okay, and perhaps it would do me good to get out, to take my mind off Marina.

But then I catch myself. That's exactly what I shouldn't be doing. She's gone missing. I can't just forget about that.

I type back:

Sorry. Already have plans for tonight.

I see his face fall as he reads it, but he recovers quickly.

Another time then.

I debate how to reply before simply adding a smiley face – friendly but non-committal.

I've just pressed send when my mobile buzzes into life on my desk. *Number withheld*, reads the screen, and my stomach flips. It's what came up when DC Hollis called me before.

I grab the phone and slip to the door. I'm not about to have this conversation with an audience. Guy, thankfully, is still engrossed in his heavy-duty perving. I answer the call en route to the loos, relieved to recognise the voice on the other end.

'I'm told you rang earlier. You have some information for me, is that correct?'

DC Hollis sounds brisk. I find myself nodding pointlessly. 'I know who it was on the train.'

There's a pause. Then, 'Okay, tell me more.'

I explain about realising the note was on a receipt. She should have done that, I want to point out, but don't. I tell her about going to the bookshop, about talking to Tabitha.

'She recognised my description. The woman had ordered a book. And she gave me her name – Marina. She didn't leave a surname. But that's an unusual name, right?'

She doesn't say anything, and I can imagine what she's thinking: *This is London. There's no such thing as an unusual name.*

'And she didn't collect the book. She said it was for her nephew's birthday, but she didn't come back to collect it.'

'You've gone to a lot of trouble.'

*Someone has to*, I want to reply. Instead I say, 'She left that note – we know that now. It was her receipt. She was the one saying, "Help me".'

'That's certainly possible—'

'And now we know she was supposed to come back for her book and never did. Something happened to her, it's obvious. So what are you going to do about it?'

I realise I've raised my voice. I'm shouting at a police officer; old habits die hard, it seems.

'Ms Fraser, I appreciate that you're upset.' I dig my fingernails into my palms to stop myself snapping back. 'But we still have no reports of any missing person fitting the description of the woman you saw on the train.'

'But the note—'

'I understand that it's unnerved you. But we have no evidence that note was left deliberately, nor indeed that it was a call for help.'

I can't help myself. 'No evidence except that it read "Help me", you mean?'

There is a long pause. I imagine DC Hollis taking a deep breath before she replies. 'As we've already discussed, there could be any number of explanations for that.'

'She didn't pick up the book. She ordered it, but she didn't go back. That's strange, right? Or at least *suggestive*? Surely it's enough for you to take this seriously?'

'Look, Laura.' It's the first time she's dropped the *Ms Fraser*, and I know she's trying to give the impression she's levelling with me. 'Do you know how many missing person reports we get in London each year?'

'I have no idea.'

'Thirty-six thousand.' She pauses to make sure I've taken it in. 'Let's think about the woman you've described. You said she was smartly dressed, healthy. She looked like she was on her way to work.'

I knew I shouldn't have said that.

'And when you went to the bookshop, they told you she was ordering a gift for her nephew.'

'Right, but she never picked it up.'

DC Hollis continues as if I haven't spoken. 'So she has family. She probably has friends, work colleagues. People who would notice if she wasn't around.'

I bite my lip. I don't know what to say. It all makes sense, but it's wrong. The certainty is like a stone in my chest.

'Listen, Laura.' First *look*, now *listen*. 'You saw something that worried you. You did the right thing – you reported it. We've investigated, and we've found nothing that would justify further action.'

She's choosing her words carefully, I realise. Everything is rational, evidence-based. The defence already prepared if it turns out they're wrong.

And they *are* wrong.

'You're abandoning her,' I say, and I'm embarrassed to hear the crack in my voice.

There's another long silence, and I wonder if she's considering hanging up on me. But then she speaks again, and her voice is gentle. 'What do you do for a living, Laura?'

I hesitate, thrown by the change of tack. 'I work for a mail order company. I'm a customer services adviser.'

'Any hobbies? Side hustles?'

I have no idea what she's getting at. 'I work with ceramics. I make pots.' My mind is racing. Could I have messed up my tax? I don't understand that stuff as well as I should do, but I've only sold a couple of pieces and I don't charge a lot.

DC Hollis clears her throat. 'You were in the newspapers recently, weren't you?'

'No. Yes. I mean, one newspaper. They interviewed a whole bunch of us.' I sound defensive.

'I saw it,' she says. 'I liked that vase of yours. Interesting title too. *Laura Fraser's History.*'

And now I start to understand. This isn't about tax.

'It's not the first time you've made the papers, is it, Laura?'

Oh God. I should have seen this coming. 'That was a long time ago. I don't see how it's relevant.'

'I've been reading about it. It must have been hard. Something like that happening in a small town. I'm from Yorkshire originally, I know what it's like. And you were so young.'

She sounds sympathetic, but I'm not the one who needs her sympathy. 'I'm sorry,' I say stiffly. 'I don't know what this has to do with anything.'

'I'm just saying: is it possible you're not the best judge of what's going on here?'

And there it is. She's not listening to me because of what I did. If someone else had seen what I'd seen, if someone else had reported it, she'd be sending out alerts right now. Finding Marina's surname, talking to her family. But she's not doing any of that, because she doesn't trust me.

I should plead with her. Beg her not to let Marina down. But my cheeks are flaming, and it's as if I'm right back in Gramwell, in that miserable police station, my mother turning up with pinched lips and her good handbag over her arm. *What's wrong with you, Laura Fraser? Why won't you ever learn?*

'Just because you believe something, doesn't make it true,' DC Hollis says.

'Fuck you,' I reply and hang up.

# SEVEN

I thrust my phone into my pocket, slam open the door of the nearest toilet cubicle and lock it behind me. Then I rest my head against the wood, push my fist into my mouth, and scream silently.

Why doesn't she believe me? Why don't they *ever* believe me?

My cheeks are wet, and I grab some tissue, scrub at my face. I can't do this, can't afford to lose it. Marina is in danger and she needs me.

I take a steadying breath then step out, just as someone disappears into the end cubicle. I recognise the silky top: it's the girl Guy was leching over. I hope she's okay.

I run my hands under the cold tap, inspect my reflection. My eyes are puffy, but I doubt anyone will notice. I smooth down my hair, rub away a couple of smudges of mascara.

The girl is still in the loo. Maybe she's gone in there to get away from Guy. I remember him leaning into her, his eyes on her chest. I should have said something – he hates me already; how much worse could it get? But I didn't. I was just grateful she'd distracted him.

I gnaw at my thumbnail. What if he's done something to her? A casual touch he'd claim was accidental if she said anything? What if she's scared to tell anyone, worried that no one will believe her?

I should tap on the door, ask if she's all right. I could offer to go to HR with her, tell them what I've seen. Help her make a formal complaint, get the union involved...

There's a flush, the rattle of a lock. The girl in the silky top strides to the sink and slaps a make-up bag on the counter, holds her hands under the tap. She catches my eye in the mirror and smiles. 'Nearly time to get out of here, thank God!'

I mumble a reply, but she's rummaging in the bag, pulling out a lipstick. I'm still standing in the same spot when she breezes past, the door squealing again on her way out. I feel my shoulders loosen, the adrenaline draining away. This woman doesn't need me to go into battle for her. She's clearly able to handle the likes of Guy.

That's good. Of course it is.

A thought worms its way to the front of my brain, but I stamp it down before it's fully formed. The situation with Marina is completely different. She asked for my help. That note couldn't have been plainer. And the way she looked at me – I didn't imagine that.

I just don't know what to do about it.

The pub is warm, dimly lit, a modest after-work crowd telling themselves they won't let things get out of hand on a school night. Sam returns from the bar, a glass of white wine in each hand. 'I got you a large one. I thought you might need it.'

He retrieves a couple of cardboard coasters from the neighbouring table, checking with the woman sitting there that it's okay. 'What happened to the others?' I ask, and I see the flush darken his cheeks.

'To be honest, Laura, I thought you wouldn't come if I said it was just me.'

I stare at him, then shrug. I guessed as much, and at least now he's being truthful. 'Why would you think that?'

He studies his wine glass. 'Was I wrong?'

There's a silence that lasts long enough for me to wonder if it would be wise to put my cards on the table, tell him I'm not in the market for a relationship. But before I can decide, he's moved on. 'So what happened to your plans for tonight?'

I'm not about to tell him there weren't any until that conversation with DC Hollis. That I couldn't face the idea of going home, spending another evening on the laptop, searching for some way to find Marina, something to make the police take me seriously. Something that, in my heart, I already know doesn't exist.

I force a smile. 'I changed my mind.'

He smiles back, and I worry that he thinks I'm flirting. I take another gulp of wine, search for small talk. But there's only one thing I can think about right now.

'How would you find someone if you didn't know anything about them?'

Sam puts down his glass. 'You're talking about that woman from the train.'

I'm surprised, but of course I shouldn't be. Sam pays attention. And I don't think I'm imagining that, when it comes to me, he pays more attention than usual.

I nod. 'She asked for my help. I feel responsible, but I don't know what to do. The police keep saying there's nothing to investigate.'

'What?' He looks shocked. 'Why would they say that?'

'No one's been reported missing. No one who looks like her. And they couldn't find anyone matching her description on the CCTV either.'

Sam knits his eyebrows. 'That's a bit weird.'

'Not really.' He blinks at my tone. 'Sorry, but you sound like that detective. And it's not weird, not when you think about it. Lots of people wouldn't be missed straight away. If someone snatched *me* on a weekend or if I was off work, no one would notice for days.'

'I'd notice.'

'How could you? You wouldn't know anything was wrong until I didn't show up at the office.'

He looks away. 'No, of course. You're right.'

'And it was the middle of rush hour. There's no way the police could have seen everyone properly on the CCTV, not in those crowds. They've missed her. They must have done, because I *know* she was there.'

I raise my glass to my lips, but it's already empty.

Sam gets to his feet. 'I'll get you another.'

When he comes back, he says, 'So what are you going to do?'

I consider not replying, making my excuses and heading home. I can't cope with someone else thinking I'm making a fuss about nothing. But it's grown dark outside, and I remember the feeling of someone following me, the prickle on the back of my neck. I don't want to be alone.

I shake my head. 'I don't know, but I can't just leave it. Marina's out there somewhere. She must be praying I've seen that message, that I'm going to help her. I can't let her down.'

He looks up sharply. 'How do you know her name?'

I explain how the note led me to the bookshop. When I get to the bit about Marina never returning for her book, Sam frowns.

'You told the detective that?'

'It doesn't change anything, apparently. No missing person report, no missing person.'

'Okay, but you saw her looking distressed. She passed you a note.'

I don't correct him.

'And now she hasn't turned up to do something she said she'd do. Surely, they should at least be trying to identify her, check everything's okay?'

'Exactly!'

Finally, someone is on my side. I look at my glass, and somehow it's empty again. 'Let me get these,' I say, but Sam's already on his feet. This time, he returns with a bottle.

'We should go to the newspapers,' he says. 'Make a fuss. Shame them into doing something.'

I refill our glasses and take a long drink. Sam's a good listener, and it's a long time since I've talked to anyone like this. I keep my distance from people, usually – I've found that's for the best, however lonely it gets sometimes. But it feels silly now, having worried about coming out with him on my own. I make everything harder than it needs to be, that's what Mum always says. Maybe she's right. I should be more open, give people a chance.

'She doesn't trust me,' I tell him. 'That's the real problem. The detective. DC Nadia Hollis.' I find I'm having to concentrate to get my tongue around her name.

His brow wrinkles. 'What makes you think that?'

'She knows.'

'Knows what?'

I hesitate, but I trust Sam. He's a good guy. 'She knows who I am.'

He looks at me blankly. Then, after a beat: 'Oh, you mean that stuff with Millie?'

I shake my head, but I'm pleased he doesn't get it. I'd half wondered if he'd done some digging after the article came out. It hadn't gone into details, but there was enough there to whet readers' curiosity. It wouldn't have taken much to find the rest online, just like DC Hollis did.

Sam didn't go looking, though. I like that.

'It was before Millie,' I whisper.

The memories are stirring, scenting freedom. I imagine how it would feel to let them out. To tell Sam everything.

'So you have a dark past?' He grins. 'Tell me more.'

His eyes sparkle, sure this is some kind of joke.

'There isn't much to tell,' I say.

I look away so he won't see the lie.

# EIGHT

*Then*

I didn't like school much. I was an indifferent student in all subjects but art, no good at sports except long-distance running (and that did me no favours in the end). The few friends I had were mostly older than me, some with less than gleaming reputations in the town. Occasionally I ran errands for them – I had a knack for going unnoticed that was useful. But I was no one's best mate, no one's preferred confidante. Until Amy.

She arrived at the start of Year 12, and I took an instant dislike to her. She was slim and pretty, with blonde hair that fell obediently into gentle waves when she ran her fingers through it. I knew at once that she'd be assimilated effortlessly into the gang of cool kids. We would, I was certain, never speak.

I was wrong.

Our paths crossed in the first English class of the term. I'd selected a table at the side of the room, expecting to claim it as my territory for the rest of the year. I'd picked it with care: not close enough to the front to be mistaken for keen, not far enough back to suggest I considered myself worthy of associating with the popular kids. The table had two chairs behind it, but I was confident I'd have it to myself. As I rummaged in my bag, I became conscious of a presence. I looked up to find Amy standing next to me.

She asked if she could sit there, and I was too shocked to do anything but nod. She took her seat with a tentative smile, and a moment later introduced herself and asked my name. I found myself nervous, tongue-tied. It was clear she'd miscalculated my position in the school's social order, that at any moment she'd realise her catastrophic error. Over her shoulder, I could see curious glances darting in our direction, as if Taylor Swift had sought out Susan Boyle for a duet.

Somehow, though, Amy's moment of realisation never came. And at the end of the class, she asked if I'd show her where to get lunch. I knew she would have been given a tour of the school already. The conclusion was bizarre yet seemingly inescapable: she wanted to have lunch with me.

From that day on, our friendship blossomed – or perhaps it would be better to say it grew roots, roots that stretched deep down into the Gramwell soil. It gave me a stability I'd never experienced before. Amy was loyal, honest, kind. She didn't bitch about people behind their backs, and if I made a cutting remark, she ignored it, as if it were beneath us both. At school, she was hardworking, anxious to do well. Her father was a self-made man, she told me, the owner of a successful haulage business who'd never been to university. He was always on her back about studying, wanting her to take the opportunities he'd never had.

Being friends with her gave me a new confidence. I began to see myself differently – as someone interesting, even fun. Someone who, like Amy, might just have a future outside the town that thought it had me pegged.

The summer that closed the first year of our friendship was hot and sticky, long sultry days and heavy nights where you

endlessly shifted position, searching for a cool bit of bedsheet.
There were few places to go in Gramwell in the holidays – a
corner shop, a couple of pubs that weren't too picky about ID.
To begin with, we mostly hung out at Amy's house, which was
modern and detached, and had a garden with sun loungers and
neatly trimmed grass. She came to mine a few times, but it was
embarrassing, seeing her picking her way around the baskets of
clothes and piles of magazines. And then came the final straw –
courtesy, inevitably, of my mother.

Amy and I were in my room, listening to music. I'd closed
the door in the hope Mum would get the message and leave us
in peace, but I should have known better. It had been perhaps a
fortnight since she'd seen Amy's mother drop her off at school,
and I'd noticed her clocking the smart car and expensive coat.
She had already 'just popped in' twice, trying to engage Amy in
chat and asking unsubtle questions about her parents. So it was
no big surprise when she stuck her head around the door a third
time.

'How are you girls getting on?'

'Fine, thank you, Mrs Fraser.' Amy smiled.

My mother beamed back. 'What lovely manners you have,
Amy.'

'No, we *still* don't want anything to drink,' I snapped, exasperated. 'And we don't want anything to eat either. Thank you.'

My mother drew herself up to her full height, five feet three
of indignation. 'I was going to tell you I'm off to the shops. So
make sure you lock up if you go out.'

I nodded, hoping to hasten her on her way. But Amy
seemed to feel she needed to compensate for my rudeness. 'Of
course,' she said, with another of those radiant smiles. 'We won't
forget.'

My mother sighed, no doubt wishing there was some kind
of swapping scheme for sub-standard offspring. 'Thank you,
Amy. Mouse has a memory like a sieve sometimes.'

Amy looked perplexed. 'Mouse?'

I glared at my mother, but she pretended not to notice. 'Oh yes! That's what we call Laura. Have done since she was a little girl—'

'You'd better hurry, Mum. The shops will be closing soon.'

'Why do you call her that?' Amy shot me a glance, her eyes bright with mischief.

'The shops, Mum—'

'Because of her hair, of course!' My mother chortled. 'They'd been talking in school about descriptions – hair colour, eye colour. Mouse – sorry, Laura' – a smile at me – 'was only little, five or six, and she asked me what the word was for her hair. So I told her, "mousey brown". And that was that! She was Mouse from that day on.'

She smiled at me again, as if this were cute, not toe-curlingly embarrassing. As if it weren't a hundred times more mortifying that she'd told this story to my beautiful blonde friend.

I felt my cheeks redden and dropped my eyes to the bed cover.

'Right then, I'll be off.' Mum lingered in the doorway. 'I'll see you later, love.'

I mumbled something back, and finally she was gone.

We heard the front door open and close. 'Your mum's nice,' Amy said.

I wondered whether to let it pass, hope Amy would forget about it. But there were too many people at school who'd love to hear that story. The idea of them laughing at me, sniggering about how even my own mother made fun of me for being plain – I couldn't bear it.

'Please don't tell anyone,' I said.

Amy pulled a face. 'She wasn't being mean. I think it's sweet.'

'Amy.'

She shrugged. 'Of course I won't, if you don't want me to.'

I nodded, but I knew then that continuing to have Amy at my house was asking for trouble. Unfortunately, her place wasn't much of an alternative. It was becoming increasingly clear that her parents weren't my biggest fans; they'd heard things, apparently, had drawn unfavourable conclusions. I'd see Mrs Linton's eyes cut to my pockets as I left the house, worried I was making off with the family silver. I couldn't feel comfortable there, no matter how nice their sun loungers were. Maybe that's why I suggested going to the quarry.

———

The site was on the edge of town, a ten-minute drive by car, but you could take a short-cut through the woods behind the leisure centre and be there on foot just as fast. There was a fence around most of the perimeter, with big signs warning of danger, loose rocks, quarry workings. For me, it was part of the attraction, but knowing that Amy would need some encouragement to break the rules, I relayed the rumour of a pool cut into the quarry walls, deep cool water, perfect for a swim.

We wore our costumes under our clothes, and the sweat trickled down my back as we walked. I knew from Will that there were places you could roll back the fencing and squeeze through; his dad was the deputy site manager, and had been in a black mood for weeks after being taken to task by his boss over yet another incident of trespass and damage. '"Bloody kids running wild", apparently,' Will said, rolling those beautiful blue eyes. I hadn't wanted to ask too many questions, both tongue-tied – as I was so often with Will – and wary of raising suspicion; but in the end it wasn't difficult to find a weak spot. A faint but distinct trail of trampled foliage led off the path through the woods, the tell-tale imprint of other teenage feet.

A triangular gap at the bottom of the fence showed me

where to focus my attention. The wire was stiff, and it took an effort to move it out of the way. Amy hovered beside me while I worked, skittish, eyes darting back the way we'd come.

'I'm not sure this is a good idea,' she said predictably.

'It's fine, Aims. Loads of people do it. Here, hold this.' I passed her my bag so I could grapple more easily with the fence.

'The water in quarry pools is really cold. I read about it.'

A bead of sweat trickled down my forehead. 'Cold sounds good to me.'

'Not this cold. You can get hypothermia.'

I gave a final tug on the wire, making the gap as big as I could. I ducked and squeezed through, then turned and beckoned to Amy to follow. 'Let's worry about finding it first.'

She hesitated a moment, then stepped through, more gracefully than I'd managed. 'Shouldn't we put the fence back?'

I shook my head. 'No one will notice.'

I led the way, tracing the faint trail through the undergrowth. After a couple of hundred feet, the ground grew stonier, jagged edges protruding from bare soil. The track petered out, but the trees were thinning too. In the distance, I could hear the rumble of an engine.

Amy heard it too. 'We should head back,' she said.

'We've only just got here.'

I thought she was going to dig her heels in. Amy could be stubborn in her own quiet way, and I knew I had limited time to get her on side. I picked up my pace.

'Mum's at her craft thing this afternoon,' she said. 'There's a bottle of vodka in the freezer.'

I gritted my teeth. 'Let's do something different for once.'

'Ow!' I looked back to see her rubbing at her leg. 'Bloody nettle.'

This was it, I thought. I could see the groove forming between her eyebrows, the one that appeared when she'd had enough.

But Amy was striding past me. 'Five minutes,' she said, flint in her voice. 'We'll keep going for another five minutes, then I'm turning back.'

I trailed behind her, grimly aware I was on a hiding to nothing. A gentle, rhythmic tapping on the hard ground alerted me that my trainer lace had come undone, and I stopped to retie it. Amy kept walking – she was playing fair, getting as far as possible in her five-minute window.

When I looked up again, she'd disappeared. Somewhere along the line, the sounds of the distant engine had faded away and I was suddenly aware of a stillness, deep and vast. Others had come this way, I reminded myself. If I turned around, I'd be back at that gap in the fence in a few minutes.

'Amy,' I said aloud, just to puncture the silence. There was no reply.

I took a couple of steps forward, then stopped, pulled out my phone. But there was no signal. We'd been walking in a straight line, I reasoned; it wouldn't be difficult to find our way back. But there were no landmarks, nothing to guide us. How easy would it be to get disorientated, to find yourself walking in the wrong direction? I knew from Will that the site was huge. How long would it take for someone to notice we were gone?

'Amy,' I said again, louder this time – but she didn't answer. I started forward, and suddenly there was a noise up ahead. I caught a flash of golden hair through the trees, and there she was.

She was laughing as she reached my side, her cheeks flushed.

I looked at her, bemused. 'What is it?'

Her eyes were bright. 'You have to see this.'

# NINE

*Now*

I give Sam the highlights of my Gramwell origin story. Heavily censored, it doesn't take long.

He tops up my glass. 'So you were a bit of a tearaway.'

I smile. 'You could say that. My best friend moved away, and I missed her. Had too much time on my hands. I guess I went off the rails for a bit. Nothing major. But you know how it is in a small town.'

He shrugs. 'Not really.'

Of course – Sam's a London boy. He's never had to live somewhere everyone knows who you are. And worse, where they know who your parents are too.

'You get a reputation,' I say. 'Then everything's your fault. Anything happened in Gramwell, and it'd be our door the police were knocking on. Mum hated it.'

How many afternoons, I wonder, had I spent hiding away in the quarry's abandoned site office? Avoiding going home. Knowing the questions that would be waiting for me when I did.

Sam's eyebrows are somewhere near his hairline. 'The police?'

'Like I said, it was nothing major.' I can see he doesn't believe me. 'The chief constable's daughter lived in our town. They *did* sweat the small stuff.'

'And DC Hollis knows about that?'

I nod. 'She didn't say it straight out, but it was obvious. She made some crack about "learning from our past".'

Sam pulls a face. 'That doesn't make any sense. Whatever you did when you were a kid, why would that matter now? Does she think you're making it all up? That's quite an assumption when a woman might be at risk.'

I like that he's annoyed: Marina deserves someone else worrying about her. He doesn't get it, though.

*You need to consider whether you're the best judge of what's happening here.*

I finish the rest of my wine in a single gulp. 'I don't care what Hollis thinks. I know Marina's in trouble. I'm not letting this go.'

Saying it out loud reminds me that I shouldn't be here. I don't have time for chitchat, no matter how comforting. I need to act.

I push back my chair and the room sways gently. Sam reaches out a hand, rests his fingers beneath my elbow.

'I'll walk you to the station,' he says.

Outside, the wind is bitter, a bite in the air that in anywhere but London might presage snow. A few steps along, I slip on a patch of ice, and Sam grabs my arm to stop me falling. We keep walking, and he doesn't let go.

I expected him to be bored of talking about Marina by now, but he keeps asking questions. When had she gone to the bookshop? How long had it been since she'd been due to collect her order?

'What book was it, anyway?'

It's in my bag, but I'm not stopping to get it out in this weather. 'Some teen thing. The title was something to do with caves.'

'So we know she's called Marina, and she has a teenage nephew who likes caves.'

I'd laugh if it wasn't so desperate. 'That's about the size of it, yes.'

We've reached the station, busy even at this hour. There's only one Tube line here, and I expect Sam to go through the ticket barriers with me, but he's lagged behind. I turn back to see him looking upwards, towards the glass orb of the CCTV camera on the ceiling. He sees me watching and quickens his pace.

He's thinking about the footage the police reviewed, no doubt, telling himself I must have got this wrong. I expect him to ask me about it, but he just presses his phone to the ticket reader. 'You're eastbound, right?' he says.

I nod. 'You?'

'Same. I'll get off with you, walk you back. It's not far to mine.'

I smile at him, knowing he has no idea where I live, that he's saying it to be kind. I should decline politely – even in my darkest days, I never bought into the narrative that a woman shouldn't walk alone at night. But seeing Marina on that train, knowing how scared she must have been, has shaken me. Maybe it's why I was so sure I was being followed when I left the bookshop. Perhaps, after all, that was just my imagination running wild.

But imagination or not, the fear was real. I don't want to feel that way again.

'Thanks, Sam,' I say. 'That's good of you.'

We get off the train together, and he takes my arm again as we leave the station, murmuring something about ice. A few minutes' walk and we're at the door of what was once a Victorian townhouse. The number of wheelie bins outside is testament to how many flats have been squeezed between its walls. One of them, the very tiniest, is mine.

I turn to face him. For a moment he continues holding my arm, and I think I feel the warmth of his body – though our winter layers mean I must be imagining it. The wine has filled my brain with a gentle fuzziness. My thoughts are syrup, slow and sweet. *It's cold out here*, I think. *It's cold, and he's walked me home.*

I open my mouth, intending to ask if he'd like to come in for coffee. But then he's bending down, and his lips brush the corner of mine.

'Good night, Laura,' he says. And he turns and strides away.


My flat is in the loft conversion, and I'm out of breath by the time I reach the top of the stairs. I go straight to the space that's the kitchen, living and dining room in one, and pour myself a large glass of water. I drink it down in one go, then pour myself another.

I am a fool. I should have come straight home, shouldn't have drunk so much. I know Sam wants more from me than I have to give – it's easy to recognise the signs when you've spent so long with the boot on the other foot. Thank God he has more sense than me. The last thing I need is to lose the closest thing I have to a friend at work.

My stomach feels bloated, but I force down another half glass of water, then flop onto the sofa. I flick on the TV, then turn it off again. I try to focus on Marina, but my brain keeps churning, dragging me backwards to Amy, to Will. I didn't explain it properly to Sam, but I know what DC Hollis meant when she asked if I was the best judge of what I saw. She hears the echoes, thinks I'm jumping at shadows.

Could she be right? I try to examine it dispassionately, but my brain is still sluggish from the wine. I reach for my phone, bring up the video from the bookshop. There she is, Marina. I watch as she talks to Tabitha, places her bag on the counter. I wish I could hear her voice, but there's no sound on the video. Tabitha is turning away, reaching for something on the shelf behind the counter. And Marina turns, raises her face to the camera...

*There.*

I tap the screen to pause the image. She's looking straight at me. I remember those eyes. I remember the way she looked at me as that man pulled her towards the door. She wanted me to help. I'm not imagining it. But I'm not any closer to doing it, either.

I stare at the picture, but it's not giving anything away. I close the video and a reminder pops up:

Prepare for meeting with Oliver Frampton.

My stomach lurches. It's the day after tomorrow, and I still haven't finished my portfolio. I shouldn't be worrying about it, not when Marina needs my help. But this is my one shot – my opportunity to take the fleeting exposure Millie gave me and turn it into something real. An exhibition at Oliver's gallery could get me noticed by people who really count. It could help me get funding, maybe even find a patron. Give me the breathing space to focus on my work, even if only for a few months.

The thought of handing in my notice to Guy, the look on his face...

And what more can I do for Marina, anyway? That receipt was my only clue, and I've followed it as far as I can. I've told the police everything I've found. I'm at a dead end. Maybe it's time to accept that and move on.

Tomorrow, then. Tomorrow I'll phone in sick and work on

my portfolio. Guy will be difficult, but that's Guy – I might as well give him a reason to behave like a dick.

My eyes are already heavy, and I need to be on my game in the morning. I finish the water and pour myself another glass for the bedside table. As I'm about to leave the room, I notice my bag where I've dumped it on the worktop. It's tipped on its side, and something is poking out of the top. It's the book Marina ordered.

I slide it out and peer at the cover: *The Caves of Agoroth*, then below it, *Create Your Own Destiny*. The picture shows three vaguely seventies-looking kids in jeans and trainers, running at full pelt into the foreground, hair flying and mouths open. A cliff face towers behind them, a gaping hole at the bottom – the entrance to the caves, presumably.

I turn it over and read the blurb on the back.

> *Dare you enter the Caves of Agoroth?*
>
> *The ancient Hapichu civilisation have hidden their most precious artifact, the golden Chalice of Eternal Life, in the caves. You and your friends have found a map to its location – but the Hapichus have laid murderous traps for anyone entering the caves. What's more, you're not the only ones on the trail. Can you escape the ruthless treasure hunters and find the Chalice?*
>
> *Create your own destiny and choose from twenty-three different endings!*

I'll read a few pages before bed. It's not going to tell me what's happened to Marina, but it feels wrong to ignore it all the same – a stone left unturned. And when I've done that, I'll be able to focus on the meeting with Oliver Frampton.

Create your own destiny, indeed. It's time I did that.

# TEN

*Help me!*

I'm running, but I don't know which way to turn. Everything looks the same.

*Help me!*

Movement behind trees, a flash of golden hair. I turn towards it, but the trees have gone. The ground beneath my feet is smooth, flat. I look up and see a woman in a black coat. Her eyes are wide. She leans towards me and I feel her breath on my face.

*Help me.*


I wake with a jolt. Around me the room is silent, but I can feel her presence. I lie there, breathing heavily, waiting for the whisper in the dark.

There is nothing. No one. Of course there isn't.

I turn my head and read the red digits on the alarm clock: 4:22.

I am wide awake, my brain buzzing. The water before bed, it seems, was not enough. I know the pattern: the wakefulness of the false dawn, the gradually building languor, the heavy head and the cotton-wool mouth. I drain another glass of water, hoping even now to avoid the worst effects.

I lean over to replace the glass on the bedside table, and feel it knock something that thuds as it hits the floor. I grope for the lamp and squint in the yellow light.

It's the book. Of course: *The Caves of Agoroth* is to blame for that dream. I followed the story through a couple of times before I settled down to sleep. Every couple of pages there was a decision to make and a direction to follow: 'turn left down the narrow path, go to page 16'; 'turn right towards the vaulted chamber, go to page 34'. The first time I finished the story pursued by bandits, escaping empty-handed as the noise of the chase triggered a rockfall that buried my pursuers and sealed the caves behind me forever. The second time, I failed even more spectacularly, stepping through a fake door and plummeting to my death down a deep chasm.

It's just a child's story, but still, I'd shivered when I read those words. And together with the evening's conversation with Sam, they'd obviously set my mind wandering in unhelpful directions.

I could lie here, try to go back to sleep, but I know that would be futile. So instead, I get up and head for the shower. The studio doesn't open until ten, but I can go through the photos again, plan what I want to say when I see Oliver.

I check my phone as I head to the bathroom. There's a text from Sam, sent just after he left me outside the flat.

*Thanks for a great evening. Sleep tight x*

My stomach twists at the intimacy of it. And it's my fault. I was the one who turned down Sam's invitation to drinks, then changed my mind. I was the one who confided in him about

Marina, who told him things about my past. Who let him walk me home. Who'd been on the brink of inviting him in.

I don't do relationships and Sam, it's clear, doesn't do one-night stands. I need to find a way to re-establish some boundaries, keep things simple. I type out a brief message:

*Feeling rough this morning! Thanks for listening to me moan.*

I re-read it and replace 'moan' with 'complain'. Then I realise the time. I can't send this now – if Sam keeps his phone next to the bed, it'll wake him.

I get into the shower, feeling more alive as the water splashes against my skin. I rehearse what I want to say to Oliver Frampton, about how much I admire the ethos of the gallery, the exhibitions I've attended there. I try saying it out loud, but it doesn't sound right. I know what Mum would say: I need to relax, stop overthinking things. I can't do it though. This is too important.

It's pitch black outside as I dress. The community centre doesn't open until ten, and I have no desire to wander the streets until then. I make coffee and sip it standing at the window.

*I greatly admire the way you support artists early in their careers.*

*I greatly admire the way you develop long-term relationships with the artists you exhibit.*

*I greatly admire...*

*I've greatly admired...*

*I've always admired...*

Movement down below. A shadow at the edge of the glow cast by the streetlamp. I move closer to the glass, but the light in the kitchen is making a mirror of the window. If there's anyone down there, they can see me perfectly. I'm backlit, as if on stage.

But all I can see is the reflection of wall cupboards, my own wary expression staring back at me.

For a moment I contemplate switching off the lights, but I catch myself just in time. I'm doing it again, imagining danger around every corner. Making this all about me, when the person I should be worrying about is Marina.

I turn away from the window. Just two days, that's all I need. Time to spruce up my portfolio, then meet Oliver Frampton and convince him to show one of my pots – maybe even two. And when that's done, I'll go back to the police station, demand to see DC Hollis's superior. Make enough of a nuisance of myself that they'll do anything to be rid of me.

I slip on my jacket, collect my portfolio case and camera. There's a café near the community centre that opens early. They run more to the croissant and Danish persuasion than the bacon butty my hangover is craving, but beggars can't be choosers.

I close the front door behind me and scan the street. Behind the rows of houses and shops, the sun has risen on some distant horizon, and the light is grey and watery. Across the road, a cat eyes me warily from atop a gatepost.

I walk briskly to the Tube station, my camera hidden beneath my coat. Inside, it's warm and steamy, already busy. I ride the escalator to the platform, overtaken by the steady stream of commuters in a hurry. I find myself scanning their faces – it's a habit by now – but none of them are familiar.

There's a train already standing at one platform, but I turn away and head for the platform opposite. That's the beauty of living at the end of the line: I can wait for the next arrival, for everyone to disembark, and choose my seat from an empty carriage.

A minute longer and the train rumbles into the station. I wait patiently for the final stragglers to get off, then take my favourite seat, the one in a group of four to the right of the door, next to the window. The same place as the day Marina sat opposite me.

The doors close, and I'm pleased the seats around me have remained empty. But a minute later we're held in the tunnel, and by the next stop the platform is heaving. I tuck the portfolio case more tightly behind my legs as bodies bundle in. The air has grown thick, and my head throbs.

I close my eyes, hoping darkness will bring relief. The engine hums, the train clatters over the tracks. Mercifully, no one speaks. I let my mind wander, remembering the shadow outside the window of my flat – a cat probably, maybe the one I saw when I left the flat. I imagine its yellow eyes in the darkness—

My head tips forward and I wake abruptly. The pitch of the engine is dipping – we're nearing a station. How long have I been dozing? I peer out of the window as the train slows and realise with relief that it's the stop before I need to get off. No damage has been done.

People are getting up, shuffling to the doors. A voice is raised in anger: 'You could at least apologise!'

I crane my neck to see what's going on. A woman near the door is berating someone in front of her. There's a trolley case involved, I see, so it's probably a case of injured toes. Nearby heads are swivelling to get a better look. And then I see one of them turn, a man with dark hair and a beard, and the breath leaves my body.

It's him. It's the man who took Marina.

*

Marina.

I like the name. It reminds me of the sea.

I know everything about her now. I live her, breathe her essence.

I know how she stands and how she walks. How she dresses. How she does her hair and make-up.

How she looks when she's afraid.

# ELEVEN

I'm on my feet, pressing against a solid wall of people. The doors slide open, and the wall moves forward – but it's too slow. I stand on tiptoes and catch sight of the back of a head in a grey hoodie. He's moving quickly, pushing aside a shorter man in front of him. He turns and I freeze: he's looking right at me.

In a second, he's gone and I'm pressing forward again, desperate not to lose him. But the woman with the suitcase is blocking half the doorway, people parting around her like the Red Sea, slowing their exit to a trickle. I want to scream at her to move, move; but instead I bob up and down, desperately trying to get a look along the platform, to spot the back of that hooded head.

Finally I'm at the door, catapulting from the train. I dodge and skip around bodies, swerve into the corridor that takes me to the exit. And then an idea flashes into my head, and I pull up short.

I could be going the wrong way. This station connects with another line – the man in the hoodie could be changing trains.

I hover, paralysed with indecision, as commuters sweep around me. On to the exit, or back to the interchange?

*You're doing it again!* screams a voice in my head. *You're wasting time!*

Sweat prickles on my upper lip. Which way do I go?

*You're letting her down, just like you always do.*

I have to choose. I run to the end of the corridor and the space opens suddenly before me, a white tiled concourse, a sea of bodies flowing to a pair of escalators. I scan the scene, trying to glimpse the grey hoodie.

I can't see him. I've chosen wrong.

I turn on the spot, rush back down the corridor. I press my body to the wall, moving as fast as I can against the tide.

*You're too late. You're always too late.*

And then I'm back on the platform, the space emptier now, room to run as I check for the sign to the interchange. The train I've just got off is still there, the doors shut. The Tannoy warns us to stand back, it's about to leave.

I feel the movement of air as the train pulls away, and something makes me turn to watch it go.

And that's when I see the figure standing just inside the door.

He's facing out, his hood up, those dark glasses in place. Common sense tells me this could be anyone.

But I know differently.

It's him.

I freeze, my mind racing. How could this have happened? I watched him step off the train. He disappeared from view, but he must have turned towards the exit then doubled back. Unless he stayed on the platform all along, and I simply missed him in the crowd?

But why would he get back on the train? People don't get off to get straight back on again.

Unless…

I know this is the man who was with Marina. He doesn't just look like him: he *is* him. And when he caught my eye across the carriage, he recognised me too. He knew I was on to him.

Why else was he in such a hurry to leave the train? Why else did he get off that platform as quickly as he could? He wanted to lead me away, then turn back when the coast was clear.

I've been so stupid. Of course he noticed me that day I sat opposite him and Marina. He would have been paying attention to everyone around them. It was like DC Hollis said – using the Tube to take Marina somewhere against her will was a high-risk strategy. It made everyone on that train a potential witness.

I shouldn't have reacted when I saw him. I should have sat there quietly, watched where he got off, followed him from a distance. I could have seen where he went, maybe even taken a discreet photo. I could have given DC Hollis something concrete to follow up.

But I didn't think, did I? I just leapt out of my seat and tried to follow him, even though I should have known it would be impossible. And now I've lost him, just as surely as I've lost Marina.

What's worse, he saw me do it. He knew I recognised him. And he knows what I look like too, that I've taken this route at least twice, at roughly the same time. How much of a stretch would it be for him to guess that it's a regular journey? He wasn't prepared this time, and he ran. But it's not hard to imagine him keeping watch, ready to act if he sees me again.

What would he do? How far would someone like that go to neutralise a threat?

He could be making these same calculations right now. Kicking himself for running away instead of dealing with the problem. I hear the echoing rumble of a train on tracks. It's coming from the opposite direction. He could have got off at the next station, jumped on the next train back, hoping to catch me off my guard. Any minute now, he could be walking along that corridor. A knife between the ribs, too quick for me to cry out. No one would even notice until they slipped on the blood.

Panic fogs my brain. What do I do? Which way do I go?

A voice echoes down the corridor. 'The next train is approaching. Please stand back from the platform edge.'

*He is coming.*

# TWELVE

I sit clutching the cup to stop my hands shaking. The department store café is bright, filled with the aroma of baked goods. But it's early, and only a handful of the tables are occupied. I should have chosen a coffee shop, full of people grabbing takeaways on their way to work. Somewhere with movement, bustle. Somewhere it would have been easy to lose myself in a crowd.

But this was the first place I came to when I raced out of the station. I've taken a table in the corner, somewhere I can keep an eye on anyone who comes in. If I see him, I'm going to scream. I don't care about making a scene. I won't make it easy for him.

I check my phone: four minutes. I've been here four minutes. If he'd followed me, surely he'd be here by now? Unless he saw me come in, is waiting for me to leave. To go somewhere quieter where he can strike.

I breathe deep, take a sip from my cup. There's a tired-looking woman with a buggy at the nearest occupied table, an elderly couple in the far corner. They'd be no help if it came to a fight. But there'll be security guards here somewhere. The woman at the counter would call for assistance if something happened. Perhaps I should talk to her, let her know what's going on.

Five minutes.

I take another sip of coffee. Maybe I should call DC Hollis. She could send someone, and they could check the store. But I know that's not going to happen. She hasn't believed anything I've told her so far. Why would this be any different?

Six minutes.

DC Hollis. I can imagine what she'd say. But then – is it possible she might be right? Is there any chance that I'm making too much of all this? That I'm catastrophising, the way that therapist said I did?

I scan the room again. There's no sign of the man from the train. And the truth is, I have no evidence that he's anywhere near me. The last time I saw him, he was standing on a Tube carriage, heading who knows where.

And what sign had he given that he even noticed me, after all? I recognised him, but he turned away again in the next moment. Yes, he looked as if he was in a hurry, but that's hardly unusual on the morning commute. And perhaps he just got off at the wrong station, then realised his mistake. Isn't that more likely than an elaborate plan to throw me off his scent?

Eight minutes. I can't sit here forever. I'm not going to phone DC Hollis. She probably won't pick up anyway. And even if she does, I can already hear her saying the things I've just been telling myself.

And yet – I'm certain it was him. Marina was scared of him; I saw it in her eyes. And now he's travelling at around the same time, on the same route, like it's part of a regular routine. But he's travelling alone.

If everything is fine with Marina, why wasn't she with him? *There could be a thousand reasons*, a voice in my head that sounds like DC Hollis replies. But I know he's taken her. I know she needs my help.

I drain my mug and push back my chair. The legs squeak on the tiled floor, and the woman with the buggy flinches at the noise, probably scared that I'll wake her baby. I raise my hand in apology as I go, and she gives me a smile of such sweetness that for a split second, she reminds me of someone else. Of how it felt to have a friend.

I quash the memory. It's not so hard when you've done it as many times as I have.

Beyond the café, the store is quiet, just a handful of browsers. I walk quickly to the doors, waiting for the moment when a bearded figure appears at my side. But it doesn't happen.

I head to a bus stop – I can't face another Tube journey. And it's not until I've got off and have turned the corner into my street that I realise what I've done.

Somewhere in this shit show of a morning, I've lost my port-folio case.

───────

I email myself the video from my phone, the one I took at the bookshop. The file is big and it takes ages to open on my ageing laptop. The first time, it freezes halfway through, and I'm ready to chuck the computer out of the window. But I force myself to take a breath, start again.

It's worth it: the video is different on the larger screen. When I pause on Marina looking towards the camera, I notice new details. She seems tired – her eyes are puffy. And there's something about the way she looks up, almost as if she knows the camera is there. As if she wants to be seen.

Was she worried, even then? Did she imagine a scenario in

which that film might be played on a news bulletin? The 'last known sighting'?

But if she knew she was in danger, why didn't she go to the police?

I restart the video and watch as she shifts the strap of her bag then removes it, places it on the counter. I keep watching until the moment she turns and goes, then rewind, watch the video a second time. This is all I have. There must be something that will help me find her.

A few seconds in, my phone beeps. I haven't called in sick, so it's probably Guy, threatening me with blue murder for not showing up. I shouldn't ignore it. Without this job, there's no way to pay my bills.

But I can't face him. I throw my phone onto the sofa without looking at it, and rewind the video, press play once again. There's Marina entering the shot. The bookshop lighting bleaches her blonde hair almost white, that sharp bob I'd never be able to carry off. She's talking to Tabitha, who checks something on the computer screen, leaves through the door behind the desk. Marina's alone. She looks up, straight at the camera – what *is* it about her expression? I freeze the video again and she's looking right at me, the way she did on the train.

*Help me.*

But I don't know Marina's voice. It's someone else I hear. Something stings my eyes and I rub them with the back of my hand. This isn't the time to go wandering down memory lane.

I restart the video and watch as she shifts the strap of her bag, removes it, places the bag on the counter.

But what's that? Movement I hadn't noticed before. A flash of white.

Something slides out of the top of the bag. It's small, rectangular. Small enough that until now, I've missed it. It sits there on the counter. I freeze the video again, peer closer.

It's flat – it looks like paper. Another note? But no, there's a second rectangle in the middle, a different colour. It takes me a moment, but then my heartbeat kicks up a notch as my brain finally makes the connection: it's an envelope with an address window.

I press my face to the screen. If there's any print there, it's too small to see. And I can't zoom in on the footage like they do in films.

There has to be a way. Could I take a screenshot, make it bigger? I try snipping the part of the image with the envelope, and open it in a photo editing app. But my laptop is too old for this kind of thing; it buzzes like a furious wasp, a blue circle in the middle of the screen going round and round. I fight back the impulse to smack the keyboard.

*Error opening file.*

No, I'm not having that. This envelope could have Marina's full name on it, her address. Even a fragment could be enough to identify her. I close the app, re-open it, try again. Again there's the buzzing, the blue circle. But something's happening – the top half of the image appears on the screen. I see part of the cash desk, an edge of the envelope. I stare at the screen, afraid that if I take my eyes off it for a second, the picture will disappear. The laptop is in a frenzy now, the fan whirring madly – and then, abruptly, it stops. I watch as the rest of the image loads.

I can enlarge it now. I hover over the icon of a magnifying glass, click on it. The picture doubles in size.

It's enough to see there's something on the envelope, a pattern of darker grey. Printed words or handwriting, surely. A name and address. But it's just shadowy smudges, nothing I have a hope of reading.

I click on the magnifying glass again, increase the zoom to 400 per cent. But it's no good. We've reached the limit of the detail. The dark smudges are just pixels now, all right angles. They don't even look like words anymore.

I stare at the image. *You're useless*, says a voice in my ear. *You're letting her down, just like you did before.*

I shake my head. I won't listen to it. There has to be a way of enhancing the image. My laptop might not be up to the task, but there'll be people with better technology. People who are experts in this kind of thing.

The police. But no – there's no point contacting them again until I've got some real evidence. So if not the police... I think for a moment, then open a new window and start to search.

# THIRTEEN

*Then*

Amy's face was glowing as she led me down the track. At first, everything looked much the same as the way we'd already come, but after a minute or so she veered sharply to the left, towards what looked like an impenetrable thicket of brambles.

'You have to be joking,' I said, and she giggled.

'Don't be such a wuss. I thought you wanted to do something different?'

'I was hoping for something that didn't involve bleeding to death,' I said.

Amy grinned and kept going. And then, just as I felt sure she was losing her mind, I saw it: a low, dark tunnel between two of the bushes. Amy pointed at it. 'Through here.'

I looked at it dubiously. 'Did you seriously go through there? What were you thinking?'

She put her hands on her hips. 'Are you coming, or what?'

I shrugged and followed in her wake. Up close, the tunnel looked bigger, but still we had to bend low to avoid the overhanging brambles. What had made her come this way, I couldn't imagine.

'Nearly there!'

And then the brambles were gone, and I stepped into a scene from a fairy tale. Before us glimmered water of the purest blue I'd ever seen. On the far side, sheer stone cliffs stretched up to the sullen Gramwell sky. Near our feet, the ground sloped invitingly to the edge of the lake. It was the perfect spot for a swim.

'How did you find it?' I breathed.

'I saw something sparkling through the bushes. It must have been the sun on the water.' There was a note of pride in her voice.

'Is it cold?' I asked her.

She shook her head. 'I haven't checked. I wanted to wait for you.'

I loved her for that.

We picked our way gingerly down the slope. I might have feigned confidence, but I had no desire to twist an ankle or find myself in the water faster than expected. After a few moments, we came to a spot where the ground flattened out, forming a ledge a foot or so above the lake edge. I bent towards the water and watched a mirror me do the same, reaching out until our fingertips met on the glassy surface. The chill of it was a balm against my clammy skin.

Amy did the same. 'It's freezing,' she said.

'We'll get used to it,' I said. 'We won't stay in long if it's too bad.'

I stood and scanned our surroundings. The spot at which we'd entered was hidden by the undergrowth. No one coming the same way would see us unless they walked down the slope. In the distance, the dull rumble of machinery was the only clue that this landscape was formed by man not nature.

I took my towel from my bag and spread it on the ground,

then took a last look around before shimmying out of my shorts and top. My swimming costume was sticking to my skin, and I adjusted the legs and straps before sitting and scooting to the edge of the ledge. I lowered my feet into the water, gasping as it crept up my calves to my knees.

Amy was watching me, so I gritted my teeth. 'It's fine,' I said. 'Are you coming?' She was looking doubtful, and I knew there was only one way to convince her. I took a breath then slid off the ledge.

The cold was an electric shock that drove every thought from my brain. For a split second, it was the only thing that existed. But then I was moving, my limbs cutting through the water, sensation returning to my skin. I gasped, spluttered, then laughed. 'It's great,' I said, waving at her. 'Come on in!'

She watched me for a moment more then, seemingly satisfied I wasn't about to expire, began undressing. I trod water, watching her out of the corner of my eye. I didn't like girls, not in that way, but Amy fascinated me. She was so different from me: golden skin where mine was milk white, blonde tresses with sun-kissed highlights that seemed to shine with their own light. I couldn't imagine how it would feel to look the way she did.

She folded her clothes into a neat pile next to her shoes before approaching the ledge. She bent one knee and pointed a shell-pink toe at the water.

'No way!' she squealed, instantly pulling back her foot.

I laughed. 'It's not so bad when you're in.'

She chewed her bottom lip.

'It's just the sun's so hot,' I said. 'It's the contrast.'

She sat down and gradually lowered her feet, wincing as they came into contact with the water.

'It's best to get straight in, get it over with,' I told her.

She shook her head. 'I don't think I can do this.'

'Of course you can! You can't come all this way and leave without a swim.'

But I could see the stubborn set to her jaw. I swam to the edge, looked up at her. 'Please, Amy. You'll love it when you're in.'

My eyes were almost level with her knees. They were sculpted, I realised, perfect. Not like mine, knobbly and prone to redness.

'You swim,' she said. 'I'll wait for you.'

I don't know what would have happened if I'd taken her at her word. We would probably never have come back to the quarry or the lake that summer. The rest of the holidays would have been spent the same way we'd spent our first weeks, hanging at Amy's house or occasionally mine, sneaking nips of her mum's vodka and listening to music. None of what came next would ever have happened.

But I didn't. Instead I reached out, grabbed her ankle, and pulled.

# FOURTEEN

*Now*

I slide my hand into my bag for about the millionth time, feeling for the sharp corners of the envelope. I'm not used to carrying this much cash. It makes me uncomfortable.

My breath forms clouds in the frigid air, but there are a surprising number of people in the park, even in these temperatures. A small girl in a woolly hat is pointing a mittened hand at the pond, and a woman crouches beside her and says something that makes her laugh. I think of my own mother and feel the familiar pang.

I check my watch, knowing already that I'm early, then scan the surroundings again. 'How will I know it's you?' I asked him yesterday, already having volunteered a brief description of myself, expecting him to tell me he'd be wearing a grey hat or carrying a copy of the *Big Issue*. 'I'll be the one asking you for two hundred quid,' he said.

I take my phone from my pocket, check my emails. There's the usual spam, but no confirmation he's received the video I sent him, no reassuring follow-up with promises of prompt action. But really, what did I expect? DDM Solutions, alleged specialists in 'forensic image analysis', had no company address, and only a mobile phone number. When I rang it, the voice at the other end – young, male – answered with 'Yep.'

'Is that DDM Solutions?' I asked, expecting to be told I had the wrong number.

A pause, then, 'Er, yeah?' Another beat. 'Yes, that's right. Er, how can I help?'

I explained about the video, trying to zoom in. There was what sounded like a snort in response. 'It's not like it is in the movies,' he said disparagingly. 'You can't just create information that isn't there.'

I bristled. 'Oh, right. I thought this was the kind of stuff you did. Then you can't help?'

'No, no, no, that's not what I'm saying.' His accent pulled apart the syllables: say-yyin. 'I mean, there's lots of stuff we can do. Brightness, contrast—' He sounded like he was looking for something else to add to the list but came up short. 'Yeah?' he finished instead.

I asked him how it worked, and he gave me an email address, told me to send him the video. Payment, he informed me, was required upfront and in cash. That made me nervous, but it wasn't like I had a lot of options. I asked how to get to his office, already suspicious that there wasn't one. He claimed he preferred to meet on 'neutral ground'.

I check my watch again: he's officially late now. Out on the pond there's a flurry of wings, splashes of water. The kid with the mittens is throwing bread to the ducks. A little way down the path, a Jack Russell pulls at his lead and eyes them beadily.

'Laura?'

I jump and turn in the direction of the voice. A tall skinny man in an oversized puffa jacket looms over me. Not long out of his teens, by the look of him.

I get to my feet, realising I don't know his name. 'You're the guy I spoke to on the phone?'

He nods. 'You've got the cash?'

It feels like being in a bad spy movie, and I hesitate. 'Have you looked at the video? Will you be able to do anything with it?'

He grins, polishes his knuckles on the front of his jacket. 'Already done.'

For a second, I wonder if I've heard him right. 'You've finished? Could you make out the words?'

His grin spreads wider. 'Cash first.'

I reach into my bag, hand him the envelope. He turns away, shoulders hunched, presumably checking it's all there.

He turns back. 'The other woman, is it?' I gawp at him, and he shrugs. 'Don't matter to me.'

'She's in trouble. I need to find her.'

'Whatever you say.' He pulls a phone from the back pocket of his jeans, and I watch his thumbs dance across the screen. He stops, and my phone jingles. 'I've emailed you the file.'

I grab my phone, but he's already walking away. 'Tell your friends,' he says.

'Sure,' I call after him, as if I have a network of mates trying to decipher clues from fuzzy photos. I jab at the email notification, and there it is – a brand new message with an attachment.

For no good reason, I look up, turn slowly on the spot. But no one seems to be paying me any attention. I click on the attachment and wait for the answer to my prayers.

*

One more push against the screwdriver, but it won't turn anymore. I tug just to be sure, but the metal box stays firm. A flick of a switch, and there's the red light, winking away. I didn't used to think I could do this kind of stuff: it just goes to show what you're capable of when it really counts.

I climb down from the ladder and survey my handiwork. The chair is utilitarian, nothing more. But the chains, I'm pleased with. They're heavy, businesslike. I got them from a well-known online retailer, the one Tabitha so despises. The padlocks came from the same place. They had 23,467 reviews, with an average of 4.2 stars.

I have also purchased: four 5-litre bottles of mineral water; one large bucket; two 3-metre lengths of stainless steel chain; one roll of electrical tape; three pairs of pliers; and one hammer. I deliberated over a ball gag, but those I found online were either flimsy or prohibitively expensive. They looked tacky too – I don't want her thinking I'm some kind of pervert.

Everything is in place. I've gone to a lot of trouble, but it will be worth it. I imagine the look on her face when she sees what's waiting for her, and it almost makes me smile.

# FIFTEEN

I emerge from the Tube station to find a missed call from Guy. There's another voicemail to add to the half dozen from yesterday too, doubtless from him, doubtless including his own inimitable take on my work ethic and manifold failings as a human being. I consider listening to it, but I have more important things to do right now. Because at last, I have something – or rather, two things: a name and an address.

Marina Leeson, 21 Flyte Gardens.

My phone buzzes again, and this time it's a text message. Sam.

*Where are you? He's going nuts.*

There's no way of replying without making Sam complicit. I'm about to stuff my phone back into my pocket when it occurs to me: what I'm about to do could be dangerous. It might be sensible to have someone who knows where I'm going, someone to sound the alarm if I don't return.

Sam would come with me if I asked, I'm sure he would. He believed me when I told him Marina was in trouble. He could find an excuse to get out of the office – Guy trusts him. And if there's any chance at all the man who took Marina is at her home, wouldn't it be about a million times more sensible to have someone with me when I get there?

*You're wasting time. It's been days. He could be hurting her right now. She could be...*

But Marina left *me* that note. It's my responsibility, and every minute I spend dithering is time I should be spending tracking her down. I'm not going to do anything crazy. I don't have any stupid fantasies about bursting in there and saving the day. I just want to get to the address, take a look around, speak to the neighbours. I'll find out when they last saw Marina, ask them if they've seen or heard anything suspicious. Find something, anything, I can take to the police. Something that will mean they'll have no choice but to investigate.

Still, there's no harm in giving Sam a heads up.

*Found address for Marina. Her name's Leeson and she lives in Flyte Gardens. Going there now. Will keep you posted.*

Five seconds later, my phone rings.

'What are you thinking?' Sam hisses down the phone with a fury that takes me aback. 'Call the police!'

'There's no point, you know that. I have to do this, Sam.'

'You know this could be dangerous, right? Really dangerous? What if that guy's there?'

He's echoing my own thoughts, but hearing them from him somehow makes me bolder. 'I'll keep a low profile. Pretend I'm collecting for charity or something.'

'For God's sake, Laura! What if he recognises you?'

'I probably won't see anyone at all. Or maybe Marina will answer the door and I'll find Hollis was right and I was wrong.'

I hear him inhale deeply; possibly he's counting to ten. Then, 'How do you know it's the right place, anyway?'

Briefly, I explain about the video. Sam doesn't say anything, and in the background I hear a door open and close, muffled voices that stop abruptly. 'You're at work, right?'

A pause, then, 'Yes. You can't keep doing this, you know.'

The words sting. Is he really criticising me for taking a day off when a woman might be in danger?

'I've got to go,' he says. 'Call me when you get there.'

And with that, I find myself staring at a silent phone. I thought he'd offer to come with me. I would have said no, of course – but I thought he'd ask. Maybe, despite his warnings, he doesn't really believe there's anything to be worried about. Maybe he's like DC Hollis after all, thinking I'm making a fuss over nothing.

My phone rings again, and my heart leaps. Sam was worried about getting out of work, but he's decided to do it anyway. Now he's calling to tell me to wait, he's coming with me.

'Sam.'

'Hello, is that Miss Fraser?'

The voice is smooth, cultured – undeniably annoyed. And suddenly I know exactly who it is, and I feel sick. How could I have done this? How could I have forgotten?

For a moment, I can't find my voice. But then desperation kicks in and the words are vomiting out of me.

'Mr Frampton, I'm so, so sorry. I had an emergency, I've been meaning to call you, trying to call you—'

'Right.' The single syllable cuts me dead. 'Then I take it you're not on your way.'

I spin my phone around, check the time. It's already twenty minutes later than we agreed to meet. I try to calculate how long it would take to get there, but my brain has stopped working. And what would I have to show him? I've lost my portfolio.

I am screwed. Royally screwed.

'I'm so sorry, today has been—' Today has been *what* exactly? But whatever it is, Oliver Frampton doesn't care.

'I realise we are a small gallery, Miss Fraser. Nevertheless, my time is valuable. I can't work with people who don't respect that.'

'I do respect that, of course—' I grope wildly for something to say to retrieve the situation. Should I tell him about Marina, try to explain what's happening?

'I understand that your celebrity endorsement may have opened other opportunities—'

'No, no, it's not that—'

'In any case, it seems best not to pursue any collaboration when you plainly have other priorities.'

'It's my mother!' The words are out before I know it, but they seem to have had some impact. There's a silence on the other end of the line, so I plough on before he fills it. 'She's been taken ill. I've been at the hospital.' The lie coils a tentacle around my chest: this is not the kind of thing you say. This is tempting Fate.

But his tone has changed. 'Oh dear, I'm sorry to hear that.'

'It was very sudden,' I say. 'They think it's her heart.' I'm making it worse, but I just can't seem to stop. 'I'm so sorry, everything else went completely out of my mind.' A moment of inspiration: 'When my phone rang, I thought you were my brother.'

'I see.' He clears his throat. 'Well, I understand, of course.'

'Can we rearrange? I know it's asking a lot.'

'Of course,' he says again. 'But perhaps we should wait for a while, until things have settled down with your mother.'

'No!' I don't want to wait too long; I know only too well how quickly Millie's reflected glory could fade. I don't want to find myself sliding to the bottom of what I'm sure is a long list of wannabe exhibitors.

But then, I have no portfolio. Even the list of shots I wanted to take was in that case. I'll have to start from scratch. Still, the pots are there – it's no more than a day's work to photograph them, clean up the images.

I try again. 'I realise you're a very busy man. I'm sure things will be fine soon. Mum's in the best place.' I hear myself and want to throw up.

'Very well, then.' Frampton sounds mollified. 'How about next week? Wednesday, 2.30, same place.'

Oh God, slap bang in the middle of the working day. How am I going to square that with Guy? He's already furious. But I'm in no position to negotiate.

'That would be wonderful,' I say. 'Thank you. And I'm so sorry again.'

He finishes the call with polite wishes for Mum's recovery. I hang up and my shoulders sag in relief. Bullet dodged, for now at least. Now it's time to find Marina.

---

Flyte Gardens is almost a half hour walk from the nearest Tube station. It's in the same neck of the woods as the bookshop, and my phone tells me there's a bus that would get you there in ten minutes. A sensible choice, then, if Marina wanted to do a spot of gift shopping without trekking into the centre of town.

Despite the London postcode, there's a suburban feel to the street. The majority of the houses here are detached and single storey, some with dormer windows suggesting loft conversions. Small gardens at the front have been mostly paved over to create off-street parking. It's quiet – eerily quiet.

I walk slowly, searching out house numbers in stained glass or metal digits screwed to front doors. I'm almost at the end of the road when I find number 21. Its garden is tarmacked on one side for a car, but the rest of it might once have been beautiful – here and there, winter skeletons of leggy roses trace dark lines through the straggly grass. It's not the kind of place I'd have pictured for Marina.

To the side of the driveway there's a wrought iron gate with a path beyond that leads to the front door. I push it and it squeals on its hinges, the noise making me wince. I wait for someone to appear at the door or a window, but no one does. The front path is overgrown, the edges of tarmac disappearing beneath blackened weeds. It slopes gently to the front door, forming a ramp, and there are handrails on both sides of the entrance. I pause, trying to make sense of it. Maybe Marina has only just moved in, has bought the house as a fixer-upper. Or perhaps she has an elderly parent who uses a wheelchair. Or maybe this is someone else's home, and for some reason, her post is being delivered here. There's only one way to find out.

Sam asked me to call him when I arrived, but it's obvious he doesn't really want to talk to me from the office. I tap out a brief text instead, then reach for the doorbell and press it.

I hear the chime echo inside, something in the quality of the sound telling me that it won't be answered. I wait anyway, listening for approaching footsteps. A minute passes and I press again, holding my finger in place this time. The chimes ding dong, ding dong urgently, but no one comes.

I look behind me, but there's no sign of anyone on the road. There's a picture window to the side of the front door, and I go to take a look. The sun casts reflections on the glass, and I press my face up close to try to see past them. But all I see is grey: someone has hung up an old-fashioned net curtain, and it's impossible to make out anything of the room beyond.

I step back and survey the house. It's a similar style to the rest of the street – a dormer bungalow, probably dating to the 1960s, white render that could do with a fresh coat of paint. The modern PVC windows aren't attractive, but probably keep it snug inside. And in London a detached house, even one that could do with sprucing up, will be worth good money.

I follow the path back to the door, then continue to where it meets the fence. Here, there's a second gate, wooden this time and taller, impossible to see over. It must lead to the side return, but when I try the latch, it won't budge. And now I see it – a small padlock securing it to the gatepost.

I head back onto the street to try the neighbours. Number 19 is an altogether neater prospect. A magnolia tree surrounded by a brick-edged border graces one side of the garden. The rest is gravel, with not an unruly blade of grass to be seen. There's no sign of a car, though, and when I crunch up to the front door, there's no response to my knock either. I retrace my steps, and head for the next house along.

Another dormer bungalow, another paved front garden. But this time, it seems my luck has changed. A Golf is parked on the drive, and a shimmer of golden light spills from the pane of glass above the front door. I press the doorbell and instantly hear thudding footsteps and a yell of 'Mum! Someone's at the door!'

'Yes, thank you, Ciaran.' A female voice, exasperated, and in the next moment the door is opening. The woman who stands there is in her mid-thirties, blonde shoulder-length hair and a guarded expression. In one hand she holds a rucksack with a picture of a web-slinging Spider-Man on it. Just back from the school run, presumably.

'Can I help you?' she says. She keeps the door pressed to her shoulder, I notice, as if worried I'm going to try to push past her.

'Hi, my name's Laura. I'm a friend of Marina's.' I pause in case this elicits anything helpful, but she's looking at me blankly. 'From number 21?' I add hopefully.

'Oh.' She nods. 'I thought she'd moved out ages ago.'

I'm disappointed, but I should have guessed as much from the state of the place. 'Yes, yes, that's right,' I say. 'Marina texted me her new address, but I lost my phone. Such an idiot. I just wondered if you knew where she'd gone?'

I smile, but I can see she's wary.

'Sorry, no.' She glances back over her shoulder. 'I'm afraid I have to get on.'

I keep the smile plastered on my face. 'Of course. I just feel so bad. She's going to wonder why I haven't been in touch.'

'I'm sure she'll contact you,' she says. Then, 'I'm sorry, I really need—'

I'm about to leave, but the memory of Marina's house is niggling at me. Those handrails next to the door – surely she'd have got rid of them if there wasn't someone in the house who needed them? Is it worth taking a risk? But I have nothing to lose.

'Did she manage the move all right?' I ask. 'It can't have been easy, you know, with...' I let the sentence trail away on a murmur of a sympathy.

She nods again. 'I didn't know them well, to be honest, but of course we all heard.' A flicker of real feeling passes across her face.

'Hmm,' I murmur encouragingly. 'So sad.'

'It's a terrible thing. Of course, a release too, in a way, though you don't like to say so.' She tails off. Then, 'Too many memories here, I expect.'

My mind is whirring. Did Marina live here with someone older, frail – an elderly parent, perhaps? But I can't think of a way of prodding at the question that won't give away my ignorance.

I play for time. 'She's been through a lot.'

'I can only imagine.' She shakes her head. 'She did such a lot for her.'

I mumble assent, trying to formulate another question – but a crash from upstairs cuts off the thought. A moment later, a wail goes up.

'Muuuum! Tell Josh to stay out of my room!'

The woman in front of me squeezes her eyes shut, as if hoping she'll be somewhere else when she opens them again.

'For the love of God.' Then, over her shoulder, 'Josh, Ciaran, don't make me come up there!'

She turns back to me. 'Sorry, I really do have to go.'

I start to reply, but the door is already closing, so instead I retreat down the path, trying to make sense of what I've heard.

Marina has moved out, that much is clear. And by the sounds of it, she left after someone close to her died. Someone who needed the ramp and those handrails.

*She did such a lot for her.*

Her mother, perhaps. That would make sense. Marina looking after her, then moving away when she died. And now Marina has been snatched by a man on a train. Are the two connected? Could the man on the train be responsible for her mother's death? Did Marina find out? Was she going to the police before he stopped her?

My mind is racing. I need to see the house again, to look at it knowing a fraction more about the people who lived there. The gate of number 21 squeals its welcome, but this time I stride straight to the front door, pressing the doorbell again because not to do so seems rude, even though I know no one will answer. I peer through the windows, but those net curtains are giving nothing away; I'm not sure what I expected to be different. But I'm not giving up.

I head for the side of the building, that tall gate with the padlock. Now that I look at it more closely, though, my heart lifts. It's a combination lock. And one of the happier legacies of my misspent youth is that I know exactly how to deal with it.

# SIXTEEN

*Then*

We returned to the lake every day that week. Amy was furious with me for approximately six minutes after I'd pulled her into the water, before admitting she'd never have got in otherwise. 'But it was stupid, Laura,' she said, unwilling to give up her point entirely. 'If I'd panicked, I could have drowned.'

'I wouldn't have let you,' I said. 'I was right there.'

We didn't stay long that day. It was beautiful, yes, refreshing, definitely. But there was no denying it was cold too. And despite the crisp blue appearance of the water from the shore, it was hard to see far below the surface. For all her earlier wariness, it didn't seem to bother Amy. But I couldn't shake the feeling that something could be down there, hidden from sight, waiting for the moment we were off our guard to strike.

It's hard to believe, looking back on it, but for those first couple of weeks, we had the lake entirely to ourselves. It was difficult to find, I suppose. The rumours of its existence might have been enough to tempt the occasional group of teens to the quarry, but the site was big enough to supply plenty of other opportunities to those not lucky enough to stumble across it.

It was a summer of record-breaking temperatures, the sun beating down day after day through clouds that seemed only to trap the heat. The icy lake was both a shock to the system and a blessed relief, and after her initial reluctance, Amy proved hardier than I was. She wasn't the strongest swimmer, but long after I'd pulled myself back onto the ledge and settled on a towel, she'd be splashing an inexpert breaststroke along the cliff walls, or floating on her back, staring up at nothing to the accompanying peck, peck, peck of distant drills.

We were in our customary positions, Amy swimming, me stretched out reading, when everything changed.

He was light on his feet, so I didn't notice him until he was standing right next to me. His shadow fell over the page of my book, and I jumped and let out a cry. I was dimly aware of splashing, so Amy must have heard me; but my attention was fixed on the boy in front of me: Will.

He looked down on me with an expression that was part amused, part cross. 'And what exactly are you doing here, Laura Fraser?' he said.

I was uncomfortably aware that I was wearing only a swimming costume and moved to pull my towel around me. 'We haven't damaged anything,' I said defensively. 'The fence was already broken.'

'Yes, I seem to remember telling you that.' But I was relieved to see a smile twitching at the corners of his mouth. He turned towards the lake. 'And who's this?'

I followed his gaze to see Amy treading water, a questioning look on her face that mirrored Will's.

'My friend Amy,' I said. 'She's just moved here.'

Will stared at her for a moment, then nodded and turned back to me. 'You know you shouldn't be here, right?'

I tilted my chin. 'Neither should you.'

'Touché.' He raised an eyebrow, and something flipped over in my stomach. 'How about a pact? I won't tell if you don't.'

I felt the heat in my cheeks and turned away so he wouldn't see. 'Deal,' I said.

He took a few steps towards the edge and placed his bag on the ground. Then he reached for the hem of his T-shirt, and I looked away again, flustered, keeping my eyes fixed to the page in front of me.

He must have been wearing his swimming trunks under his clothes, because in a couple of moments I heard a gentle slap of water as he slipped over the edge. Other boys might have taken a flying leap, cannonballed into the lake, but not Will. I looked up to see him cutting through the surface in a clean front crawl. To his left, Amy continued her breaststroke, seemingly oblivious, and he gave her a wide berth. I'd have to introduce them properly, I realised, and something about that prospect didn't please me. But it could wait until they were on dry land.

Amy got out shortly afterwards, clambering up the rocks that formed an uneven staircase near the ledge. Her tan had deepened over the previous weeks, turning from pale caramel to chestnut, and the highlights in her hair had bleached white gold. She took her time, it seemed to me, emerging with several degrees more grace than usual. I turned to see if Will was watching her, but the light was in my eyes, and it was impossible to tell.

'Who's that?' she asked, nodding towards him as she wrung the lake water from her hair.

'His name's Will,' I replied, then realised I wasn't sure how to describe him. *He lives on my road. He's in the year above us at school. He works in the bookshop. He's the love of my life.* 'His dad works here.'

She turned casually, watching him swim. 'Did he tell you about the lake?'

I shook my head. 'It's common knowledge.' As I spoke, I was aware of placing a barrier between us – Will and me, Gramwell natives, on one side, Amy, the incomer, on the other. 'But he told me about the broken fence.'

'Won't he get into trouble with his dad?'

I frowned. 'No, because his dad won't find out. Besides,' I started, then stopped. I'd been going to tell her Will had only mentioned the fence in passing, not as an invitation to come here – but I found I didn't want to do that.

Amy was looking at me expectantly. 'His dad would be okay,' I lied instead. 'He's a cool guy.'

She shivered. 'Lucky him. My dad would go mental if he found out I was coming down here w—' She caught herself, but it was too late. I knew what she'd been about to say: *with you.*

I looked at her, and she glanced down, embarrassed. I decided to let it pass: it was hardly news that Amy's parents considered me a bad influence.

*They'd probably like Will, though.*

I didn't know why the thought had come to me, but I didn't like it, and I reached for my towel. 'I'm heading back,' I said. 'I'm supposed to be getting some bits for Mum.'

'Okay, wait for me.' Amy picked up her top and pulled it over her head. Did I imagine a shadow of disappointment cross her face?

I snuck a final look at Will as we made our way up the slope. He was stretched out on his back, watching us go. I waved, and he raised a lazy hand in return.

'See you, Laura Fraser,' he called, then flipped onto his front and performed an elegant surface dive.

'Show-off,' I mumbled, fighting the temptation to continue watching until he resurfaced.

But a few steps on, I realised Amy wasn't with me. I turned to see her staring at the lake. 'Are you coming, or what?' I asked.

'Course,' she said.

But I saw the flush in her cheeks, and I knew there was trouble ahead.

# SEVENTEEN

*Now*

Combination locks are surprisingly easy to deal with when you know what you're doing. It's mainly a matter of patience and sequencing. Add in a bit of jiggling of the latch and some careful observation, and you're away. I'm both pleased and ashamed to find I still have the knack. In no more than a minute, I'm pushing open the side gate of 21 Flyte Gardens.

I find myself on a narrow concrete path leading to the back garden. At the end there's a scruffy patch of grass, a rotary washing line with sagging cables standing forlorn sentry in the middle. There are no windows at this side of the house, but when I reach the back, I see French doors overlooking the garden. More net curtains obscure any view of what's inside. There's another window further along, but it's the same story there.

I let my eyes travel to the upstairs windows. There are greying nets there too. Even in the watery sunshine, there's an air of dejection about this place. An ill parent would explain that. Poor woman. Poor Marina.

Something catches my attention and my eyes dart back to an upstairs window. The slightest movement, I could have sworn it. But the curtain remains in place. Everything is still, silent. I stare at the spot as the moments pass, then give myself a mental shake: I am letting the atmosphere of this place, the neighbour's oblique remarks, get to me.

I'll go home, regroup. Google the address, see if I can find out who lived here and who died. If there were suspicious circumstances, it might have made the news. When I reach the French doors, I pause and try the handle. It's a matter of form – no one padlocks a gate then leaves their back door open. So I nearly stumble when it starts to slide on its tracks.

I stand there, uncertain. The curtain has snagged on the top of the door, revealing a patch of dark red carpet and the bottom of a beige wall. Now that my way is clear, I find myself strangely reluctant to go inside. Yet Marina lived here – or at least, she had her mail delivered here. If this place holds a clue to what happened to her, I have to find it.

I free the curtain and slide the door wider. The room it opens onto is long and narrow, a sitting room cum dining room, I'm guessing, with a window at the far end that must be the one I tried to look through at the front. There's no furniture, just the net curtains. The neighbour was right: whoever lived here has gone. And yet, it doesn't feel empty. There's a sense of something watchful, brooding. I whistle to break the silence, but it sounds creepy, so I stop.

I walk to the front of the room and lift the curtain onto the front garden. There's nothing I haven't seen before, so I turn right through an open door and find myself in a small hallway leading from the front of the house to the back. On the opposite wall, stairs lead upwards. To my right, there's another door, this one shut up tight. I turn the knob and tell myself to relax as it creaks open.

For a moment I can't make sense of what I'm seeing. And then my stomach turns to liquid as I take it all in.

The kitchen counters are dirty, caked in dust. Lined up on one of them are three large plastic bottles of water, the kind you'd buy if you were expecting the apocalypse. Another bottle is on the floor, half-empty. Next to it, a disposable plastic cup lies on its side. There's a pile of wrappers there too, chocolate bars by the look of them. In the far corner, there's a bucket. And in the centre of the room is the chair.

It's an ordinary looking thing, grey moulded plastic seat, tapered metal legs. But it's what's attached to it that's making the hairs stand up on the back of my neck. Pooled on the floor and snaking around the legs are thick, heavy chains. And looped through one of the links is a padlock that looks a whole lot more serious than the one on the gate outside.

I gape at it, trying to rationalise what I'm seeing. But there's only one explanation: someone has been kept captive here. And that someone can only be Marina.

All this time, I was right. While I've been trying to convince DC Hollis to listen to me, Marina has been here, chained to this chair, at the mercy of that man. How long did he keep her like that? What has he done to her? Where is she now?

At least now DC Hollis will have no choice but to believe me. At least this time she won't be able to put it down to an overactive imagination, a guilty conscience, a misplaced urge for redemption. I reach for my phone to call her, and as I do so, some instinct makes me look up. For a second, I don't realise what's caught my attention. But then there's a flash near the ceiling, a dot of red light that disappears then reappears. As I watch, the shadows behind it resolve themselves into something with form and substance.

It's perhaps half a second more before I turn and run.

## EIGHTEEN

I am shivering. Night has fallen quickly, the way it does at this time of year. Perhaps it's that. Perhaps it's the shock of what I've seen.

DC Hollis has come alone, but any minute now she'll be radioing for others. They'll want to take photographs, I expect, dust for prints. I wonder if she'll apologise – but she probably won't. It doesn't seem her style.

I'm standing on the pavement just outside number 21's driveway – I don't want to be anywhere on that property now I know what's been happening there. That red light was a camera, that much I'm sure of, but I don't know whether the images were being transmitted or just stored on the device. Perhaps the man on the train isn't yet aware that I've found evidence of what he's done. Or perhaps he was watching as I entered that room, getting a good look at my face. If that's the case, I'm an easy target until they find him. I'll have to talk to DC Hollis, ask for police protection.

I pull my jacket more closely around me. Any minute now, there'll be sirens, police cars, activity. The kids at number 17 will be agog.

The door of the house is opening, and I see DC Hollis emerge. Her face is set, her jaw tight. I'd expected her to be on the radio, barking instructions, but she isn't. Maybe she's already contacted the people who need to know.

She strides down the path, making a beeline for me. There's something about her expression I'm having difficulty deciphering. She stops a couple of feet away, and I see stern lines bracketing her mouth.

'Do you want to explain this, Laura?'

Her tone is sharp, and I stare at her. This is a bit much, even by her standards.

'I think that's up to you, isn't it?' I reply. My words might be challenging, but I'm careful to keep my voice neutral. She's probably worried about repercussions when her superiors find out that she's effectively delayed a search for a woman at risk. The last thing we need now is to waste time having a row; I need her focused on finding Marina.

'Why did you call me?' she says. 'What did you expect to achieve?'

It takes me a moment to process the question, before it dawns on me that she hasn't called anyone else. What the hell is she playing at?

'What are you talking about?' I say, and this time I don't try to keep the frustration from my voice. 'Surely that's obvious? That man has been keeping Marina prisoner here. You must see that?'

She's staring at me like I'm some kind of insect she's half-minded to swat. Then she turns and walks back towards the house. 'Follow me,' she instructs, eyes straight ahead.

I don't want to go back in there, but she's steaming up the path, already at the gate. I look nervously around again, but there's no one in sight. Even if the man from the train was watching the footage from that camera, surely he wouldn't try anything against two of us? Especially not when one of us is a police officer? But DC Hollis is in plain clothes and an unmarked car. He might not know what he's dealing with.

She's disappearing through the gate, hasn't turned to check I'm following. I don't have a choice, so I set off after her. At the back of the house, the French doors are wide open, the red carpet beyond giving the eerie impression that I'm stepping into a mouth.

'Come on, then,' calls DC Hollis, her voice taut with impatience. She's already disappeared, into the kitchen by the sound of it.

I retrace the route I took earlier, through the living room into the hallway. This time the door to the kitchen is open, and I look straight in.

The first thing I see is the expression on DC Hollis's face. Her lips are pursed. She's angry. The direction of her stare suggests she's angry with me.

And even as I'm noticing that, trying to work out what it means, I see something else, something that at first my brain refuses to accept. Frantically, I scan the room, but it hasn't been moved. The chair has gone.

It's not the only thing. The chains and padlock. The bottles of water. The bucket. Even the pile of chocolate wrappers. They've all disappeared.

I gape at DC Hollis. My voice doesn't seem to be working.

'So what's the explanation?' she says coldly. 'And I'm telling you now, Laura, it had better be good.'

I swallow. 'It wasn't like this. Before, when I rang you. There was a chair right there.' I point to the spot on the floor. It's been swept, I see now, just like the counters. No footprints left behind to give him away.

'A chair,' she repeats.

'Yes, a chair. With chains around the legs, and a bloody great padlock!'

She raises her eyebrows.

'I'm not making it up. Why would I do that?'

'You tell me.'

'He must have seen me.' I look to the ceiling, to where that red light was blinking away less than an hour ago. It's gone too. 'There was a camera. He must have been watching when I came here, knew that I'd call the police. He must have come straight here and got rid of everything while I was waiting for you.'

DC Hollis pulls her phone from her pocket, checks the screen. 'It's 16.46,' she says. 'You rang me at 16.08 and I dropped everything to get straight over here.'

I understand what she's saying: he's had just over half an hour to clean the scene. 'He must have been close by,' I say, and the thought makes me feel sick. 'I ran outside to call you. He must have come back as soon as he saw me leave.'

DC Hollis shakes her head, and I want to scream. But I can't afford to lose my temper. Marina's life might depend on how I handle this.

'There wasn't much here,' I say. 'It wouldn't have taken him long. Half an hour would have been more than enough.'

'And the chair was here, right?' She moves to the spot I've pointed out and crouches down on her haunches.

'That's right.'

She looks at the floor, runs her fingertips over it. 'It's lino, Laura.'

'So?'

She gives a puff of exasperation. 'It's soft. If someone had been chained up here, I'd expect to see indentations from the weight of the chair. But there's nothing. Is there?'

I drop to my knees and pass my hands over the surface, though I can see at once that she's right. 'They must have faded. Or there weren't any in the first place. Marina isn't heavy.' I say it as if I know her, and why not? I've seen her in the flesh, which is more than DC Hollis has.

'And where was this supposed camera?'

I choose to ignore her choice of words and get to my feet again, point to the corner. 'There. Right above the cupboard.'

'But it's not there now.'

'He's moved it!'

I can almost see DC Hollis counting to ten in her head. 'And where were you when he was doing all this?'

'I was outside. I saw the camera and I was scared, so I left. Which was a pretty good decision, as it turns out.'

'Outside where?'

'On the pavement. Where I was when you got here.'

'And you didn't go anywhere else? Didn't knock on a neighbour's door to get help?'

I don't understand what she's getting at. 'No. What would have been the point? I called you. You said you were coming straight over.'

There's a buzz, and she glances at her phone. 'But you didn't see anyone. No one went in or out.' It's a statement, not a question.

'No. He must have gone out the back way.'

She gestures towards the kitchen window. 'There's no exit that way.'

'Then he must have climbed over the fence.'

And now there's something different in her eyes. It's a full second before I work out that it's pity.

'It wouldn't be that hard!' I hear the desperation in my voice. 'He's a young guy. The fence isn't tall. And he'd have had the motivation, wouldn't he? He'd have wanted all that stuff gone before you got here.'

'So he climbed the fence.'

'Yes!'

'With a chair.'

'He probably chucked it over.'

'And chains.'

'Yes!'

'And several large bottles of water.'

'He could have poured the water away, chucked over the empty bottles.'

'And he did all this in about half an hour. And no one saw him.'

'Okay, I know how this sounds.' I seem to say this to her a lot. I should know by now that it doesn't get me anywhere. 'But it's all possible, isn't it? And it must be what happened, because I swear to you, everything I've told you is the God's honest truth.'

She studies me, and I allow myself to believe there's a chance that this time I've got through to her.

'I want you to listen to me very carefully, Laura,' she says. 'I could arrest you for this little escapade today.' I feel the blood rush to my face and I open my mouth to protest – but she holds up a hand. 'Don't interrupt. Just listen.'

I feel like I'm back in school, but I shut up all the same.

'That's exactly what some of my colleagues would do. They're busy people. They'd come down on you like a tonne of bricks for wasting their time.' She glares at me. 'I'm busy too. I had to leave other work to come here. That's other people who need my help. And they've had to wait because you called me out here.'

It's too much. I can't stand it. 'Marina needs you too,' I choke. 'She's out there right now, with someone who had her chained to a chair. And no one's doing anything to find her.'

'There's a reason I'm not arresting you,' she says. 'I can see you believe what you're telling me. But trust me when I tell you, you need help.'

I gape at her. 'You're calling me crazy.'

'Listen to what you're saying. You're telling me a woman is in trouble. You see her in a crowded place, but you're the only person who notices anything wrong. You give me a detailed description, but there's no one who looks like that on the CCTV. No one answering that description has been reported missing. And now you tell me you've found evidence of a woman being kept prisoner, but half an hour later, it's vanished without a trace.'

I can't stop the tears now. 'You have to believe me. Marina's in danger.'

'I know you don't want to hear this, but just for a moment, I want you to consider that something else might be going on here.'

The words shake me. I've heard something like them before – another place, another time. DC Hollis reaches out and touches my arm, and her compassion is harder to deal with than her anger. 'You give that interview. It rakes up the past. You feel guilty.'

'No—'

'Even if you don't recognise it consciously, it's affecting your judgement.'

'That's not it—'

'So now you're reliving those feelings, trying to make it better by rescuing someone else.'

'Marina Leeson,' I sob. 'Marina Leeson at 21 Flyte Gardens. She's a real person. Look her up! Find out where she is!'

DC Hollis's voice is soft when she answers, as if soothing a frightened child. 'I've already asked my colleagues to run a check. No one called Marina Leeson has ever lived at this address.'

I stare at her, open-mouthed. This can't be right. They've made a mistake, spelled her name wrong. I'm about to tell her this, explain that they need to check again – but then my eye snags on something I haven't noticed before: a small shadow on the floor in the corner of the room, beneath the spot where the camera was mounted.

I move towards it, and DC Hollis takes my arm, tries to usher me out. I shrug her off and take another step. There's something long and thin at one end. I peer closer, telling myself that it can't be what it looks like, can't mean what I think it means. But part of me already knows that it is, and it does.

DC Hollis is talking, but her words are fading away because now I can see what's on the floor. It wasn't there half an hour ago. And there's only one thing it can mean.

The man on the train knows who I am. He knows what I've done.

And if I don't back off, he's coming for me.

# NINETEEN

*Then*

After the encounter with Will, I avoided going back to the lake for several days. Amy was eager to return, and I guessed it wasn't just the prospect of a refreshing swim that lay behind her enthusiasm. My excuses became ever more incredible – there were only so many errands I could feasibly be sent on – until eventually she tackled me outright.

'Have I done something to upset you?' she asked. She'd phoned me, but I could imagine her face clearly enough: the steady gaze, the crease between her brows that formed when she was worried.

'Don't be stupid,' I said. 'Why would you think that?'

'You know why. Every time I call you lately, you're too busy to talk.'

'Not my fault,' I said, hearing my sullen tone and wanting to kick myself for it. 'Just stuff to do.'

She was silent for a while. When she spoke again, her voice was quiet. 'I'm sorry, Laura,' she said.

'What?'

'Whatever it is I've done, I'm sorry. I know I can be—'

Her voice cracked, and I realised with horror that she was on the verge of tears. 'It's not you,' I said.

'Don't say that,' she said miserably. 'I know it is. It's always the same.'

It occurred to me then that I'd never heard her mention other friends, anyone she was still in touch with from before she came to Gramwell. Was it possible that Amy, beautiful Amy, with her elegant jewellery and her immaculate home, had been as lonely as I was?

'Honestly, Aims,' I said. 'I've just had stuff to do.'

'It's okay. I get it.'

'No, you don't.' Perhaps she was right, after all. I could guess why other girls might have kept their distance from Amy, not wanting to endure the inevitably unfavourable comparisons. And wasn't that exactly what I was doing too? Worrying that Will wouldn't look at me if she was around?

'It's just been a bit shit,' I said. 'Nothing to do with you. Just – you know.'

I knew what she'd make of that content-free sentence; I'd told her enough about my relationship with my parents for her to assume there was trouble at home. She was instantly sympathetic.

'Why didn't you say anything? I'm so sorry. And I didn't mean to hassle you. I just thought you hated me.'

She laughed as she said the last bit, but I could tell she meant it. Perhaps another person would have said, 'I could never hate you,' but displays of emotion weren't my thing. It was a reaction to the behaviour of my parents, I imagine, too long living with their cycle of passionate rows and equally passionate reconciliations. So instead I told Amy not to be silly, and arranged to meet her later that day to go to the lake.

· · ·

We rendezvoused at the end of her street, and I guessed she'd chosen the location deliberately to keep me out of sight of her parents. I arrived first, and watched as she headed towards me, a smile lighting up her face. She was wearing denim shorts and an old T-shirt, a large bag over one shoulder. It was the kind of outfit that would have had most people blending into the background; Amy, naturally, looked amazing.

'Hey,' she said, looking delighted to see me.

'Hey yourself,' I said imaginatively.

We chatted easily enough as we made our way to the quarry. But when we'd pushed through the gap in the fence and were heading along the trail towards the line of brambles, a certain reserve entered our conversation. We both had our minds on what we might find at the other end.

The path through the bushes was only wide enough for one person, and I took the lead. So when I stepped into the clearing I was the first to see it was deserted, the surface of the lake untroubled. I'd been nervous about seeing Will again, anxious about introducing him to Amy. But now that the danger had been averted, I felt disappointed, strangely flat.

'We have it to ourselves again today,' Amy said brightly, already laying out her towel. But I could tell she felt the same.

We slipped into our usual routine – a quick dip for me, then back to the ledge to read while Amy completed slow circuits around the lake. Several times I imagined I heard footsteps and turned, expecting to see Will coming down the slope. But each time there was no one there.

After a couple of hours, I was feeling hungry. Amy had got out of the water some time earlier and was lying on her stomach, eyes fixed to a book I'd told her I was planning to borrow from the library. She'd got there first, and when I'd found it already signed out, she'd countered my protests with a smile, telling me she'd mark up the good bits so I could skim through without missing anything. Now I reached for my phone to check the time, ready to suggest heading off and getting some lunch.

'I brought us something,' she said, noticing my movement and rolling onto her back, then sitting up and reaching for her bag. She rummaged inside, then held out a roll wrapped in cellophane.

'Thanks,' I said, surprised.

'I thought it might be nice to eat here. I brought drinks too.' She passed me a can of Coke and got out one for herself. There were crisps and bars of chocolate as well – and the bag, I noticed, still didn't look empty.

'How much have you got in there?' I asked, laughing.

She shrugged, and it occurred to me that she'd brought extra in case Will was around. But then I dismissed the thought, annoyed with myself. Not everything had to be about a boy.

We stayed longer that day, but Will didn't appear. That, I decided after a brief mental tussle, was a good thing. Amy and I parted with a plan to return the next day, and I promised to bring the refreshments.

Knowing the likely sparsity of the Fraser kitchen cupboards, I made a detour to the corner shop, picking up bread and cheese, then deliberating over chocolate bars. Amy seemed to have a ready supply of cash, but my funds were more stretched. I added a couple of kid-sized chocolates with cartoon wrappers, hoping to pass them off as ironic. I needed to keep back something for the other visit I'd decided to make that afternoon.

The door to the bookshop tinkled a greeting, and I felt the familiar surge of anticipation as I stepped over the threshold. I went straight to the nearest bookshelves, the ones with the new releases, and scanned the covers while I counted down in my head. *Three, two, one...*

'Afternoon, Laura Fraser.'

It was like someone switching on a light. Everything seemed suddenly brighter, more real. I spotted a title I'd heard of, plucked it from the shelf. 'Any good?'

He took it from my hand, not touching me, but for a moment we were connected: me, Will, the book. He turned it over and read the blurb. 'Haven't read it, but it's supposed to be. It's magical realism. Do you like magic?'

He looked directly at me as he said it, and I wasn't sure if he was flirting. With other boys, I'd have known, would have had a smart comeback at the ready. But with Will, my brain refused to work properly.

I shrugged. 'I haven't read any of her others.'

He feigned shock, then turned on his heel. 'Come with me.'

He was moving away before I could reply, heading towards the back of the shop. I felt my heart beat faster as I followed. Will disappeared around the corner of one bookcase, then another, and I had to quicken my pace to keep up. The shop was bigger than I'd thought, I realised, this part seemingly doing double duty as a storeroom. Piles of books sat on the floor next to bookcases, while others were heaped horizontally in front of their shelf mates, jutting precariously over the edges.

'Careful,' called Will from somewhere up ahead. 'One false move could trigger an avalanche.'

'Looks like there's already been one,' I mumbled, skirting a stack of ancient copies of *National Geographic*.

At the end of the aisle, I found myself confronted by a solid wall of bookcases. 'Will?' I called.

'Over here.'

I turned to see a hand emerge from a shelf behind me, one finger beckoning. I rounded the corner to see him smiling.

'Ta da!' he said, sweeping an arm towards a shelf of brightly coloured books.

I moved closer to examine them. There were eight or nine

novels, all by the same author as the one I'd asked him about. For a moment, I was impressed; but then I absorbed the implications. 'She doesn't sell?'

'No one buys hardbacks,' he said sagely. 'But they look good in the window.'

He ran a fingertip along the spines, then paused at one and pulled it forward. 'How about this?'

I took it from him and examined the cover. A wan-looking girl stood at the bottom, a dragon flying over her head.

'She looks a bit like me,' I mused.

He shook his head. 'Not as pretty.'

I looked up in confusion, but he'd turned away. Had he meant he thought I was pretty, or that I wasn't as pretty as the girl on the cover? Something pierced my chest at the latter idea – but it wouldn't be like Will to say something rude. So surely he must have meant—

'You could take it if you like,' he said. 'Just to borrow, mind. See what you think.'

I felt the smile threatening to envelop my face and forced my lips into a more neutral expression. 'Thanks,' I said, trying to sound as if it wasn't a big deal. I was about to ask him if I'd see him again at the lake but stopped myself. Better, I felt, that he stayed away.

He insisted on giving me a bag, telling me as I left to take good care of the book. 'No folding over the pages,' he said, and I spluttered indignantly.

'What do you take me for?'

He narrowed his eyes, and something fluttered in my stomach. 'That, Laura Fraser,' he said, 'remains to be seen.'

# TWENTY

*Now*

My mouth is dry and my head throbs. I should get up, get something to drink. But I can't move.

I don't know how I made it home. My heart was pounding, my breathing fast and shallow. I have a dim recollection of shrugging off DC Hollis, telling her I was fine. She must have thought I was crazy: one minute I was insisting what I'd seen in that room was real, that she had to investigate, the next I was apologising for wasting her time. But then, she thought I was crazy already, so what does it matter?

I open my eyes, but the light immediately makes my head thud harder, and I close them again. I keep promising myself I'll be able to make sense of all this if only I think it through, calmly and rationally. But whenever I try to remember what happened, all I see is that shape on the floor of the kitchen in Flyte Gardens.

A dead mouse. A warning to shut up. To leave things alone or I'll be next.

I gather my strength, force myself to sit up. The pulse in my head swells briefly, then subsides. I take a deep breath, then another, massage the skin at my temples. I have to *think*.

That mouse was supposed to represent me. The man on the train doesn't just know who I am, he knows about my past. I haven't told anyone in London about my childhood nickname. I've been careful not to let any part of my Gramwell life follow me here. Yet somehow he knows. This is personal. And it's linked to what happened to Marina.

I stand, walk to the window, hoping a change of view will help clear my head. It's raining, the pavement below slick. A woman hurries past, her shoulders hunched, head down. A moment later, she's gone from view. I stare at the empty street, an idea nudging its way into my brain: another few seconds in bed, and I'd have never seen her.

It was the same that day on the train. The day I saw Marina. If I'd got an earlier train, if I'd decided to queue for coffee at the station kiosk, if I'd got onto a different carriage: if I'd done *any* of those things, I'd never have seen her and that man. So how can this be about me? Am I being a complete narcissist for even considering it?

And yet, the mouse.

A dead mouse. A dead mouse on the floor of a house that's been empty for who knows how long. A dead mouse that was half hidden in a shadowy corner.

Can I really be sure it wasn't there the first time I went in? All my attention was on the chair, the chains, the padlock. Can I honestly say, hand on heart, that I *know* it wasn't?

What if I've got it all wrong? What if I'm doing what DC Hollis thinks – making this all about me, because I can't let go of what happened in Gramwell? What if no one put that mouse there, no one meant for me to see it? What if it just died?

I should find the idea a relief, but it isn't. Because if I'm jumping to conclusions, perhaps it doesn't end with a dead rodent. Is it possible I imagined the rest of it too? That I conjured up that scene in the kitchen because I desperately wanted some evidence that what I saw on that train – or what I thought I saw – was real? That none of it was there when I went back with DC Hollis because it had never been there in the first place?

*It wouldn't be the first time, would it?*

I shake my head, as if that will rid me of my mother's voice.

*I was hurting then*, I want to argue. *Damaged even. I'm not that person anymore.*

The voice in my head doesn't reply, but I feel her silent judgement. She doesn't agree.

I go to the bathroom, open the cabinet over the sink and push aside bottles and boxes until I see it: the small cardboard carton with my name on. I open it and stare at the blister pack inside. I could take one, just one. I can almost feel the cotton-wool numbness, every edge blurred, nothing mattering much. It's been a long time, but I always keep these here, just in case.

My finger presses against the plastic and out pops a capsule, one end white, the other green. I look at it for a long time. Then I replace it and smooth the foil back into place. I turn on the tap and splash my face with cold water. I need to stay sharp. I need to work this out.

*No one by the name of Marina Leeson has ever lived at this address.* That's what DC Hollis said. But perhaps Marina just used it for her post. If she was living with the man from the train, that's not hard to imagine. Perhaps she was trying to get away from him, needed somewhere to make her plans. Or perhaps she was using a fake name, setting up a new identity so he'd never find her when she ran. And maybe he'd found out before she could put her plan into action, stopped her and made sure she'd never be able to leave him.

But if Flyte Gardens was Marina's escape plan, why had the man from the train taken her back there? And why drag her across London on the Tube, in the middle of rush hour, to do it?

And if I'm not being paranoid about that mouse, where do I fit in? Did he realise Marina had asked for my help? Did he find some way to identify me so he could warn me off? Or did he know who I was all along? Was I *supposed* to see him with Marina that day? Was it a warning I'd be next?

I can imagine what DC Hollis would have to say to that idea. I'm glad the shock of seeing the mouse stopped me saying anything more. She'd been surprised when I apologised, my abrupt change of heart catching her off guard. 'Last warning, Laura,' she said. 'If you waste my time again, I'll have no choice about what happens next.' But then she lowered her voice, put her hand on my arm. 'Get some professional help. Please. There's no shame in it.'

She wasn't to know.

<hr>

*Then*

I was seated in an armchair that I imagine was supposed to be comfortable but wasn't. For once, the clouds had gone and the sun had shown its face in Gramwell, apparently working double time in a bid to remind us what it looked like. The rays streaked through the window, and I had to keep adjusting my position to avoid being blinded. The woman opposite – Janice, she had invited me to call her – had no such problem. She studied me steadily while I shuffled and blinked.

'Your mum said you had a difficult day yesterday.'

I shrugged. 'I suppose.'

She didn't say anything. It was a tactic, I had learned, to get me talking, but I wasn't in the mood. The springs of the chair were digging into my buttocks, and I shifted, rewarded with another lance of sunshine to my eyes.

Eventually, she gave in. 'Would you like to tell me about what happened in the supermarket?'

'Not really.'

'Your mum's very worried about you, Laura.'

'Are you supposed to do that?'

She looked at me quizzically.

'Use emotional blackmail to get your patients to talk?'

I'd hoped to get a reaction, but she only smiled. 'You're not my patient. I'm not a doctor. I'm just here to help you talk things through.'

'And what if I don't want to talk?'

'Then we'll stay quiet.'

I sat there, radiating belligerence. In her place, I'd have told me to sod off. But Janice was a patient woman – I suppose you'd have to be in her line of work. She sat there, hands lightly folded in her lap, while the minutes ticked past and the sun continued its silent assault. Finally, I broke.

'What did Mum tell you?'

'You're the one I'd like to talk to, Laura.'

I laughed without mirth. 'She told you I made a scene, right?' Janice didn't reply, but I was pretty sure I was on the money. 'I suppose she'd have preferred me not to say anything. Just let that kid get hurt.'

Her expression didn't change. 'Tell me about the child. It was a little girl, is that right?'

I felt the anger rise in me again. 'Her mother wasn't watching her. She was halfway up the aisle and she'd left the kid in the trolley at the bottom – in one of those seat things they have.'

'Go on.'

I could see the little girl as if she were right in front of me. She was in a carry seat, attached to the supermarket trolley by some mysterious arrangement of clips and screws. The result was too high above the floor, the drop unforgiving, the shiny surface below hard enough to shatter delicate bones.

'She should never have left her,' I said. 'The mother, I mean. It was dangerous. Anyone could see that.'

'What happened?'

'The kid tried to reach for something. There were tins on the shelves, and she was trying to grab them.'

I saw it again, the podgy arm stretched out, fingers splayed like a starfish. 'She was leaning towards the shelves. She lost her balance, started to fall.'

I'd watched in slow motion as it happened, those tiny limbs flailing like a rag doll. Heard her cry of terror. And then the terrible thud as she hit the floor. Blood. Blood everywhere.

But then I'd blinked, and the toddler was still in her carry chair. There was still time to save her.

'I rushed over there, grabbed her so she'd be safe.' I closed my eyes, remembering the softness of her arm in my grip. The toddler had stared at me for a moment, her mouth a perfect O. Then she'd let out a piercing wail. And that's when all hell had broken loose.

'That woman was crazy. Screaming blue murder, like I was trying to kidnap her kid or something. She's the one you should be talking to, not me. She's the one who needs her head examined.'

I could hear my voice rising, but Janice looked as unruffled as ever. 'Did you pick up the child?'

'No, I just grabbed her arm. Pulled her back.'

'You didn't pick her up? It would have been a natural thing to do if you were worried she was at risk.'

I could see what she was getting at. 'No, she was falling, and I saved her. I wasn't running off with her or anything! There's no way that woman could have thought that.' The injustice of it still burned. 'Anyway, I couldn't have picked her up if I'd wanted to. She had this thing around her waist.'

Janice studied me, her expression neutral. 'What kind of thing?'

'Like a strap. A belt.' Too late, I realised what she was really driving at.

'So the little girl was strapped in. Do you think that's why her mother thought it was safe to leave her?'

I shook my head. 'It wasn't enough. She was falling. That woman shouldn't have left her.'

'Was she really falling? Could that have happened if she was strapped in?'

'Yes!' But had she been? I could see it again, the blood on the supermarket floor. It had been so real, just like that day... But it hadn't happened. I'd been given a second chance.

'She was about to fall,' I amended. 'If her mother had been looking after her the way she should have been, she'd have seen that too.'

'Do you honestly think that?' She saw that I was about to reply and held up one finger. 'Just stop for a moment. Think. Is there another way of looking at the situation?'

I stared at her. 'Have you been listening to a word I've said? The kid was in danger. That woman isn't fit to be a mother. She should never have left her.'

'You've said that several times now.'

'It's true.' I leaned forward in my seat, enunciated every word. 'She. Should. Never. Have. Left. Her.'

Janice watched me, like she was waiting for something. It took me a second, maybe two. And then the air left the room as I realised what I'd said.

———

*Now*

So long ago, but the memory is as clear as ever. The kid in the supermarket was the first time it happened, but it wasn't the last. I'd see the scene unfold in front of me: a passerby stepping into the path of an oncoming car; a blameless dog attacking its owner. Blood. Always blood. And then something would shift, and I'd be left shaking with fear while people hurried past, their eyes fixed on anything but me.

But I'm not the person I was then. I'm not taking pills; I haven't since that tweet from Millie changed everything. And I left the non-prescription stuff alone years ago. I don't believe I'm seeing things that aren't there.

*You didn't believe it then either.*

I screw up my eyes, as if that will block out my mother's voice. If only I'd taken a photo of that room. If only I'd held my ground for the moment it would have taken to whip out my phone. Then I'd know for sure, and DC Hollis would too.

But then something strikes me that I should have thought of hours ago: there's another photo. The picture of the woman in the bookshop, the one with the letter addressed to Marina Leeson.

DC Hollis said no one by that name had ever lived at Flyte Gardens, that it was impossible for Marina to be the woman on the train. She thinks I'm lost in some wild fantasy, desperately trying to play the heroine. But that photo shows this isn't all in my head. There's a real woman, answering my description of the one on the train. Someone called Marina Leeson is having her post delivered to 21 Flyte Gardens. And if the woman on the train and Marina Leeson aren't the same person, they know each other, or else the woman on the train is using Marina's name.

I grab my phone. I'll send DC Hollis the photo. I won't ask anything of her, won't do anything that will let her accuse me of wasting her time. But when she sees this, she'll know I'm not a fantasist. That the woman I saw is connected to someone called Marina Leeson and Flyte Gardens. That I had good reason to go there. Maybe she'll even believe I'm telling the truth about what I saw.

I scroll through my emails, looking for the one from DDM Solutions – but there's too much crap in my inbox, and the text is blurring in front of my eyes. I type the words into the search box instead.

No results found.

Maybe I've misremembered the name. DMM Solutions perhaps? DSM? I force myself to go back through the messages slowly, methodically. But a cold finger of dread is tracking its way up my spine as I work through the emails from this week, then last.

Nothing.

Panicked, I turn to my sent items, look for the file I emailed. That image is too blurred to make out the address on the envelope, but it would be better than nothing. I go through my messages from each day, back a full week, a second, a third. I try the search function once more, my hands shaking out typos. I go back to correct them.

No results found.

The original video will be there, though. It must be. I search my phone. Videos, deleted items, folders.

It isn't.

And when I search my photos, the screenshot I took isn't there either.

I jump out of bed, run into the kitchen. My laptop is on the counter and I jab at the power button, shout at it as it stirs lazily to life. The video and screenshot were only saved to my phone, but my emails are on my laptop too. I open the mailbox, search again. But it just confirms what I already know: the messages have vanished.

There's nothing to show that photo of the woman in the bookshop ever existed.

I go back to the bathroom and open the cabinet. I take out the cardboard box and press the green and white capsule into the palm of my hand. And then I place it in my mouth and wait until it silences the voice screaming at me that I'm losing my mind.

*

*It worked. Everything hidden away in time, every incriminating detail removed. It was tight, but the preparation paid off. I only wish I could have seen her face when she walked back into that kitchen. I did consider leaving behind another camera, something small, easily concealed – but it was too risky. Mistakes get made when you're over-confident.*

*I can only imagine what that detective said. Not much chance they'll be listening to any more of her stories.*

*There'll be no help coming now, I'm confident of that. All too much like hard work. And I doubt she's enjoyed her brush with the law. Brought back old memories, I expect. She'll be telling herself she's done enough. Time to get back to her wonderful life.*

*Poor Marina. I've imagined it so many times: how it must feel to wait and hope. To tell yourself that surely, help must be coming. That someone who knows your life is in danger couldn't just walk away.*

*I almost feel sorry for her.*

# TWENTY-ONE

*Then*

It wasn't long before Will appeared at the lake again. I couldn't avoid introducing him to Amy then, trying to tell myself I had nothing to worry about. They were a little cool with each other, I thought. At the time, I found that reassuring. I should have realised, of course, that it was the opposite.

He joined us most days after that, mentioning his working hours as an apparent aside, knowing, no doubt, that I'd make sure we'd be there when he'd finished for the day. I'd been basking in the glow of his enigmatic comment at the bookshop, hopeful that it revealed at least the glimmer of romantic interest; but there were no signs of that at the lake. There, he treated me with playful good humour, much as an older brother might. He'd sit with us on the ledge, share whatever food Amy had brought for the day (I'd quickly given up attempting to compete on that front), and tease us lightly about our choice of books or music. On the surface, the only difference he made to our routine was that I swam even less than I had before. I was crippled with self-consciousness at the idea that he might see me in my bathing costume, scuttling to the water's edge only when I was certain his attention was safely elsewhere.

Amy, in contrast, seemed barely aware of his presence. She was comfortable in her skin – which, I supposed, if you had skin like Amy's, wasn't so hard. She'd stretch out on her towel and tip her face to the leaden sky, as if we were in Saint-Tropez not Gramwell. But it wouldn't be long before she'd be up again and lowering herself smoothly into the water. Truth be told, I preferred it when she was swimming; once in the lake, some of her natural grace deserted her, her strokes uneven, effortful. But Amy, I thought, didn't care what she looked like. She simply loved the water.

Will, it seemed, felt the same way. He'd swim from one end to the other then back again, a businesslike routine that seemed designed not to intercept Amy's laboured circuits. At first, they barely interacted. But then one day, I heard a sudden peal of laughter from across the lake.

I looked up in surprise to see Amy grinning while Will spluttered and rubbed his eyes. I could see from his shaking shoulders that he was laughing too.

'What's up?' I called, but they didn't reply.

I got to my feet and stepped to the edge, momentarily forgetting to worry about how I looked in my swimming costume. 'Hey!' I tried again. 'What's going on?'

Amy looked up, her eyes gleaming. 'Will's under attack,' she called gleefully.

He grimaced in mock anger. 'Not funny, Linton.' It was the first time I'd heard him use her last name like that.

'What are you talking about?'

There was an edge to my voice I hadn't intended, and some of the sparkle faded from Amy's smile. 'There's a dragonfly,' she said. 'It flew in Will's face and he ducked, got a face full of water.'

'I've swallowed half the lake,' he said, shaking his head like a dog. Droplets flew off the ends and spattered Amy's face, and she shrieked and burst into giggles again.

'Keep it down,' I hissed, uncomfortably aware that I sounded like a maiden aunt. 'Do you want everyone to know we're here?'

Will raised an eyebrow and made a mock salute in my direction. 'Quite right. Get a hold of yourself, Linton.' He stretched out his arms and kicked off into a backstroke.

I watched Amy's eyes follow him, a faint flush on her cheeks.

I tried to go back to my magazine, but it was impossible. I felt like an interloper, doomed to watch miserably while the two of them splashed about in the water. I heard Will's voice again, remembered the ease of that 'Linton'. When had he started to call her that? How had I missed their slide into familiarity?

I wouldn't have minded, though, if that had been all it was. But I remembered Amy's giggle, the colour in her cheeks. I couldn't lose her. I couldn't lose Will. And I simply refused to lose them to each other.

I watched them over the top of my magazine. Will had returned to his standard front crawl, Amy hugging the quarry walls with her ungainly breaststroke. I wasn't the natural swimmer Will was, but I was better than Amy. I should have been in there with them, I realised, not skulking on the ledge waiting for them to miss me.

My heart was beating a tattoo in my chest as I stood and strode to the ledge. *This is it*, I told myself. *Get their attention now, or watch them slip away.*

I raised my hands above my head, pointed my fingertips. I heard Will call out, a note of alarm in his voice. But my knees were flexed, my eyes fixed on the dark water. I propelled myself forward, and in that moment, I saw it. The shadow beneath the surface, the thing I'd known had been there all along. It stretched out its arms to receive me, and I shut my eyes as the icy water closed over my head.

# TWENTY-TWO

*Now*

The sound drills into my brain. I thought I'd turned my phone to silent, but I must have made a mistake. I reach for it on the bedside table and succeed only in knocking it to the floor. It lands with a smack that will annoy the woman downstairs, continuing its shrieking before falling silent.

I'm about to relax when it starts again. My eyes are glued shut, but the noise is like a screwdriver in my brain. I fumble on the floor. My fingers close around it just as it shuts up.

'Leave me alone,' I mumble, and it starts ringing again.

I want to throw it across the room, but I can guess who's calling and it's best to get this over with. I force my eyelids open and squint at the screen, jabbing at the button to answer.

'Hello?'

'Laura, Jesus. What's wrong with you? You sound like the living dead.'

'Thanks, Sam,' I say, thanking my lucky stars it isn't Guy after all. 'I've felt better.'

'You're ill then? I told Guy that would be it. Why haven't you called?' He doesn't give me a chance to reply. 'You're too unwell. I can tell. Don't worry about it. I'll tell him you phoned when he was in a meeting, so you called me instead.'

I wonder if I'd prefer to be sacked, but I don't have the energy to argue. 'Thanks,' I say again.

There's a pause, then, 'So what's wrong with you? Is it flu? It sounds like flu.'

'Yeah,' I say, 'flu.' *Or I'm going insane.*

'You sound really bad. Sore throat, right? You need a hot toddy for that. I have this great recipe. My mum used to make it for me.'

'Hmm,' I say, because it sounds like he expects a response.

'Hot water, squeeze of lemon juice, dollop of honey. You don't need to measure anything. Oh, and brandy for the grown-up version. As long as you're not taking anything you shouldn't have with alcohol. Are you?'

I'm having difficulty following him. 'Am I what?'

'Taking anything? Paracetamol or anything? Because I don't think you can drink with that.'

'No.' Not paracetamol.

'So you have it all?'

'What?'

'Stuff for the toddy? Lemon juice and honey—'

'Yeah, I'm fine. Thanks, Sam.'

'I could bring you supplies if you want. I know where you live – from the other night, I mean.'

'Honestly, I'm fine.'

'It's not a problem.' I hear the hopeful note in his voice: he'd love to come round, look after me. He's a kind man, and perhaps I should want that too. But I don't. All I want is to be left alone.

'I think I'm probably infectious,' I say. 'Thanks though. I'll see you in work.'

I let him finish saying goodbye, hoping the flu doesn't spoil my weekend, before I hang up. Then I switch the phone to silent and close my eyes. But it's too late – the call has pulled me too far from sleep and the thoughts are already flooding back, disjointed frames that stutter and jerk like an old-fashioned film. Marina, her eyes wide with fear. Whispering in my ear. Screaming silently at me across the train.

*Help me.*

Except she's not Marina. She can't be. There's no Marina at 21 Flyte Gardens. There's no one there at all. No one and nothing. No kitchen prison cell. No chair with chains and a padlock. No food wrappers or water bottles. Definitely no camera.

And no missing woman. No photograph taken in a bookshop that reminded me of the one in Gramwell.

That bookshop should have been my clue, I see that now. I should have realised what was happening the moment I stepped inside, the memories wrapping themselves like fog around my brain. They'd found a place to settle – maybe it was that interview, just like DC Hollis said, that had opened the door. And then they'd gathered, thickened, created a dream world of smoke and shadows. How much of it was real? The girl at the cash desk? Tabitha? The guy with the puffa jacket in the park?

I remember leaving the shop that evening, convinced there was someone following me. Running like a maniac down the street. The paranoia should have been another giveaway. Those were the actions of the old Laura, the one I thought I'd left behind for good.

It terrifies me that my mind is capable of doing this. Now, after all this time. When I thought I was doing fine, that I'd got my life on track. When I was hoping things were about to change for the better. That I'd be able to tell Guy where to stick his job and do something I loved. Was it all part of the delusion?

I reach for my phone, rub my eyes until the words on the

screen swim into focus. But no, there it is: the text from Oliver
Frampton. At least I wasn't imagining that. The humiliation of
missing our appointment, lying about my sick mother – that was
all too real.

I groan, cover my eyes with my hand. We'd rearranged the
meeting, hadn't we? I try to remember when it's supposed to be
happening, but draw a blank. I should call him to cancel at least,
especially after my no-show last time, but I can't summon the
energy. Maybe when I don't turn up, he'll assume Mum's taken
a turn for the worse. Maybe he'll just conclude he can't trust a
word I say.

I wonder what day it is. I should check. See how long I've
been lying here. But the tiredness is creeping over me again. I
try to lift the phone, but already I'm forgetting why I wanted to
do that. Whatever it was, it can wait. Just until I feel better.

Just until I've closed my eyes for a few minutes...


I'm awake, suddenly, completely. I lie frozen in bed, waiting for
another noise to follow the one that pulled me from my sleep. It
was a distinctive sound, cutting through my subconscious and
waking me instantly. And though a moment ago I was dozing, I
know what it was: the click of the front door.

I strain to hear more, but there's nothing. Should I lie here,
pretend to be asleep? Should I try to make a run for it? My heart
thudding, I twist my head so I can see the bedroom door. It's
shut tight, the way it always is. I stare at it for a second, then
make my decision.

I drop silently to the floor and roll beneath the bed. The
edge of the duvet is hanging down, and I pull on it to hide as
much of the space as possible. My bedroom is small. Anyone
wanting to check under here will need to get on their knees to
do it. I'm hoping the intruder isn't expecting anyone to be home,
won't bother with more than a cursory inspection.

I shouldn't have taken that pill. Should have stayed on my guard. But now fear is purging the chemicals from my system, everything flooding back sharper, brighter than before.

I rack my brains, trying to remember if there's anything in the bedroom I can use as a weapon. There's a zip-up bag of clothes under the bed, a paperback on the floor at the side. Both as useless as each other. Beyond the book, though, I see something more helpful: a high heel from a distant night out. It's not a stiletto, but with sufficient force it's sharp and heavy enough to do some damage. I hope so, anyway, because it's all I've got.

I roll onto my stomach and reach for the shoe. I'm at full stretch, but still an inch short. I draw back my hand and pause, listen. Was that movement in the hallway? Or was it just the click of the radiator? I don't have time to waste. I use my elbows to pull myself along the carpet and reach out again. My head is beyond the edge of the bed now, starkly exposed. I make a grab for the shoe and shimmy backwards as fast as I can, examining the heel as I do it.

A crack. A burning pain that makes me feel sick. My vision blurs, then kicks back into focus, but the nausea remains. I press my hand to the back of my head, where I've struck it against the bedstead. It throbs angrily, and when I remove my fingers, there's a smear of red across the tips.

Did whoever has broken into my flat hear the bump? Are they waiting outside the door, planning their next move? Are they armed, dangerous? Or do they just want to take what they can and get out of here?

I feel blood trickle down the back of my neck. The bedframe is wooden, but there must have been a screw or something sticking out. Unlucky. Head wounds bleed a lot, I know that from experience.

Another sound from the hallway. But this time it's clearer – the radiator, I'm sure of it. If someone had heard me, surely they'd have entered the bedroom by now? Or maybe they don't want trouble, have decided to beat a retreat in case I'm a six foot four karate champion.

*Or maybe there was no one there in the first place.*

The thought should be comforting, but it's the opposite. I was sure of what I heard. I know the click of that front door as well as I know my own voice.

*Unless you were imagining that too.*

Or maybe I wasn't, and whoever is out there is waiting for me to let down my guard. There have been burglaries in this street before. It's stupid to think it couldn't happen.

Or perhaps, after all, I haven't been going mad. Perhaps I was right about that mouse. Right that it was a message from the man from the train. And maybe he's followed me here, come to silence me once and for all.

I tighten my grip on the shoe. Wait. Everything is silent – no noise from the flat downstairs either. The woman who lives there works funny hours. I've no idea if there's anyone to hear me if I scream.

I should call the police. But I can't until I'm sure there's really someone here, not after DC Hollis's dire warnings.

There's another click from the hallway. The radiator, definitely the radiator. Is it possible that's what woke me? I was so sure it was the front door, but I'd been asleep. And after everything that's happened, it wouldn't be surprising if I was on edge. Made a mistake. Just a mistake – not a hallucination. Not a sign I'm losing my mind.

I feel sick, my head throbbing. I need to do something. I wait a moment more, listening as hard as I can. There's nothing. It's time to move.

I slide out from beneath the bed, the shoe held tightly in one hand, and move quietly to the bedroom door. I press my ear to the wood and listen. Nothing. But there's something on the carpet behind me – a trail of red droplets tracking my movements. There's no way I can hide while my head is bleeding like this.

I place my hand on the doorknob. Should I move fast, hope to use the element of surprise? Or should I try to be stealthy, to creep out of the flat before I'm noticed? Another wave of nausea makes up my mind. I'm in no shape to try to outrun anyone.

Gently, I twist the doorknob, open the door a crack. The hinges creak and I freeze, brace for the moment someone shoves open the door. Seconds pass. It doesn't happen.

I edge forwards, peer through the gap. I see a slice of the space beyond, cheap grey carpet and magnolia walls. I pull the door open another inch, then another. I can see the whole hallway now. There's no one there, but the chain on the front door hangs down uselessly. Did I secure it before I went to bed? Normally, I am religious about such things, but I wasn't in a good place after I got back from Flyte Gardens. It's not impossible that I forgot.

I take a final moment to gather myself, then open the door wider, step into the hallway. To my left is the loo, at the end, an archway into the living space. To the right is the front door. Every part of me wants to turn right.

But what do I do then? Call the police? DC Hollis said they could arrest me if they think I'm wasting their time. Or do I just try to wait out the intruder, hope the coast is clear when I return?

And what if there's no one here? I can't leave without knowing.

The bathroom door is ajar. I lean further into the hallway, craning my neck to see through the gap. It looks empty so I decide to risk it. Just a few steps and I'm there, slipping inside. Everything looks just the way I left it. The splashes on the mirror, the towel draped across the radiator, even the knickers escaping from the top of the laundry basket. If anyone else has been here, they've been careful not to disturb a thing.

I tiptoe across the room and place my ear to the wall that adjoins the living space. I can't hear anyone, but there's only one way to know for sure.

I adjust my grip on the shoe and return to the hallway, keeping my back to the wall as I sidle towards the arch. The sofa comes fully into view, then the TV and the window beyond. My breath sounds loud in my ears, so loud anyone in there must surely hear me coming. At any moment now there'll be a shout, a rush of movement. I raise the shoe. If someone runs at me, every second will count.

Another step. I'm almost there. The living space looks clear, but the kitchen area is behind it, hidden until I step inside. If there's someone in the flat, that's where they must be. It's now or never.

I step through the arch.

I know at once that I'm alone. It registers in some instinctive part of me before my eyes have fully taken in the space. No one else is breathing this air. No one has been lying in wait.

I collapse against the worktop, let the shoe fall to the ground. Until this moment, my hands have been steady, but now I feel a tremor in my fingertips. It spreads to my hands, up my arms. I hug myself, sucking in deep breaths.

The noise that woke me must have been the radiator. Thank God I didn't call for help. The way I'm going, being arrested might be the least of my problems. DC Hollis might have me sectioned.

I look down and see spatters of red on the laminate flooring and press my fingers gingerly to the wound at my head. The skin there is tacky, but it feels like the bleeding is slowing. I go to the bathroom, strip off my T-shirt. The back of it looks like something from a horror movie. There's probably no saving it, so I scrunch it up and run it under the cold tap, press it to my head. I debate taking a couple of painkillers, then decide against it. I've had enough pills for today.

Maybe I should call 1 1 1. But it's what's going on inside my head that I'm worried about, and that's too much to think about right now. The adrenaline is seeping away, waves of fatigue creeping in to take its place. I'll go back to bed. Sleep off whatever drugs are left in my system. Everything will be clearer in the morning. At least, I hope it will.

I follow the trail of scarlet droplets back towards the bedroom. I should try to get them out of the carpet – I can't afford to lose my deposit – but I'm too tired. It can wait until tomorrow. I'm about to go inside when something makes me pause.

I stare again at the chain on the door. An image flashes into my head: my fingers fumbling with the catch, sliding it into place. Was that the last time I came home? Try as I might, I can't be sure. But now I feel something, some subtle disturbance in the molecules of the air, a ghost of a smell that's gone before I can place it. And though my rational mind tries to tell me this is paranoia, that older, reptilian brain doesn't believe it. They might have gone now, but deep in my bones, I feel it: someone was here.

I rush to the door and pull the chain across, grab the key from its hook on the wall. I twist it in the lock, check it, twist again, check again. I go back to the kitchen, fetch a dining chair to wedge under the door handle. That always seems to work in films, but I'm not convinced. Back to the kitchen. I open cupboards, pull out saucepans, plates. Then it's into the hallway again, stacking them on the chair. If anyone tries to open the door, that stuff will go flying. There's no way I won't hear it.

I retrieve my one remaining dining chair and take it to the bedroom with the last of the plates. I repeat the process, barricading myself inside. Then I prowl the room, looking for a sign that something has been moved. The thought of someone in here while I slept makes my blood run cold, but everything appears untouched. I find a clean T-shirt and pull it on. I'm not getting undressed; I want to be able to leave quickly if I need to.

All the activity has sapped my final reserves of energy. I flop onto the bed, pull the covers over me. My eyes are fixed on the door. I should have found a proper weapon, something better than that shoe. Now I'm stuck in here, and all I've got is the other half of the pair.

I get out of bed to scoop it up. It's next to the paperback I noticed earlier. I find myself staring at the book, a germ of a thought gnawing away at my brain. Something about what I'm seeing isn't right. If I'd been reading in bed, that book should have been on the bedside table. At a push, I'd have left it on the floor next to the bed. But it's in the middle of the carpet.

It's possible, of course, that it started off next to the bed and I kicked it away without realising. And yet – I'm careful with books. If I'd kicked it, wouldn't I have noticed? Rescued it straight away?

I bend and pick it up. The cover has a title in large red letters: *The Caves of Agoroth*.

A light switches on in a dim corner of my mind. This is the book Marina ordered. I turn it in my hands and there's something sticking out of the pages: a scrap of paper, placed there like a bookmark.

I stare at it, and the memory of that day in the bookshop comes back to me with perfect clarity. Tabitha handing it to me, telling me to pay for it on my way out. That was real. But this scrap of paper wasn't there then, I'm sure of it. I would have noticed it straight away. And even if I'd missed it, surely I'd have seen it when I started reading?

My fingers tremble as I open the pages at the spot marked by the paper. It's the end of one of the stories, the one that gave me bad dreams. The main character opening a false door and falling to her death.

But there's something else here now. Something written in

pencil in the margin next to the final paragraph, the one describing the character screaming as she plummets down the rocky chasm. My heart is pounding as I peer closer. And then the book slips from my fingers as the words bypass my brain and hit me straight in the solar plexus.

*You know what really happened.*

# TWENTY-THREE

*Then*

I broke the surface of the lake, gasping and gulping. I'd swallowed a mouthful of water and knocked my leg on the way down, but I didn't care. For the moment, Will's and Amy's attention was entirely on me.

'What the hell do you think you're doing?'

Will sounded furious, but it was better than having him ignore me. 'I wanted to dive.'

'You could have killed yourself,' he bellowed. 'There's all kinds of shit down there.'

I realised I'd never heard Will swear before. I wanted to think it meant he cared about me, but his expression told me I wasn't his favourite person right now.

'You're okay, though, right?' Amy looked worried. 'You didn't hurt yourself?'

My leg twinged in response, but I ignored it. 'I'm fine. It's not a big deal.'

'Right, no big deal.' Will pulled a face. 'They leave all the broken kit in these places, you know that? All the stuff they use on the site. You just jumped headfirst into a load of rusting metal.'

I swallowed. I'd had no idea. But I'd seen something as I jumped, something lurking in the shadows. If Will was right, I'd had a lucky escape. But that didn't mean I was going to admit it.

'Why are you swimming here then?' I asked him. 'If it's so dangerous, why are you here at all?'

He hesitated. 'Swimming is okay.'

I tilted my chin in triumph. 'It's okay because you want to do it, you mean.'

'That's not it at all.'

'And I've seen you dive as well.'

He frowned. 'Surface dives. It's not the same thing.'

'Because you can't dive properly.'

'Because I'm not stupid.'

His words stung. 'Neither am I. And I'm not a coward either.'

His jaw tightened, and I thought he was going to lose his temper. But when he spoke, his voice was clipped, controlled. 'Do what you like. I'm out of here.'

'Will—' Amy looked like she was about to try to pour oil on troubled lake waters, but he was already swimming to the edge. He stopped right next to me and pulled himself out. I watched the muscles flex in his arms, tiny domes of water on his skin.

'Will,' Amy tried again, but he picked up his towel and T-shirt and started up the slope to the path.

'Leave him to it,' I said, raising my voice to make sure he'd hear. 'Must be his time of the month.'

He didn't react, and Amy and I were left there, treading water, watching until he was gone.

'He's not going to say anything to his dad, is he?'

Amy's question startled me. I hadn't considered that possibility, but it was the kind of thing Will might do if he thought we – I – had gone too far. I shook my head with a confidence I didn't feel. 'He wouldn't do that. He'd have to admit he was here too.'

For a moment, we were silent. With Will gone, everything seemed dull, pointless.

'He'll be back when he's calmed down,' I said, and Amy nodded, though she didn't look as if she believed it. 'It was a good dive, though, right?'

I forced a smile, and she smiled back. 'It was amazing. I could never do that.'

The awe in her voice made me feel better. 'I could teach you if you like.'

She bit her lip, always a tell with Amy, and I understood her reluctance at once. Bloody Will.

'Don't let him put you off. It's perfectly safe if you know what you're doing.'

'Okay,' she said. 'I should probably get back, though. Next time, maybe.'

I knew she was saying it to please me, that she didn't want me to think she was taking Will's side. I considered pushing the point, but my leg was hurting so I decided to let it go.

'Are you coming?' she asked.

I was about to say yes, but then thought better of it. 'I'll swim for a bit,' I said instead. 'You go on.'

She was dressed and halfway up the slope when she stopped and turned. 'Shall we come again tomorrow?'

I tried not to feel annoyed. This was our place before Will showed up. It shouldn't have made any difference that he'd gone off in a strop.

'Sure,' I said, as if surprised she'd asked. 'I'll meet you, same as usual.'

I waited until she'd gone, then clambered out of the water. The moment I looked down at my leg, I was glad I hadn't done it earlier. There was an ugly bruise on my calf, already turning purple. I knew I should be grateful it was my leg that was hurt, not my head. But it had been bad luck, that was all. Will was making a fuss about nothing.

I dried myself off, but I didn't want to go home. Mum and Dad had been sniping at each other for days, the house filled with barbed comments and loaded silences. I knew the pattern – it wouldn't be long before full-scale hostilities erupted. It was best to stay out of the way as much as possible.

I went back to the ledge and sat there cross-legged, staring into the water. The dark surface was keeping its secrets. I leaned closer, searching for some sign of the thing I'd seen as I dived. I'd caught only a glimpse, but the memory of it made me shiver. It must have been what Will said, some piece of discarded quarry equipment.

But hitting my leg wasn't my biggest problem. If Will told his father we'd been coming here, I was in for some serious grief. Mr and Mrs Linton already had me down as a bad influence on Amy. I wouldn't have put it past them to tell her she couldn't hang around with me anymore. If they did that, she might argue, but she wouldn't disobey them. And that would be it for my summer.

Perhaps, I thought, I should find Will, tell him I wouldn't dive again. Beg him not to say anything. But the thought filled me with a fierce resistance. What had I done, after all, that was so wrong?

No, I wasn't going to apologise. Will wouldn't tell on us. He'd probably just go off in a huff, and we'd go back to the way things were before. Just Amy and me, doing our thing by the lake. It would be nice, even, more relaxed than worrying about what he was thinking all the time.

And if I was wrong, and he tried to ruin everything? I'd just have to deal with the consequences.

# TWENTY-FOUR

*Now*

I don't know how long I stand there, staring at the book on the floor. The pages are closed, but that note is burned into my brain.

*You know what really happened.*

Those words next to that story: it can only mean I was right. Someone knows about Gramwell. Someone who's broken into my flat and left me a message. And they've left it in the book a missing woman ordered from a bookshop and never collected.

This isn't just a message. It's a threat.

And somehow, it's connected to Marina. A warning to stop searching for her, to stop stirring up trouble or they'll expose what they think they know about me. And something more too – because why would Marina have ordered that particular book? Is it really possible it's just a coincidence? And if that message was written by the man who took her, the man from the train, how did he know about the connection to Gramwell? Could there be a chance that Marina was caught up in this because she knew something about me? That *I'm* his real target, and she got in the way?

Or maybe he's targeting both of us. Perhaps he's out to punish the people he thinks deserve it. Maybe he thinks Marina falls into that category too. Something to do with the woman who died, the one her neighbour talked about. Perhaps he thinks it was Marina's fault. So he's taken her, done something to her. And now I'm next on his list.

I'm breathing hard, the panic taking hold. If this man knows me, perhaps I know him. I struggle to visualise him – those dark glasses and the beard hid most of his face. But now I think of it, perhaps there was something familiar about him. Something about the leanness of his frame, the way he held himself. Is it possible I've met him before?

A shrill ring cuts through my thoughts. I stare at my phone as if it's a wild animal. He's on the other end of the line, I know he is. He's checking I've found his message. That I've understood that he's coming for me. I shouldn't answer, and yet I watch as my arm reaches out, as my finger hits the screen to connect the call.

'Laura, are you all right? I've been ringing and ringing. I was about to send out a search party.'

I could cry with relief. Sam, of course it's Sam.

I let out a shuddering breath. 'I'm sorry.' I should say something else, try to explain – but it feels like days since I've spoken to anyone, and my mouth is dry.

'No, I'm the one who's sorry. Did I wake you?' He doesn't wait for a reply. 'I'll go. Just – are you okay? I've been worried about you.'

How to answer that question? *No, I'm not okay. I thought I was losing my grip on reality. But now I know I'm not, and that's much, much worse.*

'I'm fine.'

'You're feeling better then? Will you be in work tomorrow?'

Oh God, work. Guy. I cover my eyes with my hand, as if that will make it all go away. 'I think I'll need another day or two to get shot of it.'

'Right, sure. I'll tell Guy then, shall I? That you'll be back in a couple of days?'

I should call him myself, but I grab at the lifeline. 'If you really don't mind? Thanks, Sam.'

'Not a problem.'

'Well then, I'd better go—'

'Yes, of course.' He sounds like he's waiting for something more.

'My head is hurting a bit—'

'Right, yes. You should go. Rest up.'

'Thanks for checking in on me.'

'Laura?' Something in his tone makes me feel he's been working up to what he's about to say. 'Did you find anything?'

I freeze, the phone held to my ear. 'What?'

'At the house. The place you said that woman lived. The one from the train.' Another pause. 'Marina.'

I should never have told him I was going to Flyte Gardens. If I tell him about all that stuff disappearing, he'll think I'm crazy. If I convince him I'm not by telling him about the mouse and the note in the book, he'll want me to go to the police. And until I know what's going on here, I'm no longer sure that's something I want to do.

'Laura, are you still there?'

'Yeah, I'm here. Sorry, it's just my head—'

'Did you find anything, though?'

I grip the phone tighter. 'The house was empty. All locked up.'

'So you didn't see anything? Nothing to help find her?'

'No,' I say. 'There was nothing helpful.'

Silence. Then, 'I'm sorry. I know how much this means to you.'

'It's not about me.' *Except maybe it is.*

'Of course not. I'm sorry. I'll go. Just – let me know if there's anything you need.'

I promise I will, apologise for being tetchy. After a few more good wishes for my recovery, I manage to get him off the phone.

Finally, I have a chance to think. I stoop and pick up the paperback, *The Caves of Agoroth.* I might not have the photograph of Marina, but I have this. It proves I haven't been imagining everything. It links the woman calling herself Marina to that bookshop. But I can't take it to the police. Not now. Not with that note in the margin connecting me to what's happening here.

But what is that exactly? I need to focus. There's only one way to put together a jigsaw, and that's one piece at a time. And that note hasn't changed one important fact: Marina is missing. That's where I need to start.

If she was being held at 2 1 Flyte Gardens, where was she when I turned up there? How did whoever was keeping her prisoner know I'd found the house? And how did he manage to remove the evidence so quickly?

And that wasn't the only evidence that disappeared. There were the images I had from the bookshop CCTV, somehow deleted from my email account. How could someone do that?

I stare at my phone. There's one person who may be able to help with that, at least.

I bring up the internet and search for DDM Solutions. I tap enter, and my heart sinks. There's nothing relevant here – just a list of pages linking to a management consultancy, then a logistics company. I think for a second, then add 'digital images' to the search box.

Bingo.

There it is. DDM Solutions, specialists in forensic image analysis, complete with phone number. I start typing it into my phone, expecting the last few digits to appear automatically. But that doesn't happen. It's as if I've never called them before.

I stare at the screen, trying to work out what this means. It could be nothing, I tell myself, just my aged phone being temperamental. I press the call button.

It rings out several times before someone answers, a male voice I recognise at once. 'Yup.'

'Hi, is that DDM Solutions?'

'Laura, right?' My spirits lift. He remembers me too.

'I'm calling about that photo you looked at for me.'

'Okay.' He sounds wary, but he obviously knows what I'm talking about. Maybe he thinks I'm going to ask for a refund.

'Could you send me a copy?' Thinking it might help, I add, 'I'd be happy to pay for it.'

'No can do, I'm afraid. I don't keep copies.'

At first, I think I haven't heard him right. 'What? No copies at all? You're joking, right?'

'It's GDPR. I can't go around keeping photos of randoms, especially when they aren't my clients.' He sniffs haughtily. 'I'm a professional.'

For the love of God.

'You can send me the original file and I can do the work again. I'll give you ten per cent off, as you're a repeat customer,' he adds hopefully.

'I don't have it.'

'Then there's nothing I can do. Sorry,' he adds as an afterthought.

'I don't believe this.'

'Did you delete the email? What about your sent items? Have you checked your trash?'

'Yes.' I just about stop myself adding *Of course I have.* 'I've checked everywhere. There's nothing. Not the email you sent me, not my message to you with the original.'

'What did you delete it for?'

'I *didn't*. I'm not a complete idiot. I can't understand it. They've just gone.'

He sniffs again. 'Sounds like you've been hacked.'

The word sends a shock wave through my brain. 'What do you mean?'

'Well, if you didn't delete them yourself—'

'I didn't.'

'And nothing else has gone wrong with your system?'

I remember working through my emails. 'Everything else seemed to be there.'

'Then someone's deleted them from your account.'

My mind is racing. 'How could that happen? I haven't given anyone my phone. My laptop's been at home.'

He chuckles. 'They don't need your phone or your laptop. All they need to do is get the right bit of software on there. Have you opened any weird emails?'

'I don't know. Maybe. I get a lot of spam.'

'That's probably it then. Or a text message. A phone call, even. Have you had any calls from anyone you don't know?'

I'm trying to remember, but my memory of the last few days is foggy. A result of the pills, probably. 'Perhaps. I'm not sure.'

'That'll be it, take my word for it.' He sounds matter of fact. 'You've been hacked. I can check your phone for you, if you like.'

'Would that help? Can you get the files back?'

'Well, we could search for what they've used, what kind of malware.' He sighs. 'But look, I'll be honest with you. There's no way of getting back whatever they've deleted.'

I close my eyes. Where do I go from here?

As if he's heard my question, he says, 'Your best bet is to work out who'd want to do this. Check everything, see if any other files are missing.'

I thank him and am about to hang up, already trying to formulate my next move, but he hasn't finished. 'You can get someone to find the malware, if it's there. But this is tricky stuff. It replicates, hides itself. Your best bet is to get rid of your phone. Your laptop too.'

I laugh in spite of myself. 'I haven't got the money to do that.'

'Your funeral.' I can almost see him shrug. 'But until you do, whoever's done this could be watching your every move.'

*

*I'm surprised, I'll admit it. I thought she'd given up after that visit to the house. She went straight back to her flat and didn't leave it for days. Missed work. Didn't phone in sick. It was all about her, of course.*

*But something has changed, and I don't know why. That bothers me.*

*She hasn't been back to the police though. Perhaps she thinks they'll get interested in her if she makes a nuisance of herself. She'd want to avoid that. Those celebrity pals of hers would soon fade away if they found out what she really was.*

*And yet, she's still looking for Marina. Still seems to think she can save her. Still doesn't seem to realise how much she has to lose.*

*So I'm going to have to put that right.*

# TWENTY-FIVE

*Then*

By the time I arrived at the lake with Amy the next day, I'd convinced myself that Will wouldn't be there. So when I saw him sitting on the ledge, long legs stretched out in front of him, the shock nearly stopped me in my tracks.

'Back again?' he said, not turning, his voice floating out over the water.

'Why wouldn't we be?'

'Hey, Will,' Amy cut in, trying to stop anything before it got started. She sounded pleased to see him, I thought, and I felt a pang. Would it really have been so bad for it to have been just the two of us?

He turned to her and smiled. 'Linton.'

I threw down my towel in my usual spot. Part of me wanted to dive into the lake again, just to show Will I wasn't going to be told what to do. But my leg was sore, and I had no desire for a repeat injury. So instead I pulled my book from my bag and settled down to read. It was the one Will had let me borrow from the shop, but he didn't say anything.

Amy stripped to her swimming costume while keeping up a steady commentary on the weather (cooler that day), the choice of crisp flavours at the corner shop (a sad absence of prawn cocktail), and the speed at which the holidays were disappearing (too fast). She was, I knew, trying to paper over the silence between me and Will, hoping that if she did it for long enough, we'd forget our annoyance with each other. He replied good-naturedly enough, but he didn't direct a single comment towards me. I kept my eyes studiously on the page, not taking in a word of what I was reading, grunting now and again to show Amy I appreciated her efforts.

When even Amy's fund of small talk had been exhausted, she announced she was going for a swim. I watched her walk to the edge of the ledge and sit down, then lower herself into the water. I saw Will watching and couldn't help myself.

'That okay with you?'

He turned and fixed me with his steady gaze. 'I meant what I said yesterday. You could have killed yourself.'

I swallowed, remembering the glimpse of that thing under the water, the pain in my leg. But I remembered that 'stupid' remark too. I wasn't about to let him off the hook.

'You didn't *say* it, though, did you?' I retorted. 'You screamed at me. And you were bloody rude.'

'I wasn't the only one.'

We glared at each other, and I was about to return to my book in disgust when he raised his hand.

'Okay, I'm sorry I shouted. I was worried, that's all.'

A little spark of something kindled in my chest. I waited for him to say something else, but he was looking out over the lake again.

I cleared my throat. 'Okay then. And I'm sorry too. For what I said, I mean.'

'But not for diving in.'

I hesitated. I liked Will – more than liked him. And I didn't want to risk our brief truce. But I wasn't having him think he could tell me what to do.

He'd turned to face me again, and I could see a smile twitching at the corner of his mouth. 'It's okay, Laura Fraser,' he said. 'I know how hard you find it to admit when you're wrong.'

There was an apple core on the ground next to him, and I grabbed it and chucked it at him. He ducked and swatted it away, and just like that, we were friends again.

'Stop that,' he said, 'or I won't show you what I've brought.'

Usually, Will travelled light, just a rolled-up towel and a book. But today, I noticed, there was a small rucksack next to his cast-off trainers.

'Well go on, then,' I said. 'Don't keep me in suspense.'

He reached into the bag and drew out a yellow cylinder, a few inches long. A cord with a toggle dangled from one end.

'What's that?'

He pointed it at me, and suddenly I was blinking, a bright light in my eyes.

'I hate to tell you this, but we don't need a torch in the middle of the day.'

He rolled his eyes. 'This isn't just any torch. It's a diving torch. It's waterproof.'

I looked at him blankly. 'Okaay...'

He reached into the bag again and brought out a plastic visor. I'd never seen one in the flesh before, but I knew what it was. 'A snorkelling mask.' And finally, I started to understand. 'So, you can see what's under the surface of the lake.'

'Very good,' he said. 'I knew you'd get there in the end. These are my dad's, and he doesn't know I've got them. So keep it under your hat, all right?'

Another secret to add to our list. I nodded, pleased.

'I know what you're like. So I thought you should see for yourself, so you know why it's stupid—' He saw my expression and stopped. 'Sorry. I mean, so you can see why it's not a good idea to dive here.'

'So you can win the argument, you mean.' But I pulled a face to show him I didn't mind.

I went over to him and took the torch, inspected it. 'So what are you waiting for?' I said, nodding towards the lake. 'Get down there and tell us where Nessie's hiding.'

He laughed. 'I think you've got the wrong idea, Laura Fraser. I'm not swimming underwater in that.'

I raised an eyebrow. 'I don't get it. What have you brought this stuff for, then?'

'I told you, you need to see for yourself.' He handed me the snorkelling mask. 'I'm not going down there. You are.'


How to describe my feelings as I stood on that ledge.

I tried to pretend I wasn't afraid. But I remembered the moment I'd dived into the lake, something pale and nameless reaching out to me. I could forget about it when I was swimming, keeping my eyes on the shore, telling myself there was nothing below me but rocks and a few bits of broken equipment. But sticking my head below the water, entering its domain, searching it out – that was another matter entirely.

Yet I was excited too. I wanted to see what was down there, in that mysterious world beneath the water. A load of junk, Will had said – but what if he was wrong? The site of the quarry, it was rumoured, had been used as far back as the Iron Age. What if I found coins or an ancient piece of jewellery? It was possible, after all – I'd heard about people turning up priceless artifacts in their fields or gardens. And I'd be the first person to search here for – well, since whenever they stopped digging, which had to be a few years ago at least.

'Are you sure about this?' Amy looked nervous. 'You'll be careful, won't you?'

'Course I will, Aims,' I said, wanting to put on a good show. 'I'll be fine.'

'Don't go down too far.' I could tell Will was having second thoughts. 'You don't want to get tangled up in anything. It's easy to get a hand or foot stuck in a bit of old machinery. And we'd never know it had happened until it was too late.'

Amy's expression turned from anxious to alarmed. 'What? Then why is she doing this at all?' She turned to me, took my arm. 'Please, Laura. This is crazy. Let's just go for a swim.'

I patted her hand. 'It'll be fine, I promise. I'll just take a quick look, see what's down there.'

She looked so unhappy I tried again. 'I'll come up every twenty seconds, so you can see I'm all right.' The idea made me feel better too. 'If I'm not back at the surface every twenty seconds, Will can come and find me. Right, Will?'

'Sure,' he said, but a moment later, 'There's only one torch, though.' He frowned. 'Maybe we should wait to do this until I get another one.'

Amy looked relieved. 'Yes, let's wait. Do this properly.'

'No way.' If I didn't do it now, I'd never be able to summon up the courage to go in later. 'We only need one torch.'

I pulled off my T-shirt before I could think better of it, and unbuttoned my jeans. I felt the familiar surge of self-conscious-ness, hurrying to get into the water where neither of them would see my pale skin and bony hips.

'What's that?' Will's voice was stern, and I turned to see him pointing at my leg. 'Did you do that yesterday?'

The bruise looked even worse today, a livid splodge of crimson and purple across the side of my calf. 'Not here. I hit it on a door.'

He looked like he was about to question me further, so I grabbed the mask and torch and slid into the lake, treading water while I pulled the mask onto my head.

'Ready?' said Will.

I switched on the torch and a thin shaft of gold pierced the water. Tiny flecks danced in the beam.

'I can't see much,' I said doubtfully.

'It'll be easier with the mask,' Will said. 'You'll see better when you're under the water.'

'You do it, then,' I grumbled under my breath – but if he heard me, he didn't reply.

'Every twenty seconds, remember, Laura. I'll be counting.' Amy held out her arm, showing me her watch.

'Got it,' I said. And then, because there didn't seem to be much else to do, I rolled my shoulders forward in the water and pushed down beneath the surface.

# TWENTY-SIX

*Now*

I've never been one of those people who claim their whole life is on their phone. My life, such as it is, is in the real world – or at least, the world I think is real, which may or may not be the same thing. But now, sitting on the train heading south across the city, I feel the absence of that little bit of metal like a missing limb. It's turned off – I think it is, anyway. Darren (I eventually discovered that's what the first 'D' in DDM Solutions stands for) told me that hackers can switch it on remotely. So for good measure, it's in a kitchen drawer, shut up tight so no one can see anything if they switch the camera on. They can do that too, apparently. The thought of it makes me feel sick.

And yet, in a weird way, the knowledge that someone has tampered with my phone is a relief too. I shouldn't feel this way, I know. It means Marina's in danger and no one's doing anything to help her. But it's also proof that I can trust the evidence of my own senses. I'm not going mad. I haven't been dreaming up a whole world of fake characters and events. I know what's real and what isn't. And if DC Hollis doesn't believe me now, she will. I'm going to find a way to make her.

The train slows and I get to my feet, watching lamp posts and tarmac replace trees and the backs of houses as we ease into the station. It's the middle of the day, and I'm the only person to disembark. I wait until the train has left to be sure I'm alone; I no longer believe I imagined being followed the last time I was here. But the platform is empty, and I make my way to the exit.

I try to plan what I'm going to say as I walk to the bookshop. I can't decide if I want Tabitha to be there or not. If she is, I won't have to go back to square one to explain everything. I will, though, have to ask for a copy of an image she told me I wasn't allowed to take in the first place. It's a tough call.

I pass the ridiculous grocery shop – today's special, calçots, whatever they might be – and steal a last glance over my shoulder. There's a Lycra-clad jogger, a couple of young women engrossed in conversation. They don't seem interested in me.

I push open the door to the bookshop, and flinch at the jangling bell. There are a few customers browsing the shelves, and I check them out surreptitiously as I make my way to the back. A tall woman in the young adult fiction section briefly makes me catch my breath, but a second glance shows me she's nothing like Marina. I turn and enter the corridor of books, heading for the cash desk. There's another woman there, paying for her purchase. It gives me a chance to check who's behind the till. It's Tabitha.

A few seconds pass before she notices me, and I see something in her expression change. Last time I was here, she couldn't get me out of the door fast enough, so I wasn't expecting a warm welcome. But if I'm not very much mistaken, she *almost* smiled at me. I smile back tentatively, and sidle over to a bookcase to wait for her to finish with her customer. Maybe she's been worried about Marina too, wants to do whatever she can to help find her. Perhaps this is going to be easier than I thought.

Tabitha is handing the woman a paper bag, telling her to let her know what she thinks about her book. I step forward as she leaves.

'Hello again. Tabitha, isn't it? Thanks so much for your help the other day.'

'I'm pleased you've come back,' she says. Now this I did *not* expect. 'I was actually thinking of giving you a ring.'

'Oh?' I raise my eyebrows, my script for the meeting temporarily abandoned.

'Yes, I wanted to tell you. That customer you were asking about – Marina, wasn't it?'

I nod, my heart suddenly in my mouth. 'Has she been in touch?'

She smiles. 'She's been unwell, apparently. Covid or something, by the sound of it.'

'Marina?' I repeat dumbly.

'That's why she couldn't collect her order.'

'The book I ended up buying? The one about the caves?' I'm so shocked that for a moment the title deserts me.

'Yes, dear,' Tabitha says patiently. 'So you see, there's nothing to worry about. She's fine now, apparently. He was very apologetic about it.'

Her choice of pronoun cuts through the thoughts whirling around my head. 'He? What do you mean, "he"?'

'Her husband. He came in yesterday. It was rather embarrassing, really, that we no longer had the book.' Her smile cools a degree, and I can tell she holds me responsible. 'But he was very understanding. They bought something else for the niece, apparently.'

'What did he look like?'

The smile fades completely. 'I can't tell you that.'

'Oh, come on!' The thin thread that's been holding my self-control in place abruptly snaps. 'I've told you, Marina could be in danger. I don't give a shit about GDPR!'

I'm aware that it's gone quiet in the shop.

'There's no call for that kind of language.' Tabitha folds her arms, fixes me with a steely glare. 'I can't tell you what he looked like because I didn't see him. He spoke to one of my colleagues.'

My eyes travel automatically to the door marked *Private*. 'Okay, who was it? Can I talk to them?'

'He's not here right now.' She sees what I'm about to ask and cuts me off. 'He's not working today.'

I force myself to stay calm. None of this is Tabitha's fault.

'I'm sorry,' I say, and I lower my voice. 'It's just that I have very good reason for thinking that man wasn't Marina's husband.'

'But he was.'

'How can you know that?'

Her fingertips drum against her folded arms. 'He knew about her ordering the book. He came in to apologise for not collecting it. What possible reason would he have for doing that if he wasn't who he said he was?'

For a brief moment, I don't have an answer. But then it comes to me. 'So it would look like everything was all right. So it would look like Marina is fine, and I'm making a fuss over nothing.'

I recognise the look that comes into her eyes then. It's the same one DC Hollis wore when I told her that man must have cleared the kitchen at Flyte Gardens. She doesn't believe a word I'm saying. The time for discretion has been and gone. I can't afford to hold anything back now if I'm going to convince her.

'That video of Marina here, it was the only piece of evidence I had,' I say. 'I had the image enhanced. She had an

envelope in her bag that day, an envelope with her address
on it—'

'I'm sorry, what?'

'I went to the address, and I could see someone had been
kept chained up there—' Tabitha is shaking her head, but I keep
going before she can interrupt. 'I called the police, but by the
time they got there, everything was back to normal. Whoever
was keeping Marina a prisoner had cleared away the evidence.'

'What do you mean you had the image enhanced? What
image?'

'That's not what's important here—'

'Did you copy our CCTV file?' She's turned white.

'No, I just took a photo. But then someone hacked my
phone, and it's gone. So I need to take another one.'

She's staring at me, lost for words.

'I'm sorry,' I say. 'I know it was against your rules. But a
woman's life is in danger. And whoever has her, they're trying
to cover their tracks.'

For a moment, she doesn't reply. Then she shakes her head.
'This is unbelievable.'

'I know that's how it sounds. But please, even if you think
I'm probably crazy, wouldn't it be better not to take the chance?
If Marina has really been kidnapped or hurt, wouldn't it be
better to do everything you can to help her?'

She looks suddenly tired. I know how she feels. 'I'm sorry,'
she says, 'There's nothing I can do.'

'Just let me look at the CCTV again. I don't need the whole
file. I can just take a photo. No one will know. It'll only take a
second, and I'll leave you alone.'

She shakes her head. 'I can't help you. The CCTV has been
deleted.'

For a second, I think I haven't heard her properly. But she's
still talking.

'I did it yesterday, after my colleague told me the husband

had been in. I told you, we can't keep footage forever. It's against the law.'

I could cry. How can this be happening? The only evidence of Marina, or whatever her real name is, and it's gone. It must have been the man from the train who came here, pretending to be her husband. And he's got what he wanted, hasn't he? Any evidence connecting her to what I saw that day has been destroyed.

But then something else occurs to me. Maybe everything isn't lost after all.

'That man, the one who said he was Marina's husband. He came in yesterday, you said?'

She nods. 'He was in early. I had a doctor's appointment, so I wasn't here.'

'But there'll be footage of him, right?' I point to the camera above us. 'If he came to the desk?'

But she's shaking her head. 'No, there's no footage.' She lowers her voice to almost a whisper. 'The cameras stopped working a few days ago. We've called an engineer, but he's not coming until next week.'

I almost laugh. It's so perfect. I'm a day too late to rescue the only image of Marina. And when the man who's almost certainly holding her captive comes in here, he's not on the CCTV because the bloody equipment has chosen this week to pack up.

Except of course that's not what happened.

'He did it,' I say. Tabitha looks at me questioningly. 'The man who has Marina. He knew you had her on camera, and he knew I'd be back after he'd deleted my copy from my phone. Maybe he was planning to do the same thing to your system – find a way of hacking into it and deleting the file. Except you saved him the trouble. But before he could do any of that, he had to make sure he wouldn't be captured on CCTV himself. So he found some way of sabotaging it.'

I hear it: the manic note in my voice, the craziness of the words that are coming out of my mouth. And how much crazier would it sound if I told her the rest? That I'm starting to think the man who's taken Marina is out to get me too?

Tabitha stares at me. 'I just don't see how...' She takes a breath. 'I'm really finding this all very difficult to believe.'

And then I do laugh, because what else is there to do? 'Yeah, you and everybody else.'

On the way out, the same woman is still browsing the young adult fiction section. 'Try *The Caves of Agoroth*,' I tell her. 'It's supposed to be a real page turner.'

The doorbell jingles goodbye, and I step out onto the pavement with absolutely no idea what to do next.

# TWENTY-SEVEN

*Then*

I didn't find buried treasure in the lake that day. I didn't find a monster either. What I found instead turned out to be depressingly ordinary: a metal container from the back of a dumper truck – a 'dump box', Will told me, was its unpoetical name. It had come to rest at an angle close to where I'd dived. One step to the left, and I'd never have touched it. I'd been unlucky, and must have kicked against it as I swam to the surface.

When I first caught sight of it, looming out of the darkness in the mustard light of the dive torch, its sheer bulk had made me start. But it looked nothing like my memory of what I'd seen before I'd hit the water. This thing was solid, inorganic. A hunk of rusting metal that could give you a nasty bruise but had nothing supernatural about it. I resurfaced and reported my findings to Amy and Will, before swimming back down to take a second look.

The container was, I thought, about sixteen feet long, perhaps eight feet wide. At one corner was a jagged gash, probably the reason it had been confined to its watery grave. The surface was dark, possibly green, though it was hard to tell for sure in the dim light of the torch. And then something shifted in the darkness.

It took every fibre of self-control I possessed not to open my mouth and scream. I jerked backwards in the water, kicking hard away from the long, sinewy limbs that stretched towards me. But as I pushed upwards towards the surface, the beam of the torch illuminated the water below, showing me my mistake.

I broke the surface gasping and spluttering. Amy was instantly on high alert, demanding to know what was wrong. It took me a second to catch my breath, and when I tried to speak, I found myself laughing instead.

'What is it?' asked Will, bemused. 'What's so funny?'

'Nothing,' I said, the relief of it keeping me giggling like a loon. 'I just thought I saw something creepy down there.'

Amy frowned. 'I don't get it.'

'But it wasn't. Anything creepy, I mean. It was just some weed on the side of the container. It looked like arms, but it was just weed.' I could see from their faces this was one of those 'you had to be there' moments. 'Sorry,' I gulped. 'All fine now.'

After that, I was fearless. I circled the lake, swimming a few feet below the surface, shining my torch into the depths. I could see rocks at the bottom, but it was hard to judge how far that was. I considered trying to swim down, but Will was the expert at that kind of thing, not me. Besides, there was only one question I was interested in, and the answer to that was already clear.

'There's no problem diving here,' I told them. 'The water's plenty deep enough. And that metal thing—'

'Dump box,' Will corrected me.

'Whatever, it's the only thing down here. As long as we stand further along the ledge, we'll be fine.'

Will looked doubtful, so I held out the snorkelling mask to him.

'Take a look yourself if you don't believe me.'

He took it from me. 'We should all see it,' he said. 'If we're going to dive, we should all know where it is. Make sure we stay well away from it.'

I nodded, pleased that he'd tacitly agreed the diving was on. But Amy was biting her lip. 'I'm no good at swimming underwater,' she said. 'But it's okay. I can't dive either.' She laughed, but I could see she wasn't happy.

'That doesn't matter,' I said. 'I promised I'd teach you, didn't I? And I know where the dump thing is, so that's okay.'

Will wrinkled his nose. 'I don't think this is the place for beginners.'

'Why not?' I demanded. 'The water's deep. There's no one else here to get in the way. She can take her time. What's the problem?'

I could see he didn't like it, but he couldn't think of a reason to object either.

'What do you reckon then, Aims?' I could see she was prevaricating, so I moved to the ledge, positioned myself carefully out of the way of any potential collisions. 'It's easy. Look!'

I turned and leapt, higher than I had the previous day, hitting the water more steeply. I was showboating a bit, I'll admit it, but it was something about that moment – the air, the heat, the relief that Will and I weren't arguing anymore. I was filled with a sudden sense of freedom. *This* I could do.

When I broke the surface, Will clapped his hands slowly. 'Very good, Laura Fraser,' he said.

But Amy looked more nervous than ever. 'I'm happy just watching,' she said. 'Really, it's fine.'

I swam to the edge and pulled myself onto the rocks. For once I didn't mind that my legs were white and skinny, or that my swimming costume was losing the elastic in its straps. Will was already sitting on the ledge, pulling the snorkelling mask over his head.

'To the right a bit,' I said, and he shuffled over and pointed to the water.

'Here okay?'

I nodded, and the next moment he'd slid beneath the surface, vanishing from view in a small cloud of bubbles. I took a seat on my towel and waited for him to reappear. It took just a few seconds, and one look at his grinning face told me the argument was won.

'Fair enough,' he said, boosting himself up and out onto the ledge in a way those of us with shorter legs could only dream of. 'Time to show you what a proper dive looks like.' And with that he arched his back and flipped over in a backwards roll that sent a burst of spray glittering into the air.

A few drops landed on Amy and me, and she shivered.

'Ignore him,' I said. 'We don't have to do anything like that.' I pointed to a large rock further along. 'We could dive from there. It's a bit lower, and it's miles from that metal thing. You could go in at whatever angle you wanted, and you wouldn't hit anything.'

I saw her weighing up her options.

'You can take your time, go at your own pace. Honestly, if you want to learn to dive, you won't get a better chance than this. Up to you, though.'

I left her to mull it over, returning to what I was already thinking of as my favourite dive spot. 'Watch this!' I called to Will. I waited until he'd turned and was treading water before I attempted my own forward roll. It was inexpertly done, my body still in a ball as I hit the water. But when I returned laughing to the edge, Amy was standing there, a determined set to her jaw.

'Okay then,' she said. 'Let's do this.'

Amy, I already knew, was a conscientious student. So perhaps I shouldn't have been surprised that, having accepted my offer of diving lessons, she made sure they happened.

That first day, I'd been filled with enthusiasm, revelling in my unusual role as teacher. We started well away from the water's edge, Amy watching attentively as I demonstrated how to bend at the knees, position her arms at shoulder level. 'Point your fingers,' I instructed, as if I were an Olympic medallist instead of the graduate of a Spanish swimming club where I'd been despatched by my parents to give them more time to argue. 'You'll make less of a splash.'

She nodded gravely, copying my stance. When I suggested it was time to try it for real, she followed me to the lake with an expression that wouldn't have been out of place on a death row prisoner making the lonely walk to the executioner's chair.

'You'll be fine, Aims,' I told her. 'The first time is always the scariest.'

She ducked her head in what I took to be agreement, and positioned herself on the rock I'd selected for the occasion. Will was sitting across from us on the ledge, apparently reading; but I could feel his eyes on us as I directed her final preparations.

'That's it. Bend a little more at the knees. Look at where you're going to enter the water. Got it?' She bobbed her head again. 'Good. When you're ready, take a deep breath and go.'

She didn't move. I saw that her jaw was clenched, and her arms trembled gently. It occurred to me that she was genuinely scared.

'It's okay if you don't want to do it,' I said softly. I saw her eyes dart in Will's direction, 'And you don't need to worry about what *he* thinks—'

But I found myself talking to thin air as Amy launched herself forward.

She listed slightly to the left as she flew through the air, but avoided the belly flop I'd secretly suspected was coming. As soon as she regained the surface she struck out for the side, reaching for the nearest overhanging rock and clinging to it, blinking and opening and closing her mouth like a fish.

'Go, Amy!' I shouted. But it was Will she turned towards.

'Not half bad, Linton,' he said, and she broke into a smile of pure delight. It was like sunshine after a storm, and I saw something change in his expression. I couldn't put a name to it, but it left me with a sick, queasy feeling in my stomach.

As soon as she was out of the water, she wanted to try again.

Her enthusiasm seemed only to grow, and the next day she was back on the rock, pressing me for my view on her performance.

'I want to get better,' she told me. 'I want to be able to do that thing you did.' She gestured with her hands, miming a forward roll.

'Sure,' I replied, 'only don't push yourself too hard.'

I, of course, had no wish for her to improve too far or too fast. There was precious little in which I could compete with Amy, much less outshine her. The idea of relinquishing my slim advantage in the water didn't appeal.

Worse still was the way Will was behaving. Several times as she practised, I caught him watching her. I tried to tell myself he was just taking a friendly interest, but a little voice inside told me I was fooling myself.

Yet I still hoped that disaster could be averted. The holidays were wearing on, I reasoned, and Will would feel awkward about making a move that could only disrupt our easy friendship. We'd soon be back at school, our daily trips to the lake a thing of the past. Will and Amy would see less of each other; the danger would pass.

I suppose that's even the way it might have gone, if it hadn't been for Chloe Lambert's party.

# TWENTY-EIGHT

*Now*

Tuesday evening. The day before Sam told Guy I'd be back at work, and I have the familiar sinking feeling that accompanies the prospect of returning to the office. I turned on my phone earlier, just for a minute, and there was the predictable message from Guy. He expected to see me first thing in the morning. If I was unable to attend, I should contact him directly to explain why. It was not sufficient to inform a colleague. A note from my doctor would be required.

The message was clear: anything short of decapitation would be considered an inadequate reason for another day off work.

There followed a series of bullet points listing my absences over the course of the year, a column at the end giving a cumulative total of days off. I had to agree it didn't look good.

It doesn't change anything, though. I can't spend my time chasing someone's delayed catalogue order while Marina is out there in danger. I'll put things right with Guy when I find her, when I know she's finally safe. When I know I'm safe too.

But how do I do that? I glance at the drawer where I've stowed my phone. Perhaps even now the man on the train is staring at a dark screen somewhere, waiting for the moment I switch it on again and open a window into my life.

Now that I know he's hacked my phone, it's not hard to believe he broke into my flat too. Who knows how long he was here, creeping around my home while I slept? Yet all he did was leave that message. I try to take comfort in that, but I can't. Maybe he thought attacking me was too high risk, worried that I'd scream and wake the neighbours. Better to do what he did with Marina: make me quietly disappear, find a way to do it so that no one even believes anything is wrong.

My stomach rumbles loudly, interrupting my train of thought. I haven't eaten properly for days, can't face even the idea of food. But I know I can't go on like this. I need my strength for whatever comes next.

I'm halfway to the kitchen when an electronic trill makes me jump. The doorbell.

I freeze. It's just after six, but it's dark outside. I wait, my heart in my mouth. Seconds pass. Perhaps they've given up. But then there's another trill, longer this time, like whoever it is knows I'm in. I could pretend they're wrong, cower here and hope they go away. But what if it's the man from the train? What if he thinks the coast is clear to break in like he did before?

I grab a knife from the block on the counter and reach for the handset on the wall.

'Who is it?' I try to sound confident.

'Hey, Laura. It's me, Sam.'

I sag in relief, and it takes me a moment to find my voice.

'I'm sorry,' he says, probably interpreting my silence as annoyance. 'I know I should have called first, but I was just around the corner. Can I come in?'

I hesitate, remembering the evening I almost invited him in.

I don't want to give him the wrong idea. But he's just checking in on me, like a good friend. And there's comfort in the prospect of not being alone.

'Come on up,' I say. The moment I put down the handset, I throw the knife on the counter and rush to the front door to dismantle the barricade. I remove the pans and crockery from the chair and dump them on the bed, then pull the bedroom door shut behind me. I've just carried the chair back to its usual place when I hear his knock.

I open the door and see Sam's brow immediately furrow in concern. 'You okay? You look – harried.'

'Just moving some furniture,' I say, then realise this isn't the kind of thing a woman with flu is supposed to be doing.

He raises a hand with a carrier bag in it. 'I know you said you didn't need anything. I'll take it back with me if you don't want it.'

I take the bag. There's a loaf of bread, a couple of pints of milk, cheese, and a box of eggs. 'You're an angel,' I tell him, and he smiles awkwardly. My stomach rumbles again. 'Do you fancy an omelette?'

Too late I realise he might not want food cooked by someone who supposedly has flu – but he accepts readily enough. I direct him to a seat at the dining table while I get started on the food. He sits obediently and makes polite small talk, asking how I am, telling me there are a lot of colds going around. 'Half the office is coughing and spluttering,' he says, getting to his feet and examining the contents of my bookcase. 'Have you read all these?'

'Most of them,' I say. He runs an index finger along the spines, and I'm reminded of someone else. I clear my throat. 'Do you like a lot of cheese?'

'Just a bit, please.' Everything in moderation with Sam. 'Is one of these the book Marina ordered?'

He's still standing at the bookcase, his back to me.

'No,' I say. 'That's in the bedroom.' *Complete with a message threatening to expose me.*

He pushes his hands into his pockets. 'You're still worried about her, aren't you?'

Worried, I think, doesn't even come close. I put down the grater. 'I just don't know what to do.'

I feel myself welling up, and turn away, pretending I need something from a cupboard. When I turn back, he's there in front of me, holding out his arms. I stiffen, but then something inside me breaks and I'm crying into his shoulder, heaving, snotty sobs that are probably making a mess of his jumper.

A minute later I pull away. 'God, I'm sorry.'

He lets me go but places a hand on my arm. 'Don't be. You're allowed to be upset.'

I go to retrieve the grater, but he takes it from me.

'Sit yourself down. I'll finish these.'

I know I should argue, but I don't have the energy, so instead I thank him and do as I'm told. He doesn't say much as he cooks, and I'm grateful. It's nice just to have him here, to sit quietly while he moves efficiently around the kitchen.

He brings two glasses of water and two plates to the table, a neat golden semicircle of omelette on each one. When I touch my plate, I discover that he's warmed it. I'm about to joke that he'll make someone a lovely husband one day, then tell myself to shut up.

We eat in silence, and I'm starting to feel I should make an effort at conversation when he says, 'So tell me what really happened.'

The words are so similar to the message in the book that I put down my fork and stare at him. But he goes on cutting his omelette, oblivious to the effect he's had. As far as he's concerned, I remind myself, I've been tucked up in bed with a cold for the last few days. He doesn't know about my abortive visit to the bookshop, far less about someone breaking into the flat.

'You went to that house,' he clarifies. 'You were trying to find Marina. You sounded weird when I asked you about it.'

I pretend I'm still chewing to give myself time to formulate a reply. I thought I'd done a pretty good job of hiding my feelings when he'd phoned, but Sam's more perceptive than most. I should have guessed he'd have picked up that something was wrong.

'Did I?'

'You sounded like you were about to cry.'

I try to think of an excuse but come up blank. And then I realise: I don't want to keep this from Sam. He's only ever tried to help me. There has to be a way to tell him the truth – some of it, at least – without raking over every lurid detail of my past.

'I'm going to tell you something, and you're probably going to think I'm mad,' I say.

He shakes his head. 'I'd never think that.'

I grimace. 'Let's revisit that in ten minutes.'

And then I tell him about Flyte Gardens, about the empty house with the ramp and the handrails, the comments from the neighbour about the old lady Marina lived with. About going back there for one last look, finding the door open at the back. I describe the kitchen, that plastic chair with the chains and padlock. When I start to tell him about the camera, I realise I'm struggling to catch my breath. It rushes back again, that wave of dread: *Marina was there.* It was days ago, and the best I can hope for is that that man has moved her somewhere else. The worst? I can't think about it.

Sam has left his seat and is crouching next to my chair. He takes my hand. 'Breathe, Laura. Don't talk, just breathe.'

I struggle to comply, taking gulps of air.

'With me,' he commands, and starts to count. 'In, two, three, four; out, two three, four.'

I watch his shoulders rise and fall, and gradually I find my breathing returning to normal. Sam hands me my glass of water. 'Here, take a sip of this.'

When I put down the glass, he says, 'What are the police doing about it?'

I can't look at him. I don't want to see the moment he changes his mind about everything I've told him. The moment he changes his mind about me.

'DC Hollis came straight away,' I tell him. 'But when she got there, everything was gone.'

'What do you mean, "gone"?'

'What I said. All the stuff – the chair, the water bottles, it had gone. It was like it had never been there.'

He gets to his feet. Too late, I realise he might feel he has to tell Guy I've lost the plot, warn him I'm in no state to be at work. Unless I make him understand, I'm going to lose that shitty job. And I'm going to lose Sam too.

'Jesus, Laura,' he says. 'You do realise what you're saying?'

My mind is racing, searching for a way out, but I already know there isn't one. I'll have to tell him about the dead mouse, about the message left for me in the book. And then I'll have to tell him what they mean.

I take a deep breath. 'I know it sounds crazy, but last night—'

Sam cuts across me. 'Whoever was holding her there must have moved everything. So they must have seen you go into the house. And they must have known when you left.'

For a moment, I can't speak. He believes me. Even without knowing the rest of it, he believes me.

'You were in real danger.' He looks shaken. 'Thank God you're okay.'

'I'm fine,' I say automatically. I'm so grateful he doesn't think I'm crazy that for the moment nothing else matters.

'They must have been watching the place.' He frowns.

'That camera, I'm guessing. They must have been able to view the footage remotely. But why was it there if they'd already taken Marina somewhere else? And why bother still checking it?'

It's a good question; why didn't I think of it myself? 'Maybe he left in a hurry,' I say slowly. 'Perhaps he thought I might turn up there, so he moved Marina. He didn't have time to get rid of all the stuff, but he was keeping watch. Then he saw me arrive and knew he had to shift it straight away.'

Sam nods. 'How long did it take for the police to arrive?'

'About thirty minutes. It was DC Hollis. She came on her own. Thought I was hallucinating or something.'

'You can't be serious?' Sam looks appalled. 'But that means they – he – must have been close by.'

He's right, of course. I was a sitting duck waiting for DC Hollis outside that house. And it was the same last night, when he broke into my flat. How much longer before my luck runs out? But I don't have time to dwell on that, because Sam is still talking.

'So why did he think you might turn up there? How did you find the address?'

I explain about persuading Tabitha to show me the CCTV from the bookshop, seeing the envelope slide from Marina's bag. I tell him about paying Darren to get the image enhanced.

Sam looks up sharply. 'Who's Darren?'

'Just some guy I found online. He does stuff with photos, enhances the detail.' I tell Sam about that day in the park, handing over the money. 'It all felt a bit silly, but he did a good job. He sent me the image and I could read what it said on the envelope: Marina Leeson, 21 Flyte Gardens.'

'Can I see it?'

'If only. It's gone. Someone hacked my phone.'

Sam's jaw drops. 'You're joking, right?'

I explain about the missing photo, about asking Darren for a copy and how he'd explained my phone had probably been hacked. Sam listens carefully, an expression on his face I can't read. When I've finished, he says, 'This guy, Darren. Are you're sure he's legit?'

I laugh in spite of myself. 'Depends what you mean by "legit". He insisted on being paid in cash, so I'm not sure he's on good terms with the tax man.'

But Sam doesn't smile. 'He's the one who gave you that address, right? Then the photo it was supposedly taken from disappears, and he tells you your phone's been hacked.'

I look at him blankly. 'I'm not following you.'

'What if he's in on it?'

'What?'

'He could have doctored that photo, come up with the address to lure you there. Set up the scene, knowing you'd come to check it out, call the police. Then he – or the other guy, the one on the train – swings into action, clears it all away so when the police turn up, they think you're wasting their time. They're never going to listen to anything you say after that, are they?'

I think about it. There's a kind of logic, but it all seems so convoluted. 'That seems high risk,' I say. 'It would be easier, surely, just to tell me he couldn't do anything with the photo.'

'But what if you'd persisted, tried someone else? This way, they'd keep everything under their control.'

I'm about to voice another objection when Sam clicks his fingers again. 'How did you get into the house? If there was no one there, how did you get in?'

I shift uncomfortably. 'The back door was unlocked,' I say.

He leans back in his chair and folds his arms. 'It was a set-up.'

I stare at him. 'I googled Darren. *I* approached *him*, not the other way around. And okay, the back door was unlocked, but there was a side gate with a padlock. You had to get past that to get to the back.' I answer the question before he can ask it. 'I picked the lock.'

He raises an eyebrow but doesn't pursue it. 'Okay, just think about it though. The guy from the train knows you've seen him with Marina. He knows you're asking questions – maybe he's scouting out the bookshop.'

'Why would he do that? If he knew Marina had written a note, he'd have taken it from her. There'd be no reason to worry about anyone connecting her to the bookshop.'

For a second, he doesn't reply – but then he clicks his fingers again. 'You saw him on your way into work, right? What if he guessed you were commuting, kept an eye out for you. Same time, same route. He gets lucky. He follows you. Sees you go to the bookshop. Maybe he follows you in—'

'No,' I interrupt firmly. 'It's a small place. I'd have noticed him. And there's a bell on the door – makes a real racket whenever it's opened. No one followed me in.'

*But maybe he followed me out.*

'What is it?' Sam asks. 'Have you thought of something?'

I shake my head, remembering how sure I'd been that someone was behind me as I walked away from the shop. 'I'm not sure. Keep going.'

'Okay, maybe he goes back after you've left, gets talking to the woman in the shop. Pretends he knows you. Fishes for information. She lets slip that you've been asking about Marina. Maybe she even tells him you wanted to look at the CCTV.'

I shake my head again. 'I can't see Tabitha doing something like that. And even if she had, she'd have told me when I saw her again. Just like she told me about the guy pretending to be Marina's husband.'

Sam's eyes widen. 'What guy?'

'Let's come back to that.'

He looks like he's going to press me, but then he nods. 'Okay, so he sees you go into the bookshop. Maybe he talks to this Tabitha woman, and maybe he doesn't. But he sees the CCTV camera. And he knows Marina, knows her routines – knows that she goes there. He puts two and two together.'

'This feels like a huge stretch.' I hear myself say it and instantly feel bad. I'm used to being the one on the receiving end of comments like that. But Sam is undeterred.

'How did you get the CCTV footage to Darren? Did you message him? Email? Flash drive?'

'I emailed him. He emailed me back.' He watches me absorb the significance of what I've just said. 'I opened his email.'

'Exactly. That's how the spyware got onto your system. And at the same time, he – or the other guy – doctors the photo to give you a convenient address, somewhere he knows is empty. Somewhere he'll have time to set up a fake scene. He sets up the camera and waits. Maybe the other guy is following you, gives him the heads up when you're on your way. You get there, you see what they want you to. You call the police. The rest is history. You've lost all credibility.'

I sit there, my brain buzzing. Could it really have been like that? 'But it was Darren who told me I'd been hacked,' I say. 'Why would he do that if he was the one doing the hacking?'

Sam doesn't seem fazed. 'Maybe he thought you'd figure it out anyway. This way, he throws you off the scent. It's the only explanation that makes sense. It's a set-up. And he was in on the whole thing.'

But there's still something bothering me. 'But how? I found his number online. I called him. That was all me.'

Sam presses his fingertips to his temples. 'Okay, maybe he hacked you *before* you phoned him. The guy from the train follows you, sees you go to the bookshop, finds out who you are. He sends you an email with some kind of virus – or he gets this Darren guy to do it. Some bit of spam you click on without realising.'

Something occurs to me. 'I left my email address with Tabitha, that first time I went to the bookshop. I asked her to contact me if Marina came back.'

'There you go!' Sam slaps the table. 'So they get that virus on your system, and when you put in the right search term, you're directed to a fake website. Enter Darren.'

'Do viruses really work like that?'

Sam shrugs. 'I bet they can do pretty much anything with the right programming.'

I take another sip of water, trying to think. Bizarre though it is, there's some kernel of what feels like truth in what Sam's saying. If this is how it really happened, the man on the train has gone to a huge amount of effort. Yet if there's a chance he's known who I am from the start, why is he doing it? Why do I matter so much to him?

And then there's Darren. Try as I might, I can't see him as a criminal mastermind. I just can't.

Sam studies me from across the table. 'You don't buy it. That's okay. Just stay away from him. Don't trust a word he says.'

I tell him I'll be careful, and I mean it. The man from the train is out there, and whether he's working with someone else or not, it's pretty clear he has me in his sights. I can't afford to let down my guard.

But in spite of all that, something inside me feels lighter. Because Sam believes me. He believed me even without knowing about the dead mouse or the break-in, about the message in the book. He would have believed me even when I doubted myself. And he understands that I'm in danger. So I'm not going to complicate things by telling him the rest of it. Sam has never been to Gramwell, doesn't know any of the people I knew back then. If there's a connection between Marina and what happened ten years ago, he'll never find it. That's up to me. But at least now I know I'm not alone.

# TWENTY-NINE

*Then*

We'd been at the lake for about an hour before Amy raised the subject. The three of us were sitting in our usual triangle on the ledge: Amy, then me, a little further from the water, then Will. She'd been for a swim, and the water had crimped her hair into waves.

'What do you think of Chloe Lambert?' she asked, apropos of nothing.

I shrugged. Chloe was in our year at school, a tall girl with dark eyes and a bad case of resting bitch face. She had an older brother called Ben who sometimes collected her from school on the back of his motorbike, bestowing a level of cool that ensured we had very little to do with each other.

'She's okay, I guess,' I said. 'Why do you ask?'

Will spoke without looking up from his book. 'You're thinking of going to the party, then?'

I turned to him in surprise. 'What party?'

It was Amy who replied. 'She's having a thing at her house on the weekend.'

'Oh yeah?' I tried to sound as if I didn't care that I was apparently the only one who hadn't heard about it.

'I thought I might go. Do you fancy it?'

She was looking at me as she said it, and I shrugged. 'Haven't been invited.'

'You don't need an invitation! Chloe said to pass the word around. It's not like there's a guest list or anything.'

*Chloe said.* Presumably, then, she'd texted Amy to ask her. I felt a little stab of jealousy. 'Right,' I said.

'So what do you think? Do you want to go?'

Sometimes, I thought, Amy was too innocent for her own good. I was sure Chloe would expect anyone 'passing the word around' to understand that a minimal level of social status was a prerequisite for admission. While Amy might reach the bar, I seriously doubted I did.

'I think I've got a family thing,' I said.

'Oh, right.' Amy sounded deflated.

'I'm going, Linton.'

I turned to Will in surprise. 'You never go to parties.'

He shrugged. 'Sometimes I do.'

'*You're* going to Chloe Lambert's party?'

'It's Ben's party too,' he replied, aggrieved. Ben, I remembered now, had been in the same year as Will before leaving school. 'You can come with me, if you like.'

This last was directed at Amy, his tone light and his eyes firmly on his book. My eyes cut to Amy in time to see her blush.

'I'll come with you, Aims,' I cut in hurriedly, 'if you really want to go.'

'I thought you had a thing?' Was I imagining an edge of irritation in Will's voice?

'I can get out of it,' I said.

'Don't get into a row with your mum, though.' Amy looked concerned, but whether she was worried about my family relationships or the vanishing prospect of a date with Will, I couldn't tell.

'It's fine,' I said firmly. 'I'll just tell her I have plans.'

'The mouse can roar, can she?'

For a moment I thought I couldn't have heard him properly. 'What did you say?'

'That's what she calls you, isn't it? Your mum?' He was laughing.

I stared at Amy, but she wouldn't look at me.

'Don't sweat it, Laura Fraser. I like your hair.' I felt a warm bubble of pleasure. 'Not all girls can be blonde goddesses like Linton.'

The bubble burst abruptly, and to my horror, my eyes filled with tears. I picked up my book to hide my face, to block his view of my stupid, ugly hair. The two of them carried on talking, as if nothing had happened. And that, I finally understood as I pressed my hand to my flaming cheek, was exactly the way it was: compared to Amy, I was nothing.

I wanted to go home, to sit in my room and lick my wounds. But as I was formulating an excuse to leave, Amy stood and turned to me, flicked that superior hair over her shoulder, and pronounced it time for her diving lesson. I opened my mouth to tell her I had to get back, but instead found myself nodding dumbly, getting to my feet and following her to the rock that had become our regular dive spot.

I watched as she readied herself, then launched into the water. She was getting better, there was no denying it. She no longer listed to one side or the other, and her limbs were almost straight as she entered the lake. After one of her better efforts, she was smiling as she scrambled back up the rocks. 'That was okay, wasn't it?'

I nodded, trying to seem enthusiastic. 'Just remember to keep your head down.'

'Can we try something different?'

I knew at once what she had in mind, and my heart sank. 'You want to do a forward roll.'

Amy grinned. 'You looked so cool.'

I looked down at our chosen rock. The spot was fine for a beginner's dive, but it wasn't far enough above the water for tricks. 'Not here,' I said. 'You'd need to dive from higher up.'

I thought that would put her off, but instead she said, 'How much higher?'

In truth, I didn't know. I thought about guessing, but then common sense kicked in. 'Let me look it up,' I said. 'And wherever we dive from, I should check it out properly first.'

'But you did your dive from here.' Her tone wasn't petulant, exactly, but there was a challenge in it I hadn't heard from her before.

'I knew what I was doing,' I said. 'Trust me, you need time above the water, or you'll end up hitting your bum. Take it from me, it hurts.'

She gave me a long look, and I wondered if she might argue. But then she nodded. 'Okay. Check what you need to, and then show me how to do it.'

It was more of a statement than a question. 'Sure,' I said, but she was already walking back to the rock. I watched as she readied herself for another dive. She stretched extravagantly, arching her back, and I saw Will look up from his book. Then she reached forward, bent her knees and executed an almost-perfect dive.

It lasted only an instant, a brief flash of feeling that departed almost as soon as I'd registered it, but in that moment I think I truly hated her.


The house where Chloe Lambert lived was on the edge of Gramwell, a shiny new estate where every freshly painted house seemed to be accessorised with a manicured lawn and a spotless car. I'd agreed to meet Amy at eight o'clock at the end of her road so we could walk there together.

My outfit for the evening had caused me considerable angst. I didn't often go to parties, and as the weekend drew nearer, I'd searched my wardrobe in increasing desperation for something that might pass muster. Eventually, I rang Amy and asked her what she was going to wear. 'I haven't decided yet,' she said nonchalantly. 'Probably just jeans and a top.'

In the end, I chose skinny black jeans and an indigo vest under an off-the-shoulder black top. Not too try-hard, I thought, but still a definite step up from my usual outfits. I accessorised with purple nails and plum lipstick, and because it was over half a mile to Chloe's, my trusty DMs. I examined myself in my mother's full-length mirror. If it wasn't for the frizzy, sludge-coloured hair, I might look acceptable, I thought. I bent and rummaged in the dressing table for the ancient tube of hair serum I was sure was there somewhere, and as I did so, my fingers brushed against something tucked into the side of the drawer. A memory stirred, from the pre-Amy days. A gift from a friend I didn't see much of anymore, a reward for a job well done. I gripped the edge of the paper square and pulled it out. Perhaps it would come in useful if the evening got too much.

I was at the end of Amy's road early and leaned against the wall to wait for her. She was usually punctual, but eight o'clock came and went with no sign of her. I checked my phone, but there was no message, no missed call. I debated ringing her, but decided against it. If something had happened to change her plans, I reasoned, she'd have let me know.

It was almost twenty past when I became aware of a clack-clacking noise ringing down the street. I looked up and saw a bronzed Amazon in towering heels and a thigh-length sheath dress shimmering in gold sequins heading towards me. It took a full second for the image to connect with my brain and to realise that this was, in fact, Amy.

'Hey,' she said, while I stood there dumbstruck. 'I like your top.'

'You said you were wearing jeans!'

I saw her cheeks redden beneath her foundation. 'I couldn't find a top,' she said. 'This is okay, isn't it?'

I felt a brief, powerful urge to slap her. How dare she stand there, every inch the golden goddess Will had called her, and ask me for reassurance? It was too much, I thought. Too much for any normal person to bear.

I turned away from her. 'You look fine,' I mumbled.

She fell into step beside me, her footsteps ringing out next to the dull thud of my DMs.

'Can you actually walk in those?' I asked tetchily. 'You do know how far it is to Chloe's house?'

'They're quite comfortable really,' she said, wincing as she turned her ankle on a crack in the paving.

We walked on in silence, Amy presumably needing all her concentration to maintain her balance. Her pace slowed the further we went, and when I snuck a sidelong glance at her, her jaw was tight with suppressed pain. I took pity on her then, and insisted we stop.

'Why don't you take them off?' I asked her. There was a straggly grass verge on one side of the pavement, and I pointed to it. 'You can walk on that.'

She eyed the grass suspiciously, no doubt worried about lurking dog turds. 'It's okay,' she said. 'If I take them off, I'll never get them on again.'

Another twenty metres, and she came to a standstill again. 'I just need a minute,' she said, grimacing as she shifted her weight from one foot to the other.

I watched her silently, torn between pity and envy. She reached for my arm, held on to keep her balance as she tipped backwards on the ludicrous heels, trying to ease the burn in the balls of her feet.

'Ready to go?' I asked, and she nodded; but a minute later, we'd stopped again.

'Sorry,' she said. 'I'll get used to them in a bit.'

I reached into my back pocket and held out the small fold of paper I'd tucked away there. 'Take this.'

She looked at it suspiciously. 'What is it?'

'It'll make you feel better,' I said.

'Is it a painkiller?'

She was deliberately playing dumb, I thought. 'Yeah, Amy, something like that.'

'Where did you get it?' But then she shook her head. 'No, don't tell me. It's okay. I'll sit down when we get there.'

I rolled my eyes, put the wrap back into my pocket. 'Suit yourself.'

We soldiered on, stopping every fifty metres or so, so Amy could breathe through the pain. By the time we arrived at Chloe Lambert's house we were fashionably late, several clusters of people already dotted around the front lawn. The girls wore strappy sandals and strappier dresses, the guys, freshly pressed shirts. They were all drinking, beverages split along gender lines: plastic glasses of amber liquid with fruit floating on top for one, bottles of beer for the other. This, I already knew, would be a long night.

Eyes swivelled in our direction as we walked up the front path. With what must have been a monumental effort of self-control, Amy appeared to glide effortlessly on her torturous heels. I saw admiring looks cast in her direction and felt ever more like a Morlock clomping along in her wake.

'Ay-meee!' A shrill voice carried from a ground-floor window. A slender arm issued forth, a hand with perfectly manicured nails waving enthusiastically.

'Hey, Chloe.' Amy waved back, then half-turned towards me. 'I'll just go and say hello,' she murmured. 'Come and find me later?'

I watched grimly as she hurried into the house, aware I'd been ditched before we were even over the threshold. There was nothing to do except follow her, trying to look as if I had as much right to be there as anyone else.

Inside it was airy, bright and modern, with twinkling fairy lights and shiny wooden floors that were, for now at least, spotlessly clean. Most of the downstairs area was one large room, sofas and chairs upholstered in neutral fabrics and adorned with lolling guests. At one end, vast doors opened onto the garden beyond. Through them, I could see more well-tended grass, kids drinking and smoking. Music was playing, though not at a volume to alarm the neighbours, and a space had been cleared at one end of the room, presumably for dancing.

I headed for the kitchen, where a large glass bowl filled with what appeared to be punch was flanked by piles of plastic cups. I gave it a wide berth and took a beer from the fridge. There was no sign of a bottle opener, and I pulled open drawers, finding tea towels and an unfeasibly neat arrangement of tin foil and cling film.

'Is this what you're looking for?'

The voice sparked electricity up my spine. I turned to see Will smiling at me, the ring of a bottle opener dangling from one finger.

I advanced to take it from him, but he held it higher, just out of reach. 'Don't be a dick,' I said, and he laughed and handed it to me.

'Nice to see you getting into the spirit,' he said.

I levered off the cap and took a long swig from the bottle. 'Amy's around if you want to go find her.'

'Bored of me already, Laura Fraser?'

He was smiling, but I was tired of this, tired of knowing that as soon as Amy appeared, I'd be wallpaper again. I dodged around him, catching his look of surprise as I made for the doors to the garden.

'Catch you later, maybe,' I said.

I pushed through a miasma of cigarette smoke mixed with something sickly sweet – the fruit flavoured vapes some of the kids had started using, I guessed. A few steps led up to a terraced area where someone had erected an oversized paddling pool. It wasn't deep enough to do more than splash around in, but a couple of girls were in there anyway, skirts hitched up unnecessarily high, plastic tumblers held aloft as if to protect them from an oncoming tidal wave. I raised my beer to them and took a seat on one of the garden chairs positioned nearby, where I could give the impression of being sociable without having to talk to anyone.

As a tactic, it worked well. A steady stream of people came to check out the paddling pool before drifting away again. I leaned back and closed my eyes, telling myself I'd finish my beer, then go and find Amy. But there was still an inch or so left in my bottle when I heard a familiar laugh and looked up to see her a few metres away. She stood in a group of six or seven others, unsteady on her feet – those stupid shoes, no doubt – and hanging onto the arm of a tall guy with wavy hair. There was no sign of Will.

I watched through narrowed eyes as they edged closer to the paddling pool until Amy was in touching distance, her back to me. I was about to reach out and tap her on the arm when she swung around and placed her drink on the patio next to my feet. The next moment she was back in the huddle, clinging to her new friend's arm as she stood on one leg and massaged the arch of her foot. She hadn't even noticed me.

I sat there, slack-jawed and seething. Yet was I really surprised? I'd expected this from the moment she'd introduced herself in that English class. It had taken longer than I'd expected, that was all.

I slipped the wrapper from my pocket. I might as well take it now, float away for an hour or two and forget this stupid party.

Forget Amy and Will, the way they'd so obviously forgotten me. But then Amy laughed again, and flicked her hair, and my eyes travelled to the plastic tumbler she'd left on the floor.

Perfect Amy Linton. Blonde goddess. Just Saying No. And before I really knew what I was doing, I was pouring the powder into her drink.

I sat back quickly, just as the music changed and one of the girls in Amy's crowd whooped and raised her arms in the air. The group started to move away, heading back to the dance floor, no doubt. Amy was going with them. And her tumbler remained on the patio, untouched.

I felt a sudden, intense surge of relief. What had I been thinking? I was about to reach for it when a long arm swept down and it was gone. 'You forgot something, Amy!' called the guy with the wavy hair, and I watched her turn, a frown flitting over her face before the smile was back, and she was reaching out to take it from him.

*She won't drink it*, I told myself. Amy wasn't a big drinker, and she'd probably left the punch behind deliberately. She'd find an opportunity to pour it away. And if by any remote chance she drank any of it, would that be so bad? She might even enjoy it. At the very least, she'd forget about the pain in her feet.

I sat there for a while longer, telling myself not to worry, but I couldn't settle. I got to my feet and went to find her.

The sun was dimming now, and fairy lights twinkled in the garden. I passed a giggling couple making for the shadows beyond the lawn, a guy carrying a shrieking girl towards the paddling pool. There was no sign of Amy, so I re-entered the house, pausing while my eyes adjusted to the gloom. The numbers had swelled since we'd arrived, and I had to push through crowds as I passed from room to room, craning my neck as I went. She was nowhere to be seen, so after a quick scout of the front lawn, I headed upstairs.

A couple of girls from our year stood outside a closed door, which I guessed must be the bathroom. I nodded in its direction. 'Do you know if Amy's in there?'

They shook their heads, and I was about to move on when I caught a look exchanged between them. 'Have you seen her?' I asked.

The shortest of the two, an unhealthy looking girl with violently permed hair, gestured down the landing. 'I think she's busy.' She smirked.

I stared at her, a sick feeling in my stomach. I hadn't seen Will on my circuit of the house and gardens. Was it possible they were together?

I pushed past them and made my way along the landing.

'She wants a threesome,' cackled the other girl, and the two of them exploded in gales of laughter. I ignored them and kept going.

There were three other doors on the landing, all shut up tight. Someone had Blu-Tacked a piece of paper to each one, the first two with the same message:

No Entry. Seriously.

A third door bore the legend:

Coats

I looked back over my shoulder, but the girls seemed to have lost interest. I decided I'd start with the temporary cloakroom, but as I passed the first door, I heard a noise from inside. I stopped, backed up, and listened, but all I could hear was the music from downstairs.

I tapped softly on the door and waited. Nothing. I placed my ear to the wood, and there it was again – a low noise, half gasp, half murmur. I tapped again, louder this time.

'Amy?'

No reply, but the sound had worried me. 'Amy!' I called again. 'Are you in there?'

'Fuck off!'

The voice was male, aggressive. Definitely not Will.

'Amy, are you okay?'

I put my hand to the doorknob, but it was already turning. The door swung open to reveal the guy I'd seen Amy with earlier. He was red in the face and his shirt was untucked. He leaned towards me and growled in my face, 'I thought I told you to fuck off.'

I tried to see past him, but he was blocking the doorway.

'Yeah, well it looks like I don't give a shit what you say, doesn't it?'

His eyes darkened. 'I won't tell you again.'

'Works for me,' I said. 'Amy, are you okay in there?'

He reached out to grab my arm, and I dodged to one side. The movement afforded me a glimpse into the room, Amy slumped on the bed. It was all I needed to see.

I turned to him in fury. 'Are you serious?'

He took a step back.

'This is how you get your kicks, is it?'

For a split second I thought he might hit me, and I felt everything inside me stiffen, waiting for the blow. But then he straightened, pushed his hair from his face.

'You're not worth it,' he said, and pushed past me onto the landing.

I stepped into the bedroom to find out just how bad things were.

# THIRTY

Sam offers to stay the night. 'I don't mean – you know,' he says, blushing scarlet. 'Just, if you don't want to be alone.'

I'm going to say no. The words are already on the tip of my tongue. But then I imagine how it would feel closing the door after he'd left, using the chain that's already failed to keep an intruder out of my home. 'Thank you,' I say. 'If you really don't mind?'

He insists on taking the sofa ('You're not well,' he says, trying to make me feel better about it. 'I don't want to sleep on your snotty pillow.'). I don't have a spare duvet, so I go to the bedroom to get him the throw from the bottom of my bed. He stands in the doorway, looking puzzled.

'Why are there plates on your bed?'

I hesitate, but if he's going to spend the night in my flat, he has a right to know. I keep things brief, relating the events of the previous night, waking suddenly, thinking I'd heard a noise. I miss out the message in the book. Instead, because I don't want him to think I'm being paranoid, I say, 'The chain was off the door. I know I put it on before I went to bed.'

'Jesus, Laura.' He looks shaken. 'You have to go to the police.'

'You know I can't. What would I say? DC Hollis thinks I'm a fantasist. She's already threatened to have me arrested.'

'She can't arrest you for being scared.'

'But she can arrest me for wasting her time – or caution me, anyway. And what proof do I have that any of this is real?'

He opens his mouth, then closes it again.

'I'm sorry,' I say. 'I should have told you before. You don't have to stay if you don't want to.'

He frowns. 'What do you take me for? Of course I'm staying.'

I hand him the throw, then follow him back into the living room, wanting to make sure he's as comfortable as possible. His eyes sweep the room, and I guess he's looking for a weapon of some kind.

I go to the counter and draw out a knife from the block there.

'Here you go.'

He manages to look relieved and horrified at the same time.

'Just in case. I've got one in the bedroom too.'

He swallows. 'Thanks.'

'No, thank you. For being here. It means a lot.' We stand there awkwardly. 'Good night then.'

I leave him arranging the throw on the sofa and go to lock the door. I slide the chain into place and leave the key in the lock so no one can try to pick it. I consider replacing the chair, but I've left it in the living room, and I don't want to disturb Sam. In the bedroom, I undress quickly, choosing an old pair of pyjamas that cover me from neck to ankle. I close the door tight and stand there looking at it.

*There are two of us here*, I tell myself. *I don't need to worry.*

But I am worried, all the same. There's a chest of drawers near the door, and after another moment deliberating whether Sam might be offended if he hears me and realises what I'm doing, I decide I don't care. I push the chest of drawers so that it covers the edge of the doorframe, then go to bed and turn out the light.

I lie there in the darkness, imagining Sam trying to sleep on my lumpy sofa. He looked on edge when I left him – hardly surprising, in the circumstances. I remember the way he scanned the room, searching for something to protect himself – to protect us. He's so sure Darren is connected to Marina's disappearance, but I don't buy it. There's no way the man from the train could have known I'd try to enhance that video image. And a fake website set up just to give me a doctored photo – it doesn't seem plausible.

But someone *has* hacked my phone. The simplest explanation is that it was the man from the train. He knows where I live, so it's not a stretch to think he has my other contact details too. He must have sent me something – a text, an email – and hoped I'd open it. But who is he, and what does he want from me? And what does any of it have to do with Marina?

The questions circle my brain, but I can't get any closer to an answer. Somewhere along the line, I fall asleep.

I open my eyes to a grey dawn. In spite of everything, I've slept better than I have for days. Perhaps it's Sam's soothing presence. I check my bedside clock and realise he'll already be getting ready for work. I slide the chest of drawers away from the door and go to find him.

He's in the kitchen, hunting for something in a drawer.

'Morning,' I say, and he jumps violently. 'Sorry! Did you sleep okay?'

'Fine, fine. I was just looking for a teaspoon.'

I point to where I keep the cutlery in a caddy on the

counter, right in front of him. 'Are you sure you've slept?' I tease him.

He smiles ruefully. 'Wasn't my best night, to be honest. Do you want coffee?'

I watch him make the drinks, feeling mildly guilty that it should be the other way around. He hands me a cup, then checks his watch and raises his eyebrows in a show of surprise.

'Is that the time? I should get a move on. I'll need to get back home and change. Guy wants me at the stocktake with head office at 9.30.' He's already collecting his jacket from the back of the sofa.

I get to my feet. 'Sorry, Sam. I should have thought. I've got a cup with a lid somewhere – can I put your coffee in that?'

But he's already heading down the hallway. 'No time, sorry. See you at the office?'

'Sure,' I say, although I hadn't been intending to go in. I hurry to unlock the door for him. 'Thanks again,' I say, and he turns and waves as he disappears down the stairs.

I go back inside and re-lock the door. It's quiet without Sam, strangely empty. I've always enjoyed having my own space, but perhaps it would be nice to live with someone. To have someone to talk to when I got back from work, to share the cooking and the chores. Someone to turn to in the night if I heard a noise I couldn't explain.

I swallow another mouthful of coffee and return to the living room. Sam has folded the throw neatly and left it at the end of the sofa. He's tidied up by the look of things too. The piles of books that don't fit properly in my bookcase have been straightened, the drawer under the dining table that's stiff, and which I always leave gaping open as a result, is closed. Even the cushions on the sofa and chair have been plumped and neatly arranged. I find myself smiling. If Sam and I ever lived together, I'd drive him mad.

I finish my coffee, then shower and dress. I hadn't planned

to go to work, but I suppose I have to sometime. Seeing Sam again has made the prospect a little less daunting, and perhaps a change of scene will give me a new perspective, help me work out what to do next – like when you're struggling to remember the name of a song and it only comes to you when you think of something else.

I lock up and leave the house.

The moment I step outside, I feel it – a prickling sensation on the back of my neck that tells me I'm being watched. I keep moving, glancing around me, trying not to look scared. He'd like that, I think, and I don't want to give him the satisfaction. My eyes search for the dark hair and beard, the lean frame, that mysterious something I can't quite put my finger on but which I'm more and more certain is familiar.

He's here. I can feel him. And from now on, I'm going to trust my instincts.

I look over my shoulder as I enter the Tube station, and again as I walk down the escalators. But he's good at keeping out of sight. The platform is busy, and when a train arrives, I'm among the last to squeeze on before the doors shut. At least there's no way he's in the same carriage. I wedge myself into the corner, so when we pull into my station, I'm one of the first to get off. At the far side of the platform there's a bench, and I step onto it to survey the faces of the passengers as they disembark. A middle-aged woman in a cagoule shoots me a disapproving look, but there's no sign of the man from the train.

When the crowd thins, I clamber down and make my way to the exit. Is he behind me? Up ahead, waiting for me? What's he planning to do? Is he trying to intimidate me, hoping I'll stop looking for Marina? Or is he waiting for his moment to strike, to make me disappear like she has?

I'm shaking, and I force myself to take deep breaths. I need to concentrate, to handle this methodically. I'm on my way to work. I'm going to talk to Guy, apologise for taking time off, get things back on an even keel there. And I'll ask Sam to have lunch with me, talk everything through. Because I can only see one way to go from here, one last stone to turn, and I want his advice.

I pass through the ticket barriers and head out into the anaemic winter sunshine. I'm no more than ten steps from the exit when there's a buzz from my shoulder bag. I thought twice about taking my phone with me, but until I can get another one, it's my main connection with the world. I answer the call, my thoughts still on talking to Sam – but the voice at the other end belongs to a woman.

'Hi, is that Laura Fraser? This is Madeleine Sutton at the Frampton Gallery.'

I stop walking abruptly, and a man behind me swears as he nearly collides with my back.

'I was just calling to check that you were still available for your meeting with Oliver at 2.30?'

Oh Jesus, God, fuck. Not again. But at least she's ringing to check. At least there's still time to come up with some kind of excuse.

'Miss Fraser, are you there?'

'Yes, sorry. And yes, absolutely. I mean, I'll be there.' My vocal cords have gone rogue. My brain's AWOL and they're running riot, saying stuff they have absolutely no place saying. But there's no stopping them. 'I'm looking forward to it,' I finish.

'That's wonderful,' says Madeleine. 'Then he'll see you at the gallery at 2.30.'

That's twice she's reminded me of the time; she probably has me down as some kind of halfwit. We say our goodbyes and I return the phone to my bag. I have to assume that whoever hacked it is still interested in what I'm doing, but at least this way he won't see much if he switches on the camera.

I start walking again, then stop. What am I doing? This is my last chance with Oliver, he's been very clear about that. If I go into work, there's no way Guy is letting me out again at 2.30 – not without my P45, at least. If I call in sick again, he'll be pissed off, but I'll live to fight another day. And with my morning back, I can go to the community centre. I won't be able to replace my whole portfolio, but at least I can take some photos of my best work.

There's no competition. I take out my phone again and dial Sam's number. It goes straight to voicemail, and I check the time. He's probably in the office already, maybe in a pre-meeting with Guy before the stocktake. I only hope he hasn't already told him I'm coming in.

I tap out a quick message:

*Got ready for work, but think I've overdone it. Feeling rough again. Will call Guy later. Thanks for everything.*

I don't like lying to Sam, and I don't think he'll believe this for one minute. But it's better than telling the truth and putting him in an impossible position with Guy.

I slip my phone back into my bag, then retrace my steps to the station.

---

Forty minutes later, I'm home. It's a detour I can ill afford, but I need my good camera to take the photos. I pause in the hallway, sniffing the air like a bloodhound: everything seems exactly as I left it. Whoever was following me earlier, I don't think he came back here.

I retrieve my camera and rush out. Time is short if I'm going to get some decent shots, edit them, and print them out before I meet Oliver. I'll focus on six or seven of my very best pots – enough to show him what I'm about.

*You said you'd put Marina first.*

But this is my last chance with Oliver, I reason with my conscience. I refuse to let the man from the train ruin something else. This will take just a few hours. And with any luck, concentrating on the photos will reboot my tired brain, give it the kick-start it needs to come up with a new idea to find Marina.

When I get to the community centre, I'm in luck – the art room is empty. I unlock the cupboard where I keep my pots and remove the ones I want. The top four are easy to choose, but the remaining two or three take more thought. I take out the candidates and position them on a table near the window, rotating them slowly one by one. They're all imperfect, the gap between what I'd imagined and what my hands created only too clear. But it's their flaws that give them life, their own unique spark. I only hope Oliver Frampton agrees.

I remove my camera from its bag. I'll see how the pots photograph, and hope that helps narrow things down. But when I hold out the camera, I feel that familiar prickling sensation on the back of my neck. I spin around, taking in the space behind me in a single glance. There's no one there.

I've been spooked by the break-in. That's only natural. But now I'm being paranoid, letting the man from the train get to me when he's not even here.

I put down the camera. Coffee, that's what I need. A big cup of something strong to settle my nerves.

There's a kitchen area down the corridor, and I set off there. Salsa music blasts out as I go, no doubt coming from one of the exercise classes they run here. It makes me think of Millie's friend, that chance meeting that might yet change my life. I'm not letting the man from the train take that away from me.

In the kitchen, the music is loud, a peppy beat that in spite of everything makes me tap my toes as I boil the kettle. I spoon instant coffee into a chipped mug, the aroma filling the small space as soon as the hot water hits. I hesitate, then add a spoonful of sugar – I have a vague memory that sweet drinks are supposed to be good for shock. I take a sip, then head back down the corridor.

The music fades as I reach the art room. I've overfilled the mug and am keeping my eyes fixed on it as I enter, trying to avoid spillages.

So it's somewhat ironic that when I look up, what I see makes it slip from my hands and shatter on the floor.

*

I couldn't help myself. Seeing her in that community centre, taking her photos of those stupid pots, acting like there was nothing more important in the world – I couldn't take it anymore.

She could have come back at any moment, but I didn't care. It felt so good.

I was sweating when it was over, elated. But then I panicked. That music was loud, but someone could still have heard me. I got out of there as fast as I could – too fast, it turns out. I didn't realise I'd dropped it. It must have fallen from my pocket as I jumped around.

It doesn't matter. She probably won't find it. And if she does, it changes nothing.

Will she keep looking for Marina or won't she? That's the only thing that matters. Her choice will seal her fate.

# THIRTY-ONE

I blink at the scene in front of me, hardly able to take it in. The table below the window is empty. The nine pots I'd placed there, my finest work, have gone. They're in hundreds of pieces on the floor below.

I step forward, following the expanding pool of coffee to the graveyard of my pots. 'No,' I mumble and drop to my knees. I reach out and pick up a fragment of ceramic with midnight blue glaze. It's too small to identify which piece it came from. I pick up another shard, sea green with a fleck of brown. Next to it is a small pile of white grit, as if someone has ground their heel into the debris. I pinch it between my fingers to make myself believe it's real.

I know who's done this. The man from the train has been here, could be here right now, watching me sobbing on the floor. At any second, I could feel his hands around my neck. I should move, run, call for help. But all I can do is kneel here and know that it's over. That all my hopes for the future are destroyed.

I stay where I am, and no hands reach for my throat. I stare at the mess on the floor, knowing I should clean it up. Other people use this space. Slowly, I get to my feet, search in the cupboards and find a dustpan and brush, a roll of bin bags.

I sweep up the fragments of my work. He's been thorough; there's nothing left worth saving. I'm about to empty yet another load of broken ceramic into the bag when something catches my eye. I pick it out of the pan, shake off the chalky dust that clings to it. It's paper – newspaper, by the feel of it, crumpled up tight. I start to unfold it, but I'm interrupted by my phone ringing. I slip the paper into my pocket as I check the screen. Then I steel myself and answer.

'Hello, Guy.'

'Laura.' His voice is filled with barely suppressed rage. 'May I ask where the hell you are?'

'I'm sick.'

'So I'm told by Mr Dutta. Perhaps you can explain why you haven't had the courtesy to contact me yourself?'

'I called you, but you weren't there.' It seems best all round to use the excuse Sam's given me. 'I left a message with Sam.'

'And you think that's sufficient, do you? What was it about the email I sent you yesterday that wasn't clear?'

I barely remember the email. It feels like a hundred years ago.

'I was going to try you again—' I say, but he doesn't let me finish.

'It's now 11.45. Your contract clearly states that if you are unable to attend work, you must inform your line manager by 9.30 a.m. that day.'

I have no idea if that's what my contract says, but Guy must have checked. I don't know exactly what that means, but I'm sure it's nothing good.

'I was at the doctor's,' I try.

'For over two hours? And I presume you can send me a copy of your doctor's note right now, then? Just take a photograph and email it across. I'll wait.'

There's a note of triumph in his voice. We both know he's got me, but I can't bring myself to care.

'Look, I'm sorry, Guy,' I say. 'I've been having a really difficult time. My mum's been ill and—'

'Save it, Laura,' he cuts me off. 'I've had more than enough of your bullshit. You're fired.'

---

I sit on the sofa, nursing the bottle of wine I bought on my way home. There's a pill on the table, the white and green capsule winking at me. I should stay in control, ready to fight or fly. But I need something to blur the edges. To make what's happened bearable.

I'd dreamed of how that meeting with Oliver Frampton would go, my shining opportunity to make a go of my art. Telling myself that yes, luck might have made Millie's friend walk into the studio that day, luck might have created the opening, but it was what I did with it that counted. That I could take that bit of good fortune and craft a new life, one where I didn't have to spend Sunday evenings dreading the week ahead. One where I could make a living doing something I loved, creating work that would speak to other people, that would say something important.

Who was I kidding? People like me don't get to exhibit in Oliver Frampton's gallery. The man from the train has probably done me a favour. Saved me from humiliating myself. At least this way I can fool myself that my work might have been good enough, that it wasn't my fault things didn't work out.

I select Oliver's number from my contacts, aware that it will probably be the last time I ever use it. I hear it ring, twice, three times, before it connects to his voicemail.

'Hi, Mr Frampton – Oliver. I'm phoning to say I won't be coming to our meeting today. I'm sorry. You've been so patient, but I can't do this. I don't want to waste your time.' I'm about to hang up, but I may as well do this properly. I clear my throat. 'And I lied. About my mum. She's fine. I'm just – I'm sorry.'

I disconnect the call and a wave of nausea passes over me. That's it. An hour ago, I had an unspectacular but bill-paying job and a meeting with an important gallery owner who was thinking of exhibiting my work. Now I have neither.

I think about calling Sam, but he'll be at work. Guy's probably told him he's sacked me. And ringing him in office hours won't do him any favours. It's about time I stopped being so selfish, stopped expecting him to deal with my problems.

The truth is, I already know what I need to do. I was only planning on talking it through with Sam in the hope he'd volunteer to come with me. Or maybe what I really wanted was for him to tell me to back off, that I'd already done everything that could be expected of me. That it was for the police to decide how to proceed, and that if they weren't going to do anything, that wasn't my fault.

I've been a coward, but it's time for that to stop. I know Marina was at Flyte Gardens until very recently. I know that man was watching the house, close enough to clear it the moment I left. There's only one thing to do if I want to have any chance of picking up the trail. I need to go back there.

I get up, push my phone into the pocket of my jeans. The movement stirs a memory: that piece of paper I found on the floor of the art room. I return my hand to my pocket and pull it out, smooth out the creases.

I stare at it, and my hands start to shake. It's a scrap of newspaper, yellowed and softened with age. But time hasn't lessened its power to hurt.

Amy stares at me from the photograph beneath the headline, that dazzling smile lighting up the page. And beneath it, another photograph, another girl. For once, though, I can't compare myself to Amy. Because there's a thick black scrawl where my face should be.

———

It's cold, and that's good. It's good because I can wear my thickest coat with the big pockets that don't give any clue as to what's inside them.

I don't carry a bag. A bag is no help if I need to move fast. I can't be grappling with zips if I'm facing a weapon. Because I don't have any illusions – that's what it could come to. A man who's taken a woman prisoner, who thinks nothing of chaining her to a chair. A man like that won't hesitate to use violence.

That photograph flashes into my mind's eye, the black ink obliterating my face. It makes me shudder. The man on the train doesn't just know what happened ten years ago; that scrap of newspaper means he was there – or he knows someone who was. I can't ignore the possibility any longer: does this have something to do with Amy?

Not that she could be involved herself – but does he think he's doing this for her? She always did attract male attention.

Then of course there's Will. If this is about Amy, could he have some part in it?

But no. The idea is ridiculous. Will was gentle, kind, warm. And he cared about me, whatever other people thought. Besides, if he has a problem with me, he's had almost a decade to do something about it. Why wait until now?

None of what's happening makes sense. So all I can do is keep going, focus on why I'm here.

I've decided to try the woman at number 17 first. I don't like doing it; there are kids there, and he might be watching me. But she knows something, and I need every bit of information I can get my hands on. This has something to do with what happened in Gramwell, but Marina has to fit in somewhere. My best guess is he thinks she's done something bad too. Something that means she deserves to be punished, just like me. That older woman she lived with – her mum probably. She has to have something to do with it.

I walk briskly along the pavement, sticking close to the hedges and fences. The bungalows that line the road have big windows, but they have long front gardens too, and I can't see much of the rooms beyond. He'd see me, though. If he stood to one side and looked out onto the street, he'd see me clear as day.

I reach into my coat pocket, touch what's inside.

I turn into the drive of number 17, and immediately realise that things may not go according to plan. There's no car on the driveway.

I walk to the front door, anyway, hoping it doesn't mean what I fear it does. But when I press the doorbell, no child bellows from inside, there's no patter of footsteps in the hallway. I ring again, just to be sure, but there's no one home.

I back up, stare at the house, but it's just an ordinary dormer bungalow. There are no answers for me here.

I turn and make my way back down the path, step onto the street and head in the direction of number 21. There's no one else walking here, no cars driving up and down. I pass more blank windows, more paved driveways. My footsteps sound unnaturally loud in the crisp air.

And then I reach number 21 and I see something that sets my heart hammering in my chest. Because it might be quiet here today, but not everyone at Flyte Gardens is away from home. There, parked squarely in the driveway, is a small red car.

I stare at it, hardly believing what I'm seeing. And then I walk up the front path and, before I can tell myself this is madness, this is stupid and dangerous and I should turn around and get out of there as fast as I can, I reach out and press the doorbell.

# THIRTY-TWO

*Then*

I found Will lounging in a deckchair near the back of the house. He was with a group of boys but didn't seem to be talking to any of them. He looked up as I approached, then got to his feet when he saw my face.

'What's wrong?' he said.

'You need to help me,' I said. 'It's Amy. She's off her face and she needs to go home.'

He followed me upstairs, taking in the scene in the bedroom in a single glance. 'What's she doing here?' he said. 'Is she okay?'

He was pale, and I knew what he was asking.

'She's fine,' I said, glad that he hadn't asked the question I didn't want to answer: *has she taken anything?* 'But she needs to get out of here, and I can't move her on my own.'

For once, Will seemed uncertain what to do, and I directed matters, telling him where to stand, when to push and pull. With considerable effort – barely conscious, even slender Amy was no light weight – we got her to her feet and supported her to the door. By then, she'd started to mumble that she felt sick, so we took her to the bathroom, and Will stood outside while I held her hair and she vomited copiously.

At one point, I heard a female voice outside, and the next moment the door was being pushed open.

'You'll have to go downstairs,' I said, annoyed that Will had failed in his duty as guard.

'What the hell have you done to her?'

I looked up to see a girl with black hair streaked with purple, heavy eyeliner, and a seriously pissed-off expression. I'd met her only a couple of times before, but hers was the kind of look you didn't forget: Kate, Amy's older sister, apparently back from uni for the holidays.

'I'm trying to help her,' I protested, but she elbowed me out of the way.

'Amy, you're going home.'

Amy mumbled something incoherent.

Kate turned to me. 'Get her some water. Now.'

I backed out and did as I was told. When I returned, Kate snatched the glass from my hands, her chunky metal rings scraping my fingers.

'How much has she had to drink?'

'I don't know,' I said. 'I wasn't with her.' Somehow it made me sound more culpable, but Kate ignored me.

Amy had stopped being sick for the moment, and Kate handed her the water. 'Drink this, then we're getting you out of here.'

'I'll go with her,' I said, but Kate turned her laser stare on me.

'I think you've done enough.'

'I can take her.' Will stood in the doorway. 'I'll make sure she's okay.'

Kate looked up at him gratefully, and I wondered what it

was about Will that made people trust him. Whatever it was, I wished I had some of it.

'Are you sure?' She looked at Amy, then back at Will. 'I should do it.'

'It's not a problem.'

Kate took Amy's hand. 'Amy, Will's going to take you home. Is that all right?' Amy nodded, her eyes on the floor. 'Finish this water. Do you have your keys?'

More nodding, and with one arm draped over Will and the other over Kate, Amy stumbled to her feet. I stood to the side as they ushered her out, feeling like a spare part.

Downstairs, the crowds parted before Kate's glare. I followed, but as I got to the door I felt a hand on my arm. I turned to see the girl with the perm who'd been outside the bathroom earlier.

She held something out to me. 'Is this Amy's? It was on the bed.'

I recognised the purse and took it from her. 'Thanks.'

'Is she all right?' She bit her lip. 'I didn't realise she was so out of it.'

I stared at her, and she dropped her eyes.

'No harm done,' I said, and turned away.

But the short conversation was all the time it had taken for the crowd to thicken again, and by the time I manoeuvred my way to the gate, Amy and Will were already halfway down the road. I set off after them.

I was relieved to see that the fresh air seemed to have brought Amy to her senses. Will held her arm, but while there was the occasional wobble, she didn't stumble. She'd removed her shoes, I noticed, and they dangled from one hand. Perhaps, after all, she'd ditched that doctored punch and it was alcohol alone that was to blame. For all I knew, she'd already had too much to drink by the time I saw her at the paddling pool. I shouldn't have done it, though. The drinking could have made things worse – the two weren't designed to mix. What had got into me?

But then maybe it wasn't so bad. She'd been sick, after all, purged the worst of whatever she'd had from her system. It was a reminder not to let my temper get the better of me, but there was no need to dwell on it. The important thing was that she was okay.

I'd closed the distance and was about to call out to them when something stopped me. Amy was talking, and I watched Will turn and bend towards her as though to hear her better. There was something in the way he moved, the tilt of his head, and for a second I froze, thinking he was going to kiss her. But then the moment passed, and they were walking on just as they had before.

My heart pounded and I felt sick. I no longer wanted to join them, but couldn't bear the idea of leaving them alone. I slowed my pace and let the distance between us grow. I'd wait until they were at the end of Amy's street, I decided, then race up to them with the purse, pretend I'd just caught them up. But somehow, when they reached that point, I didn't do it. Instead I followed from a distance, keeping to the shadows.

Amy had clearly sobered up because they were talking, voices low. I strained to hear what they were saying but couldn't catch the words. I watched as they walked up the drive, forced into single file to negotiate the narrow space left by the Lintons' car.

When they reached the door, I saw her draw out her keys, then rummage in her bag again. I couldn't see her well in the darkness, but I imagined the look of panic on her face. This should have been my moment to step forward, present her with her missing purse, but still I didn't move. She buried her face in her hands, and I heard Will say something, probably reassuring her that someone would find it, get it back to her. *Just give her the purse*, I told myself – but I stayed where I was.

Amy was nodding, placing her key in the door. Then she turned, and everything went into slow motion as I waited for the moment I'd been dreading.

She looked up at him, took a step forward. Maybe she smiled. Maybe she didn't. I watched her raise her hand, place it on his shoulder, stretch her face towards his. He didn't move. Her silhouette joined his briefly as she kissed his cheek. A chaste kiss, but she waited a moment before drawing back. Then she was opening the door, slipping inside, one hand raised in a final wave. The door closed. Will was alone.

Neither of us moved. My mouth was dry, an empty feeling in the pit of my stomach. *She kissed him*, I told myself. *But he didn't kiss her back.*

Slowly, he turned and began to walk towards the drive. Then he paused, put his hand to his cheek and touched the spot where her lips had been. I watched him from the shadows and felt my heart break into a thousand pieces.

# THIRTY-THREE

*Now*

The doorbell rings out its synthetic chime. I slide my hand into my pocket and clamp my fingers around the handle of the knife. It's too late to back out now.

I count in my head, trying to stay calm as I wait for signs of life from inside. When I get to twenty, I press the button again, but there's no response.

I step back, run my eyes over the front of the house. It looks empty, but I'm not fooled. It looked the same way the last time I was here, yet someone managed to smuggle out a pile of evidence from under my nose.

The memory injects me with a stream of panic – the same thing could be happening right now. I run to the gate at the side of the house, ready to do battle with the padlock again. But the padlock has gone, and the gate swings open at my touch. The ease of it unsteadies me, and I check my pace, proceed more cautiously. When I reach the corner, I stop and peer around it, but the garden is empty, and there's no sign of anyone at the French doors.

I check over my shoulder before moving towards them and tugging on the handle. They don't budge. I press my forehead to the glass and cup my hands around my face. The lace curtain that obscured the interior when I was here last has been pulled to one side, and I have a clear view into the room beyond. It looks much the same as it did before, and I'm about to move away when I catch sight of something that lifts the hairs on the back of my neck.

It's to the right of the French doors, tucked into the nearest corner. If I'd been standing a couple of steps away, it would have been invisible. There are no chains around the legs now, no sign of a lock. But I'd recognise that grey plastic chair anywhere. If it isn't the one I found in the kitchen on my last visit, it's its identical twin.

I step away from the door, almost stumbling on an uneven paving slab. I swear and right myself, then spin around, convinced that someone has snuck up behind me while I've been staring in the window. There's no one to be seen, but every inch of my skin tingles with the certainty that I'm not alone.

He's playing with me. Whoever has been keeping Marina here knew I'd come back. That chair is a message: *I know what you've seen, and you know what you've seen, and it doesn't matter because no one, least of all the police, is ever going to believe you.*

A surge of anger overtakes my fear. I clench my fist and the handle of the knife digs into my palm. He thinks he holds all the cards. Thinks he can take Marina and parade her in front of me. That he can make me run in circles, question my sanity. That I'm going to just wait for my turn to take whatever sick punishment he has planned for me.

He's wrong. I'm going to find Marina. And I'm going to make him pay.

I back further into the garden, keeping my eyes on the

house. There are no lights on inside, no movement at any of the windows. If the man from the train is here – or his accomplice, if Sam's right that he isn't working alone – he's keeping out of the way. But why do that, then leave a car on the drive for anyone to see?

I return to the front of the house, but the net curtains are still in place. With nothing else to do, I head for the drive.

The car is a Polo, old and a little battered. I make a note of the registration on my phone, not sure what I'm going to do with the information. The driver's window is grubby, and when I peer inside, someone has left a bobble hat on the passenger seat. It throws me; I can't imagine the man from the train wearing something like that. Perhaps whoever owns this car has nothing to do with any of this. Maybe they're visiting someone else in the street and parked here knowing the owners had moved out.

The back seat is clear, but there's something on the parcel shelf: a luminous yellow tabard of the type worn by construction workers. I take out my phone and snap a photo, just to feel I'm not leaving empty-handed.

Again, the prickle of unease. I return the phone to my pocket and turn slowly, casually, to scan my surroundings. And there it is: a shadow at an upstairs window, a suggestion of movement that's over before I can be sure of what I've seen.

Every muscle tightens, the urge to run almost overwhelming, but I force myself to stay where I am. I gaze upwards, letting my eyes roam slowly over the building. Three dormer windows are spaced evenly along the roofline. And as I watch, I see it again: a sliver of darkness at the edge of the one on the left.

The darkness shifts, retreats. I stand there, uncertain what to do. My options are limited. Knife or not, I'm not fool enough to try to force my way inside when they know I'm coming. Whoever has Marina must have managed to overpower her, and

I'm not deluded enough to think they won't be capable of doing the same to me.

'Excuse me?' A woman in her mid-twenties stands on the pavement looking into the garden, a small white dog snuffling at her feet. 'Can I help you?'

'I'm fine, thanks,' I say tersely. I don't need this.

'Do you know the people who lived here?' she asks. The dog has stopped its snuffling and looks at her, then at me, alert to the challenge in her voice. 'They moved out a while ago.' The hands on her hips convey the rest of her meaning more clearly than words: *so there's no need for you to be hanging around here.*

'I know,' I reply. 'I was just in the area, and I promised them I'd take a look at the place. They wondered if the new people had moved in yet.'

She narrows her eyes. 'Did they now? I'm surprised to hear that.'

I swallow. Evidently I've mis-stepped, but I have no idea how.

'Is that your car?' she asks, pointing at the Polo.

I shake my head. 'I just tried the house, but no one's answering.'

She raises an eyebrow. 'No, it's still empty. Who did you say your friends were?'

I glance up at the windows, but there's no sign of the shadow. Perhaps this annoying woman and her diminutive dog have given whoever was there time to beat a retreat.

'Sorry, I have to dash,' I say, and her expression darkens – my attempt to duck the question hasn't gone unnoticed. But then I have a flash of inspiration. 'You live around here, I'm guessing? Say hi to Josh and Ciaran for me. I popped by to see them too, but I'm missing everyone today.'

I see her shoulders relax, and before she can ask more questions, I step past her onto the pavement. The dog gives a low growl, and I smile as if I haven't noticed. 'See you, then.'

I stride purposefully in the direction of the main road. Perhaps I should have tried to pump her for information – she's clearly the sort of person who notices things. But she's already suspicious, and I don't want her reporting me to the police. I can't afford to waste time on another unsuccessful attempt to get DC Hollis to take me seriously.

A little further on, the road curves around to the right, taking me out of sight of the inquisitive dog walker. I stop and pretend to retie my shoelace while I consider my options. My best bet, it seems to me, is to find somewhere I can watch the house unnoticed. If the Polo belongs to someone connected to Marina, I'll get at least a glimpse of them as they're driving. And if it doesn't, whoever I saw lurking in that upstairs window will have to leave the house on foot. I can follow them, see where they go. Maybe they'll lead me to her.

I'm about to turn and head back the way I've come, when my phone bursts into life. I grab it before it alerts the whole street to my presence.

'Hello?' I hiss, scanning the road behind me, expecting the dog walker to appear at any moment and demand to know what I'm still doing there.

'Laura. Laura Fraser.' The voice is low, male.

'Hi, yes, that's me.'

There's a rumble at the end of the line. 'Get out of here and don't come back.'

I snatch the phone from my ear and stare at the screen. *Number withheld*, it reads.

For a moment, I can't breathe. 'You're the man I saw on the train.' I swallow. 'I know you have Marina. Let her go.'

'You sound scared.' The voice is smooth, unruffled – but there's something strange about it. 'That's very sensible,' it continues. 'So keep being sensible. Because if you don't—'

There's a noise, a succession of sharp knocks. The line falls silent, but when I check the call is still connected. A hum of background noise, then he's speaking again.

'Stay away. Forget all about Marina Leeson, or you're going to get hurt. That's not a threat. It's a promise.'

# THIRTY-FOUR

*Then*

I made a last-ditch attempt to change the way things were heading, but I think I knew even then that it was doomed to failure. Will and Amy getting together was like the setting of the sun or the changing of the seasons, both natural and inevitable.

The day after Chloe's party was a Sunday, our weekly non-swimming day, since both of them usually visited their grandparents. My head was full of everything I'd seen and done, and I was desperate to see them together, to gauge how things stood. Several times I started to compose a text to Amy, but each time I abandoned it. I expected her to message me herself, hoped for something from Will, but by Monday I'd heard from neither of them and my anxiety was at fever pitch.

I set off early for the corner of Amy's street, our usual meeting place to walk to the quarry. I'd barely left home when my phone pinged. It was a text from Amy. She wasn't going to be able to make it. No reason was given, and I'd have worried what might have been behind it if she hadn't closed by saying

she'd see me tomorrow. A couple of kisses assured me that whatever it was, she wasn't upset with me yet.

 After the initial surprise, I felt a surge of excitement. Everything had changed, and I'd have Will to myself for the day. I'd
be able to talk to him, have an honest conversation for once.
We'd known each other so much longer than either of us had
known Amy. It was time to put my cards on the table, find out
how he really felt.

 I hardly remember the walk to the quarry. My head was so
full of everything that had happened, the words I'd use to
explain how much I cared about him, how honest and real and
important it was. Before I knew it, I was at the ledge, looking
out over the water.

 Will wasn't there, but when I checked my phone, I saw it
was still early. I spread my towel on the ground, then paced
back and forth along the ledge, full of nervous energy. Looking
for a distraction, I walked to the spot where Amy and I usually
had our diving lesson, examined the rock. It was large and flat,
perfect for a beginner's dive. But I still believed it was too low to
try anything fancy.

 I scanned the perimeter of the lake, looking for an alternative. The best-looking candidate, I thought, protruded from the
cliff face opposite; but while it was the right shape, it was too
high for my liking. If either of us hit the water at the wrong
angle, we might do ourselves a serious injury. And getting to it
in the first place would be challenge enough; there was no path
that I could see.

 With still no sign of Will, I set off to examine the rocks more
closely. There was a narrow trail around the edge of the lake,
dotted with a few weeds and brambles which had found a
foothold in the stony ground. I picked my way along it carefully.
At the end, I was met by the cliff face soaring upwards, thirty
feet of grey stone a shade darker than the sky above. Scree
fringed the lower edges, and I could see at once that it wouldn't

take my weight. A little further along, though, looked more promising. A few larger rocks jutted out from the water, presumably the top of a pile that had either fallen or been blasted from the cliff. They weren't far from my potential dive board, and if I could climb to the highest one, it might be possible to jump across. There was no way of reaching them on foot though; I'd have to swim.

I'd half expected Will to interrupt my survey, but he still hadn't put in an appearance as I headed back to the ledge. I checked the time again. He'd never been this late before, but I told myself that didn't mean anything.

I settled on my towel and tried to distract myself by reading. But after an hour of inventing increasingly elaborate excuses for his lateness, I had to admit he wasn't coming. Maybe he'd had to work, I reasoned, perhaps someone was off sick. But set alongside Amy's no-show, I couldn't prevent a dark suspicion entering my head. Were they together? I didn't want to believe it, but the idea had taken root in my brain, and I couldn't shake it.

Staying at the lake seemed pointless without Will, but I had nowhere else to go. Hot and anxious, I stripped to my swimming costume and lowered myself into the water. I'd swim to the rocks at the base of the cliff, I decided, check their potential as a route to the dive site.

The chill of the lake temporarily drove thoughts of Will and Amy from my mind, and for a moment I enjoyed the feel of the water on my limbs. I flipped onto my back, exchanging a view of the dark surface for one of grey sky, then back again. When I reached the rockfall, the going looked good. A long, flat boulder had come to rest at a shallow angle just above the water, a smaller rock below it allowing me to pull myself up. From there, it was relatively easy to clamber from one to the next, gradually ascending above the lake.

I took care, moving slowly, making sure my footing was

secure before transferring my weight. I was beginning to think it wouldn't be as hard as I'd thought, when my progress came to an abrupt halt. I'd reached the edge of the rock fall, and there was nothing but sheer cliff face between me and the flat rock I'd selected for our dive. I considered whether it might be possible to continue upwards, then jump down onto my target, but it was too high and too far.

I climbed back down and slipped into the water again. It was less of a shock to the system this time, and I swam for a few minutes, trying to clear my mind of imagined scenarios in which Will and Amy fell into each other's arms and headed into the sunset. When the sky began to grumble, I decided to call it a day, and I'd just started back when the first penny-sized drops of rain began to fall. By the time I got home, I was soaked to the skin, my hair plastered to my scalp and water running in rivulets down my face. I went straight to my room to brood on what might be going on without me.

I was still in bed the next morning when my mother called up the stairs that Amy was there to see me. I was pleased; after the previous day's abrupt cancellation, I'd decided peevishly that I wasn't going to the lake again until I heard from her. Part of me had harboured the secret fear that she wouldn't even notice, that I'd already been consigned to the status of third wheel – but here she was after all. Perhaps I'd got it all wrong.

I hadn't.

As soon as I saw her, I knew. She sparkled with happiness. She took me by the hand and whispered urgently that she had something important to tell me. I led her upstairs to my room, my legs feeling as though they belonged to someone else. The moment the door was closed behind her, she flung herself onto my bed, eyes shining, desperate to tell me everything.

'Will came to see me yesterday,' she said. 'You'll never guess what he said.'

He must have arrived early, I realised, in time for Amy to send me her message. It spoke of a restless night, a decision he couldn't wait to communicate. It couldn't have been clearer: I meant nothing to him. And although part of me wasn't surprised – who, after all, wouldn't have preferred Amy to me? – the realisation was crushing.

I tried to disguise how I felt as she talked. Will hadn't quite declared undying love, but he'd told Amy how special she was, how being with her was the highlight of his day. I nodded along, wanting nothing more than for her to shut up and leave, but she was so wrapped up in what she was telling me that my less-than-enthusiastic reaction seemed to register not at all. She and Will had spent the previous day together, of course, and there she turned coy; but if she was expecting me to press her for the gory details, she was disappointed.

Finally, she stopped talking.

'So,' I said, 'you're an item now.'

Something in the tone of my voice must have finally penetrated her self-absorption, because a faint frown darkened her brow. 'This is okay with you, though, right? I mean, you don't like Will that way?'

'Course not,' I said. 'I'm happy for you.'

She smiled, looked as if she was about to speak again, to find new and devastating ways to tell me how wonderful he was, what an amazing time they'd had together, how I was surplus to requirements now.

'Actually, Amy,' I said, 'I was about to go out.'

Her face fell. 'Oh,' she said, deflated. 'Where are you going?'

I wished I could present her with some grand plan, something that would show her I didn't need her or Will, that there were a million other ways I could spend my summer. 'I promised Mum I'd pick up a prescription,' I said.

I thought she'd offer to come with me and was already groping for an excuse to fend her off, but perhaps she'd got the message after all.

'Okay, then,' she said, and got up to leave.

'I'll see you tomorrow,' I said automatically.

She bit her lip. 'I'm not sure, actually. Will said something about a picnic.'

It stung all over again, hearing her say those words, knowing I wasn't included.

'Sure,' I said, not meeting her eyes as I held open the door. It took every ounce of self-control I had not to slam it behind her.


I didn't return to the lake that week. I couldn't bear the thought of turning up there and finding myself alone, like a lost puppy abandoned by its owners, desperate for some scrap of attention. I imagined Will and Amy together, lost in each other, not thinking of me for a moment, and I hated it. And I imagined them discussing me, how they should probably go back to the lake, just for an afternoon, because I didn't have any other friends and they were sorry for me – and I hated that even more.

Amy tried ringing every day at first, but when I saw her number appear on my phone I didn't answer. The calls were followed by texts asking if I was okay, hinting that I shouldn't feel uncomfortable about joining her and Will at the lake, reassuring me that my presence would be welcome, pretending everything was as it had been before. I replied briefly, giving vague excuses I knew she'd correctly interpret as a brush-off, and after a while the texts stopped.

For my part, I stayed mostly in my room, wallowing in self-pity. I composed long messages to Will that were alternately brilliantly furious or coolly detached. I imagined him reading them and realising that he'd been a fool, that he'd given up something extraordinary, that our meeting of minds was more powerful than anything he'd ever have with Amy. But then I remembered the way he'd touched his cheek where she'd kissed him, and I deleted the messages unsent.

With radio silence from Amy, I might have spent the end of the holidays in self-imposed exile, dreading the return to school where, I was sure, the news that Will and Amy were now an item would be the subject of feverish gossip. But after a few days without hearing from her, I received a message:

*Coming over. Need to see you.*

The first thought that leapt to my mind was that she and Will had split up. It was that which made me hesitate before replying with yet another excuse, and in the time it took me to realise that this was likely wishful thinking, there was a knock at the door.

I heard my mother inviting Amy in, cooing over how pretty her hair looked. I wondered if I'd have been able to count on any maternal loyalty if I'd told her that Amy had stolen the love of my life, but in my heart, I knew the answer. It was why I hadn't shared the story in the first place.

Amy was despatched upstairs ('Try and get her out of that room. I think she's decided she's allergic to fresh air') and I had just enough time to check my face in the mirror before she was tapping at the open door.

'Knock, knock,' she said. 'Can I come in?'

I closed the magazine I'd been reading, which she took as assent. She settled herself on the end of the bed. 'I've missed you,' she said, without preamble. 'You don't answer my messages.'

I wouldn't meet her eyes. 'I've been busy. I thought you would be too.'

'You mean with Will?'

'I suppose.' I could smell coconut on her skin, a sharp reminder that I hadn't set foot in a shower for days. 'It's fine,' I said, hearing the bitterness in my voice.

'Have you got your stuff for next week?' she asked, trying to pretend there was nothing wrong. I let her talk about buying new uniform, speculate about the timetable and how many free periods we'd get. Her words washed over me, while I drew patterns on my duvet with my fingertip. *If only she'd never come here*, I thought. *If only she'd never moved to Gramwell.*

Eventually, she must have seen she was getting nowhere. Silence budded, blossomed, filled the air between us. She was, I thought, on the verge of giving up and leaving. The prospect filled me with equal measures of relief and despair. But then something seemed to occur to her.

'You made me a promise,' she said.

I looked at her, perplexed. We'd never made solemn vows of friendship, held hands and sworn that nothing would come between us, we'd be sisters to the end, etc, etc. That kind of thing, I firmly believed, happened only in books, or possibly in boarding schools. Yet Amy was staring at me as if about to invoke some kind of ancient oath.

'What are you on about?'

She leaned closer, and I caught another whiff of coconut. 'You promised you'd teach me how to do that dive.'

I would have laughed if I hadn't felt like crying. 'I don't think so,' I said. The idea of standing next to Amy, watching Will's mesmerised expression as she took something else I'd thought was mine and made it hers – I wouldn't do it. I refused. 'It's not safe,' I added, hoping that would shut her up.

'You'd make it safe,' she said. 'I'd do what you told me. We could go on our own. Just you and me.'

I was going to say no, but I was lonely, I suppose; that's the only explanation for it. Even knowing things could never be the same between Amy and me, I hoped for the impossible – that if we went back to the lake, we could reset our friendship. That without Will there I would remember the things I loved about her, could forget what she'd stolen from me and simply take pleasure in her company.

'I can't teach you to do that dive, Amy,' I told her firmly. 'There's nowhere safe to do it. But if you want to go back to the lake, I'll come with you. Just us two.'

She clapped her hands and gave a little cheer, and in spite of myself, I felt my spirits lift. I was pleased that she hadn't argued, gratified that she still wanted to spend time with me.

I should have realised it was never going to be that simple.

# THIRTY-FIVE

*Now*

The street slides past outside the windows of the bus. A manicurist. A betting shop. A Turkish barber. The red-bordered roundel of the Tube station appears, but I wait until the last minute to get to my feet, jumping off just as the doors are about to close.

I look around, keep looking as I enter the station, as I run down the escalator. There's a train waiting on the platform, but I keep walking until the doors start to beep before running to the next carriage and hopping on board. It is middle-of-the-day quiet. I count eight people, inspect each of them in turn: woman, older woman, man with dreadlocks, man in scrubs, man and woman with toddler, older man with walking stick.

Is the man from the train working with someone? Do dreadlocks or scrubs count those men out? Is there a chance it could be a woman?

I scan my surroundings as I get off at the next station, follow the signs to the exit, every nerve ending crackling with adrenaline. At the ticket hall, I turn and go back down the escalators, take the next train in the direction I've just come from. I travel two stops, repeat the process. I can't see anyone following me, but that means nothing. I switch to another line, then another. I get off at Oxford Circus, because it's busy and has multiple exits. I take one, walk along the road and re-enter the station. Then I take another train, get off at Marble Arch, make for a burger place, buy coffee.

I find a table in a corner at the back, facing the entrance. I sit there, feet tapping, watching it like a hawk.

The words of that phone call run round and round my head. *Forget all about Marina Leeson, or you're going to get hurt.* Meaning, perhaps, that I *won't* get hurt if I abandon her. Does that mean she's the one the man on the train is focused on, after all? But what about the message he left me in that book? The newspaper cutting with my face scribbled out?

I take a gulp of coffee, try to focus. He could have found out who I was, googled that article about ceramics and followed the trail of breadcrumbs to the stories about what happened in Gramwell. Maybe he chanced his arm, thinking no smoke without fire, that some vague threats would be enough to make me shut up about Marina.

But that newspaper cutting was the real thing, not a printout or a copy. Only someone who was there at the time would have had it. Someone who cared enough to keep it for all these years. And someone who hated me so much, they couldn't bear to look at my face in that photograph.

Who? I don't have any answer that makes sense.

And if this is about Gramwell, why is it happening now, after all this time? And where does Marina fit in? If she's just another wrongdoer the man on the train is out to punish, why did she order that book with its eerily relevant story? If it was just a coincidence, how did the man on the train know to write his message on that page?

I'm going round in circles. But I'm not giving up.

No matter how hopeless this feels, I must be getting closer. That's why he's upped the ante, calling me directly to warn me off. I think back to that phone call: there was something about it that bothered me. What was it?

There was no question the voice belonged to a man, surely the one I saw with Marina. I cast my mind back to that day, trying to remember what he looked like. His face was mostly hidden by those sunglasses and that beard, his hair covered by the hoodie. But he was white, roughly the same age as me. Not much to go on, but there was no reason the voice wouldn't fit. And yet there *was* something about it that had struck me at the time, something that had seemed not quite natural.

It's getting busier in the burger bar, the background noise gradually climbing. There was noise in the background of the call too, I remember, that staccato series of knocks, abruptly cut off. Then it fell silent until the voice started speaking again. Why was that?

And then it comes to me: *he muted the call.* But why? There can only be one explanation. There was something about that background noise he didn't want me to hear. Something he worried might give me a clue to where he was.

I thought he was at Flyte Gardens, that he was the dark shape watching from the upstairs window. But what if I was wrong? What if my anxiety was making me jump at shadows? What if he'd rigged up another camera somewhere, was watching from another location?

Or perhaps there really was a figure upstairs, but it was his accomplice, someone he instructed to keep watch on the house while he stayed with Marina? Maybe they told him about my visit. It had been a few minutes, after all, since I left the garden before I received the call. Perhaps that was explained by the time taken for his spy to report what they'd seen?

I concentrate, try to recall the noises. Harsh knocks, one following the other in rapid succession. There was the ghost of an echo too, as if the sound had travelled a distance. Something about it is familiar to me, but try as I might, I can't put a name to it.

I finish my coffee, but I'm still no clearer what to do next. So I pick up the phone and call the one person who might be able to help me decide.


Sam arrives an hour later. By then, I've drunk three more coffees, and I'm wired. He looks jumpy too, checking over his shoulder twice on his way from the door to the small table where I'm sitting with an array of empty cardboard cups.

I surprise myself by getting to my feet and giving him a hug. I suppose it's relief that he's here, that he hasn't decided he can't associate with me now I'm officially persona non grata with Guy.

'Are you okay?' he asks as he pulls out the chair opposite and glances behind him again. 'You haven't seen anyone?'

I've told him about the phone call, about how somehow the man from the train knew I'd been back to Flyte Gardens. I haven't said anything about the broken pots or the newspaper article with its defaced photograph. I tell myself I don't want him distracted, focusing on the wrong things – but the truth is, I can't see a way of telling him without explaining what happened ten years ago. And I can't bear the idea of looking at him and seeing the moment whatever he feels for me turns to disgust.

Now I shake my head, reassure him that, as far as I can tell, we're not being watched.

He nods. 'So tell me again what he said.'

I repeat the conversation, as close to word for word as I can remember it. He frowns. 'That doesn't give us a lot to go on.'

I like the sound of the 'us', but there's not much else that's comforting. 'There was something else, though,' I say, and he looks up quizzically. 'Well, two things, actually.'

I explain about the noises in the background, about how they were cut off. Sam understands immediately. 'He muted the call. So there's something he didn't want you to hear.'

'That's what I thought.'

'So tell me more about the noises.' I try to describe what I heard as accurately as possible, but I'm aware as I'm saying the words that they're not much help.

Sam wrinkles his nose. 'A drum, maybe?'

'No, I don't think so. It sounded harsher than that. Like something hitting something else, but fast.'

'How many times?'

I think about it. 'Four or five, maybe? But then the sound cut out, so there might have been more.'

'Someone knocking at a door?'

'Maybe, I guess. But why would he care if I heard that?'

'True, it doesn't make a lot of sense.' He sighs. 'You said there were two things you noticed. What else?'

'His voice. It sounded odd.'

Sam shifts in his seat. 'Odd how?'

It's the same question I've been asking myself, but I don't have a clear answer. 'Something about his accent, perhaps. It didn't sound quite right.'

'What, like he wasn't British?'

'No – more like, it changed as he was talking. As if maybe it wasn't real. Like he was faking it.'

Sam stiffens. 'I knew it.' He prods the tabletop with his finger. 'It was Darren.'

I groan. I know it's his favourite theory, but I still don't agree. 'It sounded nothing like him,' I tell him.

'Exactly! Because he was disguising his voice! He didn't want you to recognise him.' He leans back in his chair, confident he's hit the nail on the head. 'Let's look at the evidence. Who comes into your life after you see Marina and this guy on the train? Who feeds you an address where you find a bunch of incriminating stuff that miraculously disappears when you call the police? Who has a good idea of when you're likely to turn up there? Who emails you just before your phone is hacked?'

'But I googled him, Sam! I still don't see how anyone could have known I'd do that.'

He continues as if I haven't spoken. 'Who has your phone number?' He pauses, then: 'He does have your phone number, right?' I nod. 'Okay, then. And who has to disguise his voice, so you won't recognise him when he calls? Did you ever hear the guy on the train speak?'

'No.'

'Then why would he have to put on some weird accent?'

He sits there, waiting for an answer I don't have. But he doesn't know about the newspaper article, the connection to Gramwell. Darren's accent is south London born and bred, and he's barely out of school into the bargain. Why would he care about what happened almost a decade ago at the other end of the country?

Unless he's the accomplice. Someone helping out the man on the train in order to make a fast buck. That, I find less difficult to believe.

'Let's call him now,' Sam says.

'What?'

'Let's ring Darren. You can see if he sounds like the guy who phoned you.'

I think about it. Maybe it's worth doing, even if it's just to rule him out.

Sam is already getting out his own phone. 'Put him on speakerphone. I'll record his voice, so you can listen to it back afterwards.'

'Okay.' I reach for my phone, find the number. 'I'm not saying anything about today, though. I don't think he's involved in any of this. But if I'm wrong, I don't want him thinking I'm onto him.'

Sam slides his phone across the table, already recording. I select speakerphone and hit the button to connect the call. Two rings, three, then the ringing stops. A recorded voice says, *'Please leave a message after the tone.'*

I hang up. 'It's the generic voicemail woman.'

'He's ignoring you,' says Sam. 'He's worried you've recognised his voice so he's not picking up.'

'He's probably just busy.' But I'm uneasy; he's always answered before.

Sam stuffs his phone back into his pocket. 'We can't sit here forever,' he says.

He's right, but I have no idea what else to do, or where to go. I'm not going back to my flat to wait for the man from the train to pay me a visit. Perhaps I should go to my parents'? But if I announce I'm staying, they'll have questions. Answering them honestly is unthinkable, and I don't have the energy to lie right now.

'Could we go to yours?' As soon as I've said it, I wish I hadn't.

Sam's face lights up like a Christmas tree, and he's already on his feet, retrieving my coat from the back of my chair and holding it out to me.

'Sure,' he says. 'I mean, it makes sense.'

I should say something, make it clear this is a friends-only thing.

'Do you need to go back to yours first, get some stuff?' He's piling up the empty cups, using a paper napkin to wipe a smear of coffee from the table. 'You will stay, right? You can't be in that flat on your own.'

'Thanks, Sam. That would be great, if it's okay with you. Just for a few days, until I've figured out what to do. I'll take the sofa, of course.'

It's come out clumsily, implying that he was expecting something different. I see him colour, and I turn away, busy myself picking up my bag and scarf. When we get to the door, I pause, checking the street for anyone who looks suspicious. But despite his wariness when he came in, Sam walks straight out onto the pavement, apparently not worried about who might be watching. It's a guy thing, I suppose – they're not trained to be afraid. I pull my coat more closely around me, and hurry to catch up.

*

*We're nearing the end now; I can feel it. The warning has been given. She knows the risks.*

*Will she do the right thing? Or will she crawl back under her stone?*

*I see her in that chair, chains around her chest, around her feet. Nowhere to hide. Nothing to do except tell the truth.*

*How will I feel when it's over? I rather think I'll miss it. The challenge, the anticipation. It's given me something to fill the days. A sense of purpose, I suppose.*

*I'll miss Marina too, strange though that sounds. I'll be alone again. There's no escaping that.*

*But what good's a sense of purpose if you don't fulfil it?*

# THIRTY-SIX

*Then*

The day after Amy came to my house I was back in my usual spot, leaning against the wall at the end of her road. I'd hoped it would be like it had been at the beginning, before Will turned up at the lake, but something about Amy was off from the start. She walked down the road right on time, but her greeting was stiff and formal.

Our conversation as we walked was stilted. The pressure of not mentioning Will made everything seem forced, unnatural. When we arrived at the lake, it seemed wrong to be there without him, impossible not to acknowledge his absence. But neither of us did.

For the first hour or so we read, swam and pretended to relax. When lunchtime came, Amy reached for her bag and extracted Tupperware boxes of sandwiches, salad and fruit. She'd even brought plastic plates and cutlery for us to eat with. She'd gone to some trouble, I thought, and was touched.

'I've brought something too,' I said, smiling tentatively as I pulled the bottle of white rum I'd liberated from my parents' drinks cabinet from my own bag. I twisted off the cap and handed it to her. 'No cups, though. Sorry.'

We handed the bottle back and forth between us as we ate. Amy wasn't usually much of a drinker, but that day was an exception. Perhaps, I thought, she was nervous. Perhaps we both were. And perhaps it was the rum that loosened my inhibitions enough to raise the subject that until then we'd steadfastly avoided.

'So, you and Will,' I said, my tone determinedly casual. 'How are things going?'

She looked down at her plate. 'Okay. Good.'

I waited, but she seemed intent on spearing a cherry tomato. I laughed lightly. 'Is that it? Just "good"?'

'I thought today was going to be about you and me,' she said. 'We don't need to talk about Will.'

I shrugged. 'I don't mind. He's your boyfriend now. It would be strange not to talk about him.' She didn't answer, but it was like picking a scab – I couldn't help myself. 'What do you talk about when it's just the two of you? Or perhaps you don't have much time for talking.'

It was meant to be a joke, but it sounded crass. I thought Amy would take her usual tack of refusing to dignify it with a response, but instead she put down her fork.

'Actually, we talk about you. We did yesterday, anyway.'

There was something about the way she looked at me as she said it that made me uncomfortable. 'Oh, yes?'

She nodded. 'I told him that we were going to spend today together, just you and me. I think he was worried.'

I was taken aback. 'Worried how?'

'Worried that you might say something.' She looked at me for a long moment, then picked up her fork again. 'Tell me something.'

She speared a cherry tomato, and I watched amber pulp

slide up the tines. I laughed again, louder than I'd meant to, the sound echoing off the cliff face.

'Is something funny?'

I shook my head. 'This is a weird conversation. I don't know why Will would be worried about us talking.'

She pushed her plate away. 'I think I've had enough.'

My appetite had gone too. I went to take another sip of rum and was surprised to find the bottle nearly empty. 'Want to finish this?' I asked her, expecting her to say no, but she took it and drained the last few drops.

'And now it's time for my lesson.'

She said it as if it were a pre-arranged thing. 'What lesson?' I said, blankly.

'You said you'd teach me how to do that dive. I want to do a somersault.'

Not this again. I sighed in exasperation. 'Amy, I've told you, it's not safe. You'll hurt yourself if you try to do it too close to the water.'

'Then we go further up.' She pointed to the cliff. 'There are plenty of places. You said you'd find somewhere.'

'No, I said I'd look into it. I did. There's nowhere the right height.'

'I don't believe you.'

I turned to her in surprise. She pointed to the flat rock jutting out from the cliff face, the place I'd identified myself as a possible dive site. 'What's wrong with that?'

'I checked it out the other day, when you cancelled on me at the last minute.'

I thought the reminder might chasten her, but she started walking to the track at the edge of the lake. 'So what's the problem?'

I got to my feet and followed her. 'You can't get up there.'

She ignored me, started picking her way along the trail. When she reached the cliff, she inspected it closely, hands on hips. 'What about if we swam across? We could climb up those rocks.'

She pointed to the rockfall I'd scrambled up with the same thought.

'I've tried it. You can't get close enough.'

She turned and gave me a hard stare. 'You just don't want me to do it.'

'Don't be ridiculous. I told you, you can't get to that rock.'

She mumbled something I didn't hear, and made her way back to the ledge, sitting down and dangling her feet in the water.

'I could teach you to do a forward roll in the water instead,' I said. 'You know, like a racing turn.'

She looked at me coldly. 'I'm doing that dive with or without you.'

She pushed off the ledge and started swimming to the opposite side. I watched her find the same rock I had to haul herself from the water. She was out quickly, striding confidently up the sloping face of its neighbour.

'You can't get up there,' I said. 'I've told you, you're wasting your time.'

She ignored me. She'd slowed now, looking for a path between the rocks; but still she moved faster than I had the previous day. I wondered if it was the rum, giving her false confidence. And just as I thought that, she stumbled.

I ran to the water's edge. 'Amy! Are you okay?'

But she was on her feet again. 'I'm fine,' she said. 'Completely and utterly fine.'

'Maybe you should come down.'

'Maybe you should stop telling me what to do.'

I gaped at her. 'What's wrong with you?'

'I could ask you the same thing.'

She was slurring now, I realised. 'You need to come down from there,' I said. 'You're going to fall.'

She didn't reply, continued climbing the rocks. I could barely look, but I reassured myself that in a moment she'd see she couldn't go any further. Sure enough, a few seconds later she came to a standstill, hands planted on her hips as she surveyed the edge of the rockfall.

'I told you,' I said. 'There's no way to get over there.'

But now she was looking towards the dive site, measuring the distance and angle with her eyes.

'It's too far, Amy,' I said, and I could hear the panic in my voice. 'Don't be stupid.'

'Too far for you, maybe,' she said.

I was too scared to be annoyed. 'This is madness. Why do you even want to do this?'

She took a step towards the edge of the rock and stopped, one leg in front of the other.

'Please, Amy, please come down.'

She looked down at me then. 'I know what you did,' she said. 'After Chloe's party. Will told me.'

The breath left my body. I opened my mouth to reply, then closed it again. Did this mean he'd seen sense at last, that he'd told her it was over?

'He told me you threw yourself at him.'

I gaped at her in disbelief. 'What? No, it wasn't like that.'

'Don't try to deny it.' Even from this distance, I could see her eyes glisten. 'I thought you were my friend, but all you care about is yourself. You're disgusting.'

She gritted her teeth, bent her knees. She was going to make the leap, and fear drove every other thought from my head. 'You're pissed!' I screamed at her. 'Just come down. Let's talk about this.'

For one terrifying second, I thought she was going to jump. But then she straightened her knees, and the tension left her shoulders. She took a step back from the edge.

'Okay, just take your time—'

And that's when her foot slid out from beneath her.

# THIRTY-SEVEN

*Now*

Sam's flat, it turns out, is just a few streets away from mine. Funny, I never knew we lived so close. The interior is just like Sam himself – neat, self-contained, stylish in an understated kind of way. I stand in his tiny front room with the bag I hastily filled with a toothbrush and change of clothes. There is an exceptionally healthy pot plant in the corner; Sam looks after the things he loves.

'That's Melissa's,' he says, seeing me eyeing it. 'My flatmate. She's the one with the green fingers.'

I'm surprised. He's never mentioned a flatmate before, but of course it makes sense. I can only afford my place because the landlord is a sweet older lady who keeps the rent low 'to support the young people'.

'Will she be okay with me staying?' I ask.

He nods. 'Of course. She's out and about though, so I'll take the sofa. I don't want her having a heart attack if she comes home and finds some strange woman sleeping in the sitting room.'

I'm annoyed with myself. I should have thought this through, asked more questions. Now I'm turfing Sam out of his bed and imposing on some woman I've never met.

'It's fine, Laura, honestly,' Sam says. 'Let me get you a coffee, then I'll go and get your room ready.'

I ask if I can help, but he waves me away, disappears to make the coffee. I've already drunk a vat of it and to be honest I'd prefer something stronger, but I'm not going to complain. He returns with only one mug, and bustles off again immediately. I settle myself on the sofa, but the phone call and the caffeine have left me jittery, and a second later I get up and circle the room. In addition to the sofa and the pot plant, there's an armchair with wooden armrests, a small round table, a TV on a cloth-covered chest, and a bookcase in the corner. I stop in front of the bookcase and inspect its contents.

The top two shelves are non-fiction – a few reference books, a handful on mindfulness and yoga, others on management and business. A couple of poetry anthologies are stacked at the end, and I find myself wondering if this collection belongs to Sam or Melissa. Both, maybe.

The remaining shelves are fiction, and again there's an eclectic mix. Literary fiction, thrillers, a series of detective novels. And then I see something and my head swims so that I have to put out my hand to steady myself. I pull out the book, stare at it. It's the same edition as the one I have in my bag, the book the man from the train left his message in: *The Caves of Agoroth.*

'They're good fun, aren't they?' Sam's voice breaks into my buzzing brain, and I jump, almost drop the book.

He comes over and takes it from my hand, reading from the blurb on the back. '"Dare you enter the Caves of Agoroth?" I couldn't resist when you told me about it. I used to read these books all the time.'

I try to return his smile, but I'm on edge. It's the shock, I suppose, seeing that book here. But there's no reason Sam shouldn't have bought it. No reason it should mean anything more than he's said.

'My favourite was set in the Wild West,' he continues. 'But it was more a ghost story than a Western. Pretty gory, as I recall. I've been trying to find a copy, but I can't remember the title.' He reaches past me and slides the book back onto the shelf. 'Do you want to see where you'll be sleeping?'

I nod, not quite trusting myself to speak, and follow him down the hall.

'Shower room,' he says, pointing to a door on the left. 'And this is my room. Well, your room, of course. For the duration. For as long as you need it.'

He stands back to let me inside. The room is a decent size, clean, minimalist. The bed, though, is a departure – a black cast iron frame that immediately and inappropriately makes me think of handcuffs. It's been made up with white sheets that have obviously been ironed. There's a faint smell of fabric softener in the air.

'This is great. Thanks, Sam.'

He beams. 'I'll leave you to settle in. I'm just going to pop to the shop and get us something for dinner.'

I try to tell him I don't want to put him to any more trouble, that I'd be happy to go to the pub or get a takeaway, my shout. 'It's the least I can do,' I say. But Sam isn't having any of it. He insists he wants to cook, that I need to eat properly and keep my strength up. I give in because Sam is a good person, and doing things for other people genuinely makes him happy – and because I'm not a good person, and having other people do things for me makes me happy too.

He goes off to get provisions, and I close the door to the bedroom in case Melissa comes home. I sit on the bed and find the mattress is firm, the way I like it, and the sheets crisp. I could almost imagine ironing my own bedding to be able to sleep in a bed like this. I shift a couple of cushions that are propped against the pillows and rest my head. I'll close my eyes, just for a moment, just to see how it feels...

*It's a promise.*

I open my eyes. The room is as dark as it gets in London, ochre light suggesting there's a streetlamp just outside the window. The temperature has fallen a few degrees, and the flat is silent save for the rumble of distant traffic. I reach for my phone to check the time, but it's not in my pocket. I sit up in sudden panic, only to find it's next to me on the mattress. I must have left it there before I went to sleep.

The screen reads 01:28. I've been asleep for over five hours, slept right through dinner. I hope Sam didn't go to too much trouble.

I settle back onto the pillows, but lying down stirs the echoes of my dream. The voice is as clear as if the phone were next to my ear: *Forget about Marina Leeson or you'll get hurt. And that's not a threat. It's a promise.*

I'm cold, and I wriggle beneath the duvet. Is it possible that Sam was right and the man on the phone was Darren? Try as I might, I can't explain how he could have known I'd want someone to look at that image of Marina, or how he could have made sure that I'd contact him. But what if I do as Sam suggests, and set that to one side for the moment? If the case against Darren is compelling, there has to be an explanation that makes sense of everything.

And it's true – Darren was the one who presented me with the Flyte Gardens address. I only have his word that it was really what was printed on the envelope that fell from Marina's bag. He could have superimposed it there. And Darren knew I'd open whatever attachments he emailed me, so he'd have had the perfect opportunity to plant a virus. He'd probably get some kind of alert when I opened the file, firing the starting gun for my visit to Flyte Gardens.

Then there's the weirdness of that voice on the phone, the accent I couldn't place and that seemed to drift in and out. Sam's right that only someone I knew would have had to worry about me recognising his voice. Who else could possibly fit the bill?

And then an answer comes to me and I jolt upright in bed, my heart pounding.

*Sam.*

I shake my head, but the thought won't budge. I told Sam I'd found Marina's address, told him I was going over there. It's been Sam I've confided in every step of the way. Sam, with all his questions, his offers of help, turning up just after someone had broken into my flat. Was it really to check how I was feeling? Or was it to make sure I'd found his message, that I was taking his threat seriously?

An image flashes into my mind: Sam rummaging in my kitchen drawer, claiming to be looking for a teaspoon. But there'd been a caddy of cutlery right in front of him. And after he'd left, I noticed the bookshelves tidied, the cushions on the sofa plumped. Is he really that much of a neat freak? Or was he searching for Marina's note? Trying to remove the last piece of evidence that could have corroborated my story about what I'd seen on the train?

And what's he doing with a copy of *The Caves of Agoroth*? Has he known all along what happened in Gramwell? He said he'd never looked into my past, but how believable is that? Someone who's pretended to like me, who showed that interview in the newspaper to Guy but has never been curious enough to follow up the hints there about my past? And if it's true that he'd simply loved those books as a child, why didn't he say so when I told him what Marina had ordered from the bookshop?

Sam knows my phone number, my email, my address. And suddenly I remember that first time he offered to walk me home. He'd said he lived near me, and I assumed he was being polite, trying to give the impression it wouldn't inconvenience him. But what if he was simply telling the truth? What if he knew where I lived, had moved close by deliberately? What if he knows more about me than I ever imagined?

I don't know Sam from Gramwell, I'm sure of that. But the man on the train must have been there, the man who went to so much trouble to hide his face behind those dark glasses and the thick beard. He was the one who enlisted Sam's help, needing another pair of hands to carry out his plan. It makes perfect sense: from the moment he started at the firm, Sam singled me out – trying to get me to talk, asking me for after-work drinks. Trying to get close.

And it worked, didn't it? I've been telling him what I was thinking at every stage, feeding him information he could pass straight back to the man on the train. It was Sam I told about the note on the receipt, finding out Marina's name, getting her image from the bookshop CCTV. Sam who knew I was going to Flyte Gardens, who asked me to call him when I arrived. Did he want a heads up, to make sure the coast was clear if I found my way inside?

I've opened Sam's texts, answered his calls and emails. He's had every bit as good a chance of putting spyware on my phone as Darren. And he's been trying to throw suspicion on Darren from the start. I should have seen through that tactic straight away, should have seen that he was trying to distract me from the truth – that the accomplice to the man on the train was someone much closer to home.

The phone calls checking in on me, the visits to bring me shopping. No one is that kind without an ulterior motive. And now he's got me exactly where he wants me.

I push back the duvet and swing my legs out of the bed. I'm

fully dressed apart from my shoes, left in the hallway to protect Sam's pristine carpet. I go to the window and look out. The street is deserted, a terrace of Victorian two-up two-downs that stretches in both directions. The window is a sash, the roof of a bay directly below. I could try to climb out, but there's a light on in the house opposite. Someone might see me and think I'm a burglar, alert the police – or worse, Sam. Besides, the drainpipe to the side of the window is plastic and looks disturbingly fragile. I don't trust it to hold my weight.

I could try to brazen it out. Just walk out of here and if Sam asks where I'm going, tell him I know exactly what he's been up to. I don't see Sam as the violent type – but then it seems I don't know him at all. And what of this 'Melissa' person he supposedly shares his flat with? I've never set eyes on her. For all I know, she doesn't exist. For all I know, his flatmate is the man from the train.

Despite the cold, I feel sweat trickle down my back. As far as Sam is concerned, I'm tucked up fast asleep in bed, blissfully unaware of what he's been doing. I should make the most of that advantage – leave quickly and quietly, and get as far away as I can.

I pick up my bag and open the door to the hallway. Everything is still and silent. I switch on the torch on my phone, taking care to keep the beam pointed at the front door. There's a metal door guard, and a bolt at the top and bottom, but only one keyhole. Slowly, I sweep the torch beam around the end of the hall, illuminating coat hooks and a small table with a vigorous pot plant on top and a drawer underneath. I grab my shoes and pull them on, then position the strap of my bag across my body. Silently, I creep towards the table and open the drawer, praying to a god I'm not sure I believe in that I'll find what I need.

I see it at once – a small yellow fob with two keys attached. I separate it from pencils and scraps of paper, a car key with a Ford key ring. I'm surprised that someone capable of doing what

Sam has done could live somewhere so ordinary. But then I catch myself: I, of all people, know how much can lurk beneath the surface.

The plain fob suggests the keys are spares. I just hope they don't open doors at a neighbour's, or Sam's parents' house. I tiptoe to the front door and retrieve my jacket before gently sliding back the bolts and the door guard. I select the Yale and it slides smoothly into the keyhole, producing a soft click as the lock gives. I pause, listen, but nothing moves. I slip the keys into my pocket and step onto the landing, pulling the door closed behind me. Then I'm stealing down the stairs, moving as fast as I dare. The floorboards protest and I freeze, wait for the shout, the opening door. I'm about to continue when I hear it: a stealthy creak from above.

Someone is awake.

I fly down the remaining stairs, throw myself at the front door. It doesn't move. I fumble for the keys in my pocket, my fingers all thumbs. At any moment, I expect to feel arms dragging me back. But I have the keys, and I shove the longer one into the keyhole. It doesn't turn.

I rattle it in the lock, no longer caring how much noise I make. It has to fit, I have to get out of here. And then by some miracle I feel it slide further in, and it's turning, and the door is open and there's cold air on my face. I'm sobbing as I run onto the street, and when I look back the doorway is a gaping hole, leaking its darkness onto the path.

I don't wait to see who'll come through it.

———

The night bus is half-empty, quiet. We are away from clubland here, this route the realm of night shift workers and homeless people. A man dozes on the back seat, his hat pulled down over his eyes. Beyond the window, the street is grey and blue. Is

Marina out there somewhere? I reach for my purse, take the slip of paper from the coin section, stare at the words.

*Help me.*

Sam knew. He must have done. All this time I was confiding in him, telling him how worried I was, he knew what had happened to Marina. Every time he asked me a question and I replied, I was betraying her. I'd thought he was my friend, but all the time he was monitoring me, feeding me red herrings, checking I didn't get too close to the truth. How could I have been so stupid?

And it's Marina who's paid the price. While I've been running around getting nowhere, she's been trapped, maybe hurt, maybe worse.

I want to curl up in this seat and never move again. But I close my eyes and I see Marina's face, the way she looked at me as that man pulled her from the train, begging me for help. And I know I can't abandon her. I have to put this right.

The bus is slowing, the interior lights switching on and off, the silent signal to sleeping passengers that it's time to rouse themselves. We're at the end of the line, and the symbolism of it is almost too much to bear. I get to my feet, make my way to the door. The bus station is brightly lit, and even at this hour there are a few people perched on plastic benches, awaiting their ride. They all have places to be.

I should get another bus, keep myself around people until day breaks or I work out what to do. There's a Routemaster pulling in at a shelter across from the station, so I set off to catch it. The passengers are already disembarking as I get there, most heading towards the road. One, though, is lucky enough to have a lift. She walks towards a red car parked near the bus station entrance, raises a hand to the driver in greeting.

Something about it presses a switch in my mind. *A red car.*

Slowly, my brain kicks into gear, making the connection. There was a red car parked outside Flyte Gardens that day. I took its registration number, but the conversation with Sam distracted me, turned my focus back towards Darren – just the way he'd intended it to.

I board the bus and take a seat near the front, pulling my phone from my pocket. I find the registration. I've never checked a plate before, but it turns out it's simple. The DVLA tells me the car is a red Volkswagen, which at first, I think, gives me nothing I didn't know before. But that's not true, I realise. It means the plates match the car – they're the real deal.

There's plenty of other information too. It's taxed and insured, like the car of a good, law-abiding citizen. It was manufactured in 2016, registered the same year. There's stuff on fuel type, cylinder capacity, wheelplan – whatever that is. But there's nothing about who owns it.

My mind goes back to the car key in the drawer at Sam's house – but that had a Ford logo on it. Perhaps, after all, the Polo has nothing to do with Marina or the man who took her. I remember the bobble hat on the front seat, and I can't help feeling that men who kidnap women don't wear bobble hats. There was something on the parcel shelf too, I recall, some kind of fluorescent tabard.

I check the photographs on my phone, and there it is. Bright yellow, like the kind of thing worn by builders or lollipop ladies. It's folded neatly, an emblem in black print across the front. I zoom in and read what it says: Thorstone.

Time stands still. And then it speeds up, hurtling backwards so fast my head swims and bile rises to my throat.

I should have known this was coming. There was only ever one way this could end.

If I'm going to have any chance of saving Marina, I have to go back to the place I'd hoped never to set foot in again.

# THIRTY-EIGHT

*Then*

Amy didn't cry out. There was just a sick sound of flesh striking stone again and again, until her body came to rest on the sloping rock just above the water. She didn't move, and for a moment I could only stare at her, watching the red pool blossom from her head.

And then something clicked, and I was diving into the water, swimming as fast as I could to the other side. I reached the rock where she lay and hauled myself upwards; but with her body draped across the surface there was no way to climb out without risking hurting her or me. Her arm was hanging down and I grabbed her by the wrist, shook her.

'Amy!' I called. 'Amy!'

She groaned, and relief flooded through me.

'Stay where you are,' I said. 'You could have broken something.'

She didn't seem to hear me, was struggling to turn her head. Her lips moved, but no sound came out. I reached for her hand, squeezed it.

'I have to go,' I told her. 'I need to get someone, but I'll be back as fast as I can.'

Her lips were moving again, and I leaned forward as far as I could. This time I just made out what she said: 'Help me.'

'Yes,' I said. 'That's what I'm going to do.' I let her go, dropped back into the water and swam for the ledge.

The moment I was on dry land I grabbed my phone. I knew already there was never a signal here, but I dialled 999 anyway, stabbing out the numbers one-handed as I dragged on my shoes. But the phone just gave a dull chirrup: *No service*.

I threw a T-shirt over my swimming costume and ran up the slope, back to the track. I was about to turn and go back the way we'd come, to run to the leisure centre, but then I heard the noise of the quarry works, a revving engine and the boom of machinery. The workers were closer, I thought, and they'd prob-ably have someone trained in medical emergencies. I ran towards the sound of the machines.

I expected to reach the works at any minute, but time stretched by and the trees I'd thought would soon thin out remained as dense as ever. It was impossible to see more than a few metres ahead. Then the noise of a drill rang out again, and I stopped. It had come from my right, not straight ahead as I'd expected. I must have got turned around in my panic.

I tried my phone, but the cross at the top of the screen showed it was a waste of time. I set off again, telling myself I'd be there soon and that Amy would be all right. But still there was no sign of anyone. My leg had started to ache and I looked down to see a bruise darkening on my thigh. I hadn't checked my position before I'd dived into the lake: I must have struck it on the dump box. I kept moving, trying to ignore the pain, but with every step it got worse. In my mind's eye, I saw Amy lying on the rock, her skin gradually turning blue. I had to keep going.

I limped along the stony ground, but the drill had stopped. I wasn't sure if I was going in the right direction. I paused, listened, but there was nothing but the sound of crows chattering in the trees above. Though the day was hot, I was suddenly cold, shivering. *Shock*, I noted, in a detached way, *I must be in shock.*

I remembered what Will had told me about the size of the site. I must have misjudged how close the works were. Perhaps, after all, the best thing was to go back the way I'd come. I'd wasted time, but I could cut my losses.

I turned, wincing at the pain in my leg, and started back. The trees crowded in on every side – everything looked the same. I caught my toe on a root and stumbled, arrows of pain streaking up my bruised leg. I gasped and bent double, trying to get my breath. When I looked up, I knew it: I was lost.

My knees gave out and I crumpled to the ground. An image of Amy flashed into my head, that red pool spreading slowly from her head. *She could die*, I thought. *If I don't get up and find help, she'll bleed to death.* I thought of Gramwell without Amy in it, and the rush of emotion was so intense I could hardly breathe.

*I have to do this*, I told myself. *I have to.*

By the time I reached the leisure centre, it was starting to get dark. I stumbled into the foyer and collapsed, the woman at reception running around the desk, calling for help. I managed to tell her that Amy had fallen, that she needed help. There were phone calls, a blanket that looked like tin foil, a police officer in a yellow jacket crouching in front of me, asking what had happened. My parents arrived, my mother exclaiming in horror when she saw me. I felt removed from it all, as if the sounds and pictures were coming at me through thick glass.

I was taken to hospital, lights shone in my face, my blood

pressure taken, my leg X-rayed. It wasn't broken, they said. I was fine, they said.

I asked about Amy. She was in ITU, but I couldn't see her. There were rules, apparently. Her family was with her.

I think that's when I first detected it: a subtle shift in the way people spoke to me. A degree less kindness, a degree more suspicion. Another police officer came, asked me why we'd been at the quarry, had we been drinking, whose idea was it to climb the rocks. She made me go through every detail of what had happened, returning to each part of the story again and again. I was exhausted, in pain, and finally my mother asked if this was really necessary, couldn't I go home and talk to her after I'd had some sleep? I'd never been more grateful to her in my life.

It was late the next morning when we eventually arrived home, and it seemed the news was already out. I trudged up the stairs to bed and pulled the duvet over my head, but I could still hear the telephone ringing downstairs, the anxious chirruping of my mother, the low rumble of my father's voice. I must have slept, because some time later I was woken by my mother opening the curtains, telling me I had to get up, that the police wanted to talk to me.

It was more of the same. Why had we gone to the quarry, who had brought the rum, where had I got it? (I could feel my mother's eyes on me as I confessed to taking the bottle from the drinks cabinet, but she stayed silent.) Why was Amy climbing the rocks, when had she fallen, what had happened then, why had it taken me so long to get back to the leisure centre?

'I heard people working,' I said. 'I thought they were nearer. But I'd hurt my leg. I was limping. And I must have panicked. Lost my bearings. I tried using my phone, but there's no signal.'

'She has a very nasty bruise,' my mother broke in. 'Have you seen her leg? I don't know how she managed to walk at all.'

But it went on. It hadn't been the first time I'd been to the quarry, had it? How many times would I say I'd been there?

With Amy or on my own? Did anyone else go? Why wasn't Will there that day? How long would I say it took me to walk to the leisure centre – on a normal day? On that day?

'Please,' I said, 'can you just tell me how Amy is? Is she okay?'

'You're good friends,' the officer said.

'She's my best friend.' It was an effort not to choke on the words.

She studied me, as if trying to make up her mind about something. 'The doctors have induced a coma,' she said. 'Amy fractured her skull and there's swelling to her brain. It's too early to say for sure, but there's a strong likelihood of permanent damage.'

I heard my mother make a strangled sound, but I couldn't speak, couldn't move. It was as if I were back at the lake, looking at Amy on that rock. The blood bloomed from her head and her lips moved as if in prayer: *help me*.

The officer looked down at her notebook. 'Let's go back to when you left her.'


When school restarted, I stayed home. I heard my mother on the phone to the headmaster, telling him I'd had a lot to deal with. 'A lot more than she should have, as I'm sure you're aware,' she said icily. But after that call she came up to my bedroom, sat on the bed. 'You can't hide away forever, Laura,' she said. 'You need to show them you have nothing to be ashamed of.'

So a week later, I was walking back through the school gates. Everywhere I went, I felt eyes on me, whispers behind my back. When I didn't react, the whispers grew louder, turned to comments. I did my best to ignore them. They weren't the people whose opinion I cared about.

I hadn't heard anything from Will since the night of the

party. Despite everything else that had happened, I couldn't stop thinking about him. I remembered the way he'd looked at me when I'd taken his hand, led him to the alley behind Amy's house. The way he'd tasted, the feel of his fingers in my hair. The exquisite combination of desire and fear as he'd pushed inside me, the terror that at any moment someone would round the corner and see us.

I'd thought about texting him, but nothing I typed sounded right. I told myself that he was staying away to protect me, that he didn't want to add fuel to the rumours. I told myself I should follow his example, wait to see him until people had found something else to talk about. But the loneliness and the longing grew inside me like a cancer.

When Saturday rolled around, I told my mother I was going out.

She was baking and paused in the middle of pouring flour into a bowl. 'Where?' she asked.

'I want to see Amy.' According to the school grapevine, Amy had been brought out of her coma after forty-eight hours. As far as I could tell, that was good news.

Mum put down the bag of flour and dusted her hands against her hips. 'I know it's hard,' she said. 'I know it's unfair. But they're her parents, and you should respect their wishes.'

'She's my best friend. I don't want her to think I don't care.'

'She won't think that. She'll be in and out of consciousness. She just needs to rest.'

I felt the tears welling up and couldn't reply. Mum sighed and reached around her back to undo her apron. 'Give me five minutes,' she said. 'I'll drive you.'

It wasn't what I wanted, but I didn't have the energy to argue.

. . .

At the hospital, Mum asked if she should come in with me, and to my surprise I found myself agreeing. ITU, it turned out, was on the second floor, and one step down from a maximum security prison. You had to be buzzed into the area, then admitted to see a patient. If your name wasn't on the list, you weren't getting in. And my name, it was clear, was very definitely not on the list.

'I'll talk to Veronica,' Mum said, meaning Amy's mother. 'See if you can go in just for a minute.'

I saw the look on the nurse's face. 'It's okay,' I said, then to the nurse: 'But could you tell Amy I came? Tell her I send my love?'

She nodded, tight-lipped. I walked with Mum back to the lifts, but as we were about to be buzzed out, I caught sight of someone going into what seemed to be some kind of visitors' lounge. 'Would you mind if I walked back?' I asked her. 'I could do with some fresh air.'

There was a pause, but she must have decided it was better to pick her battles. 'I'll see you at home, then,' she said.

I left her with the excuse of needing the loo and walked back along the corridor. The door to the visitors' lounge had a glass window in the top, and as I looked in, the girl inside glanced up. I pushed open the door and stepped inside.

'Hi, Kate.'

'What are you doing here?' she snapped.

'I wanted to see how Amy was.' She half-rose from her seat, and I shook my head. 'Don't worry. They wouldn't let me in.'

She subsided, her jaw tight. 'Good.'

'I miss her,' I said.

'Don't you dare.'

I sniffed. 'Okay then. How is she? I heard she was out of the coma.'

'Like you care.'

I stared at her. 'Of course I care. How can you say that?'

She was on the verge, I could tell, a hair's breadth from letting go and unloading all the accusations I knew her family had stored up for me. And why? Because I wasn't good enough for Amy. Because my parents didn't have as much money as hers did. Because I didn't speak with the right accent. I waited for it to come, but she got up and walked to the window. 'Just go, Laura,' she said.

The weather had finally broken and the rain fell in fat cold drops as I crossed the car park. I was drenched before I got to the road, but I didn't care. I had to see Will. I had to talk to him.

The high street was all but deserted as I splashed my way to the bookshop. I saw the corner shop, picking up my pace as I passed the shelves of newspapers displayed behind clear plastic windows. But I didn't avert my eyes in time and caught sight of the headline in the *Gramwell Courier*:

'SHE LEFT MY GIRL': AMY'S MUM SPEAKS OUT

My stomach churned. The other local rags would be more of the same. The story had even made a few inches in the national tabloids. It wasn't discussed at home, and I might never have known if some kind classmate hadn't gone to the trouble of cutting them out and leaving them on my desk. I pretended to ignore them, crumpling them up and tossing them in my bag. But later I locked myself in a toilet cubicle and read every word. I had the starring role, but Will got a mention too. Quotes from people I barely knew. Events that 'have rocked this quiet town'. And the phrase I wanted to laugh at but somehow burned itself into my mind: 'a dark love triangle that ended in tragedy'.

The bookshop was almost empty, just one older couple browsing near the window, probably waiting for the rain to pass. They glanced at me, then turned back to the shelves. I was surprised: apparently not quite everyone in Gramwell knew who I was.

Will was seated behind the counter reading. He looked up as I approached, and I saw dark circles beneath his eyes. I smiled at him but he didn't smile back and I stopped, stranded in an expanse of blue carpet. 'Will?' I said.

'Laura.'

I took a step closer. 'I tried to visit Amy, but they wouldn't let me in.' He wouldn't meet my eyes. 'Have you seen her?'

He nodded, and I saw a muscle throb in his cheek.

'How was she?'

He took a shuddering breath. 'Not good.'

'But she'll get better, right?'

He didn't reply. I tried to absorb the implications of that, but my brain wasn't working properly.

'Everyone blames me,' I said. 'It doesn't matter. I know it's Amy who matters.'

I wanted him to tell me that I mattered too, but he didn't speak.

'I miss her. I miss you.'

He shook his head. 'Don't, Laura. Please don't.'

My throat tightened. 'Amy's so special. To both of us. I hate this. I don't know how to be without her.'

He wiped his hand over his face, looked up at the ceiling.

'I'd like to talk to you sometimes. Maybe you could talk to me too. We could be there for each other.'

He looked at me then. 'I don't think that would be a good idea.'

A black, cold despair descended on me. 'I can't go on like this, Will,' I said. 'I can't stay in this place, in this shitty town, with everyone acting like it's my fault. Like Amy's so perfect and I'm some kind of demon.'

He came towards me, and I waited for him to take my hand, to tell me he knew I wasn't to blame, that people would understand that in time. But then I realised he was looking over my shoulder, and I turned and saw the woman I'd noticed browsing on my way in. She was holding a book in one hand, a purse in the other.

'Can I take that for you?' he said.

I dropped my hand and went back out into the rain.

# THIRTY-NINE

*Now*

I am back on the pavement outside Sam's flat. The front door is closed. Everything looks normal.

I've timed my arrival carefully. Almost every house here has a burglar alarm on the front; it's the kind of street where people worry if someone hangs around for too long. I waited until 8 a.m., then positioned myself a way up the road, ready to duck between parked cars if Sam came out. I worried my disappearing act might trigger a change of routine on his part, but it seems not. He set off at ten past the hour dressed for work, no sign that anything was wrong. I thought he must be confident that, whatever suspicions might have driven me from his flat before he woke, I was no closer to finding Marina. But as I was plucking up the courage to go in, my phone buzzed in my pocket. I pulled it out to see a message from the man himself.

> *Gone to work – didn't want to wake you. Help yourself to food – eggs in fridge, cereal in cupboard, bread in bread bin. Hope you slept well. See you later.*

I must have closed the door of my bedroom behind me, just as I closed the door of the flat when I left. Despite what I thought then, it seems my departure has gone unnoticed. It's a stroke of luck that's bought me time. I must use it well.

I take one last look around before striding purposefully to the front door. I do my best to appear confident, like someone who has every right to be here. I let myself in with the keys I took last night and close the door softly behind me. In front of me are the stairs leading to Sam's flat. I'd never have believed when I made my escape that a few hours later I'd be walking up them again. But there's something here I need.

I ascend to the first floor, not trying to avoid the creaking floorboards. Sam's message means he's sticking to his charade, which suggests I'm not likely to run into the man from the train here. And if Melissa is home, I can simply explain that Sam's letting me stay for a few days. It'll be awkward if he hasn't already told her that, but he'll confirm my story if she contacts him. No one needs to know why I'm really here.

I push the key into the door and step over the threshold. The flat is silent, but I'm not taking any chances. I head straight for the table in the hallway. The drawer is open a crack – I was lucky Sam didn't notice that on his way out. I pull it open fully and there it is: the car key. I grab it and I'm gone, running downstairs and back outside. The whole thing has taken no more than a couple of minutes and I haven't seen a soul. Perhaps my luck is changing.

I point the car key into the road and push the button. There's a beep and the clunk of doors unlocking. I turn my head in the direction of the sound just in time to see the final flash of a headlight.

My heart is pounding and I'm half-expecting some kind of alarm to go off the moment I place my hand on the door. But then I'm shuffling into place and putting the key in the ignition, and no one seems to be giving me a second glance. I pull out cautiously, still hardly daring to believe it can be this simple, and point the car in the direction of the main road.

If I had time to stop and think about what I'm doing, I'd be paralysed with terror; but I don't. Driving in London demands every ounce of concentration. The heaving traffic has me moving at a snail's pace, which at least gives me time to obey the directions from my phone. According to the app, I should be there in three hours and twenty-one minutes. But it said the same thing ten minutes ago.

My head is throbbing by the time I make it to the motorway. At last, the traffic opens up and I put my foot down, my phone counting down the miles. It doesn't feel real: driving someone else's car, returning to a place I'd hoped I'd never see again. I would almost believe it's a dream if it weren't for the pounding headache and the sick feeling in the pit of my stomach.

Thorstone. Deep down, I've always known this was coming. That there would be a reckoning.

Maybe it's why I've kept my distance from people, never wanting to get too close. Worried that they might see the real me, the person I tried so hard to keep hidden. I used to think that what happened in Gramwell changed me – but perhaps that's not true. Perhaps it was those first few months with Amy that were the aberration, a temporary reprieve from my true nature. Before and after that, I was the girl everyone thought was trouble and had to prove them right. And now, all these years later, I'm driving back to Gramwell in a stolen car. If it weren't so desperate, the symmetry of it might make me smile.

The road seems to stretch on forever. The monotony of the motorway and my tightly strung nerves suck the energy from my bones. I'm not sure how long I've been driving, but my head is pounding, and my eyelids are heavy. I pull into the services and go to the loo, buy painkillers and the biggest bottle of water I can find. Then it's back on the road again. I can't afford to waste time.

It's another hour before I see white letters on a blue sign:

## GRAMWELL 22

I sit up straighter, tighten my grip on the wheel. Not far now. The sign comes up quicker than I expected:

## KELVERDALE QUARRY

I slow down, indicate. There's no other car on the slip road, and when I reach a roundabout it's the same story. I turn left, obeying the disembodied voice on my phone, reassured to see another sign. Every other time I've been here I've arrived on foot, taking the illicit route through the broken fence. Belatedly I realise I've been imagining going to the spot I shared with Amy and Will, the lake where we spent so many hours. But that's madness. If the man from the train is keeping Marina here, he's not going to have her camped out in the open.

*Unless he's hurt her. Unless what I'm really looking for is a body.*

'No.' I've said the word out loud. I can't think like that. I'm not giving up on her.

*You could already be too late. Just like you were before.*

I reach for the radio to drown out the voice in my head. Marina is fine. She's going to be fine. All I need to do is find her and get her out of there.

The appearance of yet another sign interrupts my thoughts:

## SITE ENTRANCE, 200 YARDS

I ease off the gas and switch off the radio. To the left there's a break in the hedge, a pair of tall metal gates standing open. Above them, another sign welcomes me to Kelverdale Quarry, home of fine quality aggregates, an arrow beneath directing me to a car park. At the bottom, in thick black print, is the company's familiar logo: Thorstone.

The road is strewn with small grey stones that crunch beneath the car tyres. Anyone nearby will hear me coming, but I tell myself that doesn't matter. Sam thinks I'm still holed up in his flat in blissful ignorance, an assumption I've no doubt he'll have passed on to Marina's captor. They have no reason to suspect I'm here.

The car park is big, mostly empty. One end is busier, and I slot the car into a space there; if this is Sam's vehicle not Melissa's, it's possible it will be recognised. I don't want it standing out like a sore thumb.

I switch off the engine and release the wheel. My hands are shaking and I clasp them together to make them stop. So far, I've been operating on adrenaline, but now I feel a deep lethargy spreading over me. I need to keep moving, but I don't know where to go. And if I run into the man from the train, I don't have any kind of weapon.

I unbuckle my seat belt and reach across to the glove compartment. If this were a film, I'd find a gun, or at the very least a screwdriver. What I actually find are a packet of tissues, a small plastic pot of coins, a biro, and a hairbrush. I pull out the latter and examine it. It's purple with black bristles smothered in long, red hairs. Melissa's car, then. I send her a silent apology.

I get out of the car and lock it behind me. There's a single path leading towards the site office, but I've no intention of going there. Instead I make for the trees at one side of the car park. One final check to make sure no one is watching, then I plunge into their shadow.

There's no sign of a trail, and the ground beneath my feet is treacherous with exposed tree roots. But the trees are spaced wide enough apart that it's easy to find a way through, light enough to see where I'm going. After a few minutes, I find myself in a clearing, a wall of rock rising in tall steps before me.

I turn right and follow the line of the wall, looking for signs of a path.

A series of cracks in the air around me. Someone's shooting. I duck, cover my head with my hands, crouch against the rocks. I wait for the pain to hit, but it doesn't come. Seconds pass before I come to my senses and realise what I'm hearing. It's quarry machinery, the thing Will told me they call a pecker drill, boring into the rock.

I straighten, breathing heavily, angry with myself. I should have recognised that noise the moment I heard it. It's louder here, yes, but that series of bangs is the sound I heard in the background of that phone call, the one warning me to stop searching for Marina. I'd thought that call was from Sam, the strange accent intended to disguise his voice. But he couldn't have made it here and back in time to meet me after I rang him. It must have been the man from the train, after all.

I turn on the spot, survey the surroundings. There's nothing to see except the trees on one side and the wall of rock on the other. All I can do is keep moving, hope to find a building where Marina might be hidden. Yet I know only too well that in a site this size, it's like looking for a needle in a haystack.

Except that it isn't. Because when I reach the end of the wall and turn the corner, the ground falls away. In front of me, stretching into the distance, is a huge crater, stepped walls climbing to the sky. At the bottom, a yellow vehicle raises an arm and lowers it again, the noise of metal against rock ringing out across the space. Other vehicles are parked at angles next to piles of shale that dot the crater floor.

It's not the same as it was before. Standing here, the angle is different, and the dig site has deepened and spread in the intervening years. But I recognise this landscape. And suddenly the memory comes to me in glorious technicolour, and I know, *know*, I'm right.

I know where Marina is.

*

I watch the blue dot on the map. Every few seconds it disappears, reappears a little further along.

She is coming.

I pace the floor, unable to rest. My skin itches with anticipation. I thought she'd have given up long ago. Is it possible she'll find us? Is it possible—?

No. There's only one way this ends.

Part of me is afraid of how it will be then. The unknown is always frightening, even for someone like me. Someone with nothing to lose.

It's been a long time since I felt as alive as I have these last few months. Learning new skills – the art of disguise, how to manipulate an image, hack a phone, track a person. Sometimes, I'll admit it, I forgot myself. Almost enjoyed it. Like that quick change in the station, stuffing Marina's coat and bag into a scruffy laundry sack, pulling that woolly hat over her hair. I almost smiled as we walked through the ticket gates, knowing they'd never spot her on the cameras.

But it's time for it to stop.

*Poor Marina. I feel sorry for her, strange though that sounds. I've spent so long with her, discovering her secrets, her fears. She's almost a part of me. But she's served her purpose.*

*Now it's all about Laura. Just the way she's always liked it.*

# FORTY

Even after all these years, I remember how lost I felt after Amy moved away. Her new home was somewhere down south, apparently within easier reach of the specialist medical facility where she had regular appointments. I wrote to her several times, extracting her new address from Will with the promise it was the last thing I'd ever ask of him. A letter, I thought, would show how much I cared, would allow me to craft the words in a way I could never have managed on the phone – but Amy never replied. My mother told me not to take it personally; she'd probably need help to write back, it would be difficult and tiring for her. She might not be able to express herself in the way she wanted to. She might find that limitation painful and embarrassing.

I didn't believe any of it. Amy didn't write back because she blamed me for what happened. And she wasn't the only one.

I'd never been as lonely in my life as I was after she left. I barely ate, couldn't sleep. I saw danger around every corner, for me and for others. My father was of the school that believed such problems were best ignored. It was my mother who insisted on counselling to go with the pills, who drove me every week to visit the ever-patient Janice.

It helped, up to a point. If nothing else, I learned to recognise the signs of my hypervigilance, to occasionally pause the pattern of thoughts that made every minor risk a potential crisis. But there was nothing Janice could do about what other people thought. I was a pariah to the whole town, treated as if I had some kind of contagious disease. The day the girl at the newsagent refused to serve me was the day I shoplifted for the first time since Amy had come to Gramwell. It served them all right, I thought: if my money wasn't good enough for them, I wouldn't offer it again.

I was caught, inevitably, and more than once. My renewed reputation for petty crime saw my old friends resurface, ready to make use of me. I stole to order, everything from lipsticks and nail varnishes to printer cartridges and bottles of vodka. I traded them for cash and sometimes for weed, sometimes something stronger. And to conduct our business, my collaborators directed me to a location away from the town's prying eyes.

The path is overgrown now, no more than a slight indent in the vegetation. You'd never spot it unless you knew it was there. It skirts the edge of the crater then turns its back on it, leading into scrubby grassland and brambles. At night, you could bring someone along this track and never meet another soul.

It's perhaps half a mile before I see it. The single storey building must have once been white, but I've only ever witnessed it in its grey period. The window frames, always peeling, are now almost bare of paint, a layer of white flakes resting like dandruff on the ground below. A tile is missing from the roof, and green leaves sprout from the gap. But as I draw closer, I see that not everything here is old and decrepit. Someone has attached a gleaming new padlock to the door.

I tell myself not to jump to conclusions. I stop, inhale, count to ten, try to do the things Janice taught me to keep the anxiety at bay. And when that doesn't work, I move forward anyway. What choice do I have?

As I near the building I duck, trying to keep out of sight of the windows. That padlock suggests whoever is using it isn't here right now, but I'm not running the risk that I'm wrong. When I reach the wall, I straighten slowly and peer in at the edge of the windowpane.

It's so dirty that I can't make out what's inside. But I can see enough to know that the room is empty. I clear a coin-sized circle in the grime, then place my eye to the spyhole.

The room I'm looking at runs the full length of this side of the building. There's a table topped in peeling Formica against one wall, a dilapidated kitchen area below a second window further along. A door opposite indicates a room beyond.

I creep around the rear of the building. There are no windows here, and when I reach the corner, I see an enormous pile of logs stacked along the other side. I can't see beyond them from where I'm standing, but if memory serves, there's a window further along. I drop low to shuffle past, and sure enough, the window comes into view.

I move forward quickly, staying as low as I can. When I reach the corner I stand, my back to the wall, conscious even in my fear that there's something ridiculously *Mission: Impossible* about all this. The thought brings an urge to laugh that Janice's voice tells me is hysteria. I gulp down a calming breath, then another.

I make my way to the front of the house. There's a concrete step up to the front door, and standing there, I feel horribly exposed as I check out the padlock. It's all business, securing a thick metal bar that connects the door to the wall beside it. Why bother with this to protect a few bits of decaying furniture? I need to get inside, take a proper look around, but without the right kit, picking a lock like this isn't an option. I search the ground and find what I'm looking for – a rock the size of my fist. I wrap it in my jacket, then creep back to the first window I looked in. Then I draw back my arm and smack the rock against the corner of the window.

The sound of shattering glass echoes around the clearing. If the man from the train is nearby, he'll have heard – but I can't do anything about that. I use the rock to knock out the shards of glass that cling to the window frame, but the edges remain jagged and vicious. I won't be able to pull myself through without cutting myself to ribbons. I turn my attention to the window frame. A few hard thumps with the rock and the rotten wood gives way, leaving a space I can work with.

After all the noise I've already made, there's no point trying to be discreet. I check behind me one last time, then grab the window frame and haul myself inside.

I take care where I'm putting my feet, trying to avoid the glass and stray nails scattered on the floor. I mentally add trespass, criminal damage and breaking and entering to my latest Gramwell rap sheet. It's almost like old times.

The room I'm in has white walls, grey vinyl floor tiles. I make my way to the sink in the kitchen area, try turning the taps, but they're stiff with disuse. At either side there's a worktop, chipped at the edges, with cupboards below. I swing open the door of one, but it's empty. The other will be the same – except that it isn't. Inside are two large plastic bottles of water. Just like the ones I found at Flyte Gardens.

I leap back as if they're going to bite. My eyes travel to the ceiling, checking for a camera. There's nothing. But was there anything outside, tucked under the eaves, perhaps even secured to a neighbouring tree trunk? Is it possible that I'm being watched, that the man from the train is on his way here right now?

I reach for my phone and take a photograph of the water bottles. Then I bring up my contacts and find DC Hollis's number. I don't care what happens to me anymore. Let her arrest me if she wants to. Just as long as she gets up here and finds Marina.

The number rings out three times, then switches to voice-mail. Is she deliberately ignoring me? I try again with the same result: *'This is DC Nadia Hollis. Please leave a message after the tone, and I'll return your call as soon as I can. In case of emergencies, hang up immediately and dial 999.'* For a moment I contemplate doing just that. But how could I explain what's happening here? I don't even know myself. I disconnect the call, dial DC Hollis again, wait for the recorded message. Then I speak.

'It's me, Laura. Laura Fraser. I'm at Kelverdale Quarry, near Gramwell. I've found something – I'm sending you a photo. He's got her, Marina, and she's somewhere near here. Please, I know what you think of me, but get someone over here.' I pause, knowing as I say the words that they won't work. I can't afford to have her ignore me. I take a breath. 'I'm not going to let him hurt me. I have a gun.'

I hang up, shaking, realising what I've done with that lie. But there's no going back now. I send the photo, adding a caption:

*The same bottles were at Flyte Gardens.*

I wonder how long it will be before DC Hollis gets my message. I wonder if the man from the train will get here first. And then I tell myself to stop wondering, because none of that will help.

I open the door and step through into a smaller room next door, looking for any sign of Marina. The front door is on the left. I used to come in that way, leave the stuff in that corner. Sometimes I'd stay for a while, just sitting. Books reminded me of Will, so I no longer read. But here, in this sad little room, I was out of the way of the world. For an hour or two, that felt almost like peace.

There's another doorway to my right. There was a loo there, I remember, but even back in the day it was unusable, the water cut off. The door has gone, and I step through the gap into a space with a cracked WC, the bowl black with mould. Next to it is a sink with a metal panel above it that in better days might have served as a mirror. The missing door hasn't gone far – it's leaning against the wall.

I return to the other room, look out of the window. From here I can see the edges of the woodpile. There's something about the view that niggles, a detail that isn't quite right. I step to the side, crane my neck, but it's just a pile of wood. What's wrong with what I'm seeing?

I walk into the loo, stare at the far wall, the one the wood is stacked against outside. Except that it can't be.

It's too narrow, I realise. The building is a simple rectangle. This room should be the same width as the one next to it. But now that I look at it, it's obviously narrower. There's space behind that wall.

I step towards it. It looks different, I see now, the paint here nowhere near as dirty as the rest of this place. I reach out tentatively and rap it with my knuckles. The sound is hollow.

There's a silence so deep I can almost hear my heart beating. And then something raps back.

# FORTY-ONE

The blood freezes in my veins and for an instant I can't move. But then I'm banging on the wall and screaming Marina's name. There's no reply, but I hear a scrape like chair legs against a hard floor, an indistinct mumbling. He must have put tape across her mouth.

Cold fury jolts me into action. I haul the door away from the wall, jumping back just in time as it topples and falls. Behind where it stood, a smaller door is cut into the plasterboard, bolts across the top and bottom.

I draw them back, my nails scraping against the metal, and tug open the door. The space in front of me is in near darkness, a thin trickle of light seeping in from a window that's been mostly blocked by the woodpile. But I feel it instantly: there's someone here.

Slowly my eyes adjust to the gloom and I see her, a shape slumped in a chair. She's dressed in the same dark coat she wore on the train. The horror of it hits me like a bullet: she's been a prisoner since that day. She raises her head and there's a cloth tied around the bottom of her face. I rush forward, try to pull it off.

She flinches as if my touch burns her. I step back, hold my hands up so she can see I don't have a weapon. 'It's okay,' I tell her. 'I'm here to help you. I'm getting you out of here.'

She nods and I move forward again, fumbling with the knot in the scarf. Her hair is tangled in it, and I feel it pulling. 'Sorry,' I say, 'I'm so sorry.'

Finally, the knot gives, and I pull away the fabric from her face. I can barely see her in the half light, but it's enough to confirm it's Marina.

'You,' she says, and her voice is strong. 'You came.'

Suddenly my vision blurs and there are tears running down my cheeks. This time I've done it. This time I'm going to save her.

I switch on the torch on my phone, trying to see how she's being held to the chair. The beam illuminates a sight that's sickly familiar. A silver-coloured chain is wound around her body and the back of the chair, trapping her arms to her sides. There's another around her ankles, wrapped around the legs of the chair. Both chains are secured with padlocks.

'I'll be back,' I tell her. 'I need to find something to break these locks.'

I run out, scanning the space for anything I can use – but there's nothing heavy enough to do the job. Back in the kitchen area I check the cupboards, peering into the corners in case by some miracle he's left a key here. But I'm not that lucky. My eye falls on the hole where there was once a window. I dropped the rock I used to break the glass outside, but perhaps it would be heavy enough. I lean out of the window and it's there, sitting innocently on the ground below. I reach down as far as I can, but it's just out of reach.

I reposition myself, rest my stomach on the window ledge and tip my body forward. My feet paddle in the air, and for a moment, I think I'm going to fall; but then my fingers are closing around the rock and I kick backwards, hard, and I'm in the room again.

I'm about to rush to Marina when I stop, turn back towards the window. Was that movement outside? My eyes sweep the clearing, my heart thudding. I see nothing but scrubby ground, a few trees. I have to get back to Marina, get her out of here as fast as I can.

I run back through the building. She's sitting quietly, waiting for me. I wouldn't be so patient in her place.

'This should do it,' I say, holding up the rock with more confidence than I feel.

'Can't you pick the locks?' she asks, and I look at her in surprise. But she must see me as her saviour; she thinks I can do anything.

'Not these,' I tell her. 'I'm going to have to try and break them. Hold still.'

I raise the rock above my shoulder, then bring it down hard on the padlock near her ankles. The noise is like a bomb going off, but when I inspect the lock it's as secure as ever. I glance nervously over my shoulder.

'Have you done it?' Marina shuffles her feet.

I wipe the sweat that's gathered on my top lip. 'I'm going to break the chain instead,' I tell her. 'It won't be as strong.'

Hitting the chain without hitting Marina, though, will be difficult. The best place to try seems to be behind her heels. A few links rest against the floor, which I'm hoping will give me a better chance of breaking through.

'I need you to stay still,' I tell her, and she obeys. I raise the rock again, but the chair's in the way and I can't get much of a swing. It connects with a thud, but the chain holds firm.

'Is it done?' Marina sounds oddly calm. She must be in shock, I realise.

'It will be soon.' I lift the rock, bring it down again. And again. And again.

I shine the torch at the chain. There are a few scratches, nothing more. I need to find a sharp corner of the rock. Aim carefully and hope to find a weak spot.

And then I hear a noise.

Marina hears it too. I feel her whole body stiffen. 'It's him,' she whispers. 'He's coming.'

I wait, listen. And there it is again: a footstep on concrete. He's at the front door.

I grab the chain around her legs, pull at it frantically. It hurts her and she stifles a cry, but that chain's not going anywhere. I hear the rattle of a key in a lock. At any minute now, he'll be here, and we're like rats in a trap. I have to get out. It's the only hope for both of us.

My eyes flicker to the window. There's no time to run back to where I got in earlier. But if I manage to open this window, push hard enough, perhaps I can dislodge the logs, scramble through.

Marina follows my eyes. 'No,' she says. 'You can't leave me.'

I put my finger to my lips, whisper urgently. 'I'll come back, I promise.'

'No!' she shouts and strains at the chains.

I grab the piece of fabric from the floor. She twists her head from side to side, making it hard for me to retie it. 'Please, Marina,' I beg. 'He can't know I've been here.'

With the gag back in place, I can only see her eyes. They burn with anger and fear. 'I promise I'll come back for you,' I tell her again. But there's no time to try to convince her: I hear the front door open.

I hurry to the window, trying to be quiet, and twist the catch. The window opens upwards, but it moves only an inch, then stops. It's blocked by the logs on the other side.

I push again, as hard as I can. I feel something move, but I'm running out of time. From towards the front of the building, I hear the squeak of shoes on a vinyl floor. He's moving away from us, towards the kitchen, but that won't buy me long. It'll take him only a moment to notice the smashed glass, to realise someone's been here.

I slam the window into the logs again, wincing at the noise, and this time I feel them shift. The gap is just big enough for my hands and I reach through, gather my strength and give a mighty shove.

There's a noise like thunder as logs tumble and fall. And over the rumble, I hear another sound: footsteps running.

Panic floods my brain, and I stretch through the window, trying to pull myself out, though the gap is still too narrow. I thrash wildly at the logs, pushing more of them to the ground. The window opens another inch. I'm so close.

Stars burst in my head. A rush of sound. A voice that rises and fades on the tide.

Then all is darkness.

# FORTY-TWO

The sky is white and grey, cold as marble. My head hurts, my back too. How long have I been here? I was trying to get somewhere. I don't remember now. The absence of memory bothers me, like an itch I can't reach.

There's a low murmur nearby. It sounds like the sea. But there's no ocean here, only the lake.

The lake. Yes, that's where I am. I feel the rock beneath my back. She lay here once, but that was a long time ago. Amy. She wanted me to help her, but I didn't.

Something brushes against my face. A bird, its wing across my cheek. Strange for a bird to fly so low.

'Don't. Please.'

Could it be? I thought for a moment I heard his voice. But he won't return, no matter how long I wait.

Here comes that bird again. The rush of air.

'She needs to wake up.'

A sharp sting and I gasp, open my eyes. My cheek is burning and I place my hand against it. The skin is hot beneath my fingertips.

'Get up.'

I try to turn in the direction of the voice, but my head swims.

'Get up.'

And then the fog lifts and I remember. I'm back in Gramwell. I'm at the quarry.

*Marina.*

It's dark. My vision blurs. Someone's grabbing my arms, hauling me upright.

'On the chair.'

I feel a seat beneath me, something wrapping itself around my chest.

'No.' My voice sounds as if it's coming from a long way away.

'Tighter.'

'Is this really—?'

'Tighter.'

I blink, try to focus. At the end of the room, a tall figure stands motionless, half-shrouded in shadow. The second voice came from behind me, from the person tugging a chain around my body. I try to pull free, but the movement brings a wave of nausea.

I moisten my lips. 'What have you done with Marina?'

'What do you care?' The voice comes from the end of the room. But something about it is wrong. It's not like the voice on the phone, the one who told me to stay away from Marina. This person isn't putting on an accent. Yet something doesn't fit—

'You were going to leave me here.'

The figure steps forward and there's something in the way it moves that doesn't fit either.

'It's always the same, isn't it, Laura?'

Another step, and the shadows recede. And now I realise why the voice didn't make sense.

'You always look out for Number One.'

The voice belongs to a woman. She stops right in front of

me and bends forward so that her face is next to mine. I see lines around her eyes, shadows underneath.

My brain is whirring, trying to make sense of this. But I can't. There's a name on my tongue and I struggle to free it.

'Marina?'

She closes her eyes, as if disappointed in me. Then she moves closer still. 'Take another look.' Her breath is on my face. 'Don't you recognise me at all?'

And finally I see it. Even though this woman is too old. Even though she's walking, talking, no sign of what happened to her. It can't be her – and yet the eyes, the shape of the lips...

My voice is a whisper and a prayer. 'Amy.'

She blinks, straightens. 'Amy's dead.'

'What?' I can't have heard her properly. 'No, Amy's fine. She moved house. She doesn't live in Gramwell anymore.'

'And why did she do that?' She's in my face again. I feel spit on my cheek.

'Who are you?' I stare at her, trying to make sense of what I'm seeing. She's so like Amy, but there's a hardness in her eyes.

She says again, louder, 'Tell me why she moved away.'

'There was an accident,' I say. 'She was hurt. Her family moved so she could be nearer the doctors.'

She stands, turns away from me. 'An accident. Is that what you tell yourself?'

'Kate, she came.'

I've been so focused on the woman in front of me that I've forgotten there's someone else here. I try to twist my head to see them, but they've positioned themselves out of sight.

She shakes her head. 'It's not enough.'

Belatedly, the penny drops. 'Kate?'

Oh, God. How could I have been so stupid? But finally I can see past the blonde hair and the sophisticated make-up. The woman in front of me has nothing in common with the intimidating goth who barely acknowledged I existed. But of course she looks like Amy: she's her sister.

Yet I don't understand why she's here. I don't understand any of it.

'I don't look the same these days, I suppose,' she says.

'You – you look good,' I stammer. But she doesn't, not close up. The heavy eyeliner and purple-black hair have gone, but something else has gone with them. The old Kate was a force of nature. This one looks exhausted.

She laughs, and the sound makes my skin prickle. 'I'm sure I look great. That's what a decade of not sleeping through the night will do for you.'

'Kate.' The voice behind me is soft.

'Not going on holiday. Not going out, except when you risk an hour away to get food. No boyfriend. No friends at all, really.'

I look at her blankly.

'Not like your life, eh, Laura?' She crosses the floor in three easy strides. 'You've been doing well for yourself, haven't you?'

I shake my head. 'I don't know what you mean.'

'Course you do. Hobnobbing with the stars. That Millie woman. That's right, isn't it?'

I'm about to reply, to explain I barely know her, but Kate continues before I can open my mouth. 'I loved the article, by the way. So inspirational.'

'What—?'

She raises her arms, as if addressing a crowd. '"There's a redemptive quality to Fraser's work. The promise that even our darkest moments offer the hope of renewal." I've got that right, haven't I?'

There's a chill settling over me. This is the woman who broke my beautiful pots. The woman who kept that newspaper article all those years. Who took a pen and obliterated my face.

'What was your darkest moment, Laura?'

I don't answer.

'Was it when you left my sister here? When you left her alone and bleeding?'

I can't speak.

'Was that it?'

I swallow, try to form words around the grief that's lodged like a stone in my throat. 'I'm so sorry, Kate. I know I let her down.'

She makes a sound somewhere between a snort and a sob. 'You wanted her to die.'

'What? No, I—'

'He told me what you said.' I see her eyes travel past my shoulder, and again I try to turn my head.

'Who did? I don't understand.'

'I think it's time you introduced yourself.'

I hear movement behind me, and a shadow moves in the periphery of my vision. A man steps forward. He's tall and spare, wide shoulders. He moves into the light and I see dark hair, a full beard. I should have guessed the moment I realised Marina wasn't who she seemed to be. This is the man she was with that day. This is the man from the train.

'Hello, Laura Fraser,' he says.

It's like the breath has been knocked from my body. My brain tries to reject the truth, to come up with something that doesn't mean what this must surely mean. But it's no good. This is a voice I'd know anywhere.

His name is like a magic spell. If I say it, everything will be different.

'Will.'

# FORTY-THREE

Kate laughs, and I recognise the edge of hysteria in the sound. I might be the one chained up, but she's barely keeping it together.

'Surprise, Laura! Still a good-looking guy, isn't he? Did you really think you stood a chance?'

Even now, after everything, the words sting.

'We all saw the way you trailed after him. Like a puppy, only not so cute. It was embarrassing to watch. And you couldn't stand it, could you? Couldn't stand that he chose Amy not you.'

I can't look at Will. 'That's not true,' I mumble.

'Oh, really? But you went to see him, didn't you? When Amy was in hospital? Your supposed best friend was fighting for her life, and you were trying to make a move on her boyfriend.'

'It wasn't like that—'

'Go on.' Kate turns to Will, and I'm still trying to process that now, after all this time, in this terrible place, he's less than six feet away from me. 'Tell us what she said.'

'Kate, I don't think—'

'Tell us what she said!'

'She said we could be there for each other.'

Was that how I'd put it? It was so long ago, I can barely remember. 'I meant as friends,' I say, looking at Will, wanting him to understand.

'Please. Do you think I'm stupid?' Kate's anger won't let her keep still. She paces back and forth like a caged tiger. 'That's why you left her there, wasn't it? You thought if you waited long enough, she'd die. You thought you'd have him all to yourself.'

'No,' I say. 'I loved Amy. She was my best friend.'

Is it possible I'll see her again? Is Kate setting the stage, leading up to the moment Amy walks in here and tells me she hates me? I'd take that, I realise. I've missed her so much.

'Where is she?'

Kate stares at me. 'She's in the lake.'

'What?'

'That's where she wanted her ashes scattered.'

'No. You're lying.'

'She said she'd spent some of the happiest times of her life there. With you, if you can believe that. She was too good, that's the problem. She could never see you for what you were.'

'No, it's not true. Will, it's not true, is it?' But he's looking down at the floor.

'Save the act, Laura. You killed her. It might have taken you nine years, but you did it in the end.'

The tears run down my face.

'It killed my parents too, what you did. They split up – did you know that? Mum tried, but she couldn't cope. Her heart gave out in the end, and then it was only the two of us. Me and Amy, day after day.'

'I didn't forget her,' I cry. 'I thought about her all the time. I wrote to her, but she never answered.'

She strides towards me, and I think she's going to slap me, punch me, scratch out my eyes. But she stops right in front of the chair and when she speaks, her voice is low, and I hear exactly how much it's costing her not to do any of those things.

'You're a liar. You lied then, and you're lying now.'

'No, I wrote again and again...' And then it comes to me. 'Your parents must have taken the letters.'

'Of course!' She slaps her forehead. 'It wasn't that you didn't give a shit. It was my parents' fault. That's right, isn't it? You're never the one to blame.'

'Please.' I have to make her understand. 'I tried so many times. I only stopped because I thought she hated me. I didn't want to upset her.'

She laughs, and it's like nails down a blackboard. 'So you were putting her first?'

'It's the truth! You can ask my mum.' I rush on before she can pour scorn on how pathetic that sounds. 'She was the one who told me to stop writing. She told me...'

I grind to a halt, realising where this is taking me. But it's too late; I've piqued Kate's curiosity.

'What? What did she tell you?'

For the first time, she sounds like she's interested in what I have to say.

I swallow. 'She said Amy might not be able to write back.'

Kate blinks slowly. 'You stopped writing because you thought Amy was too badly hurt to reply.' She bends so her eyes are level with mine.

'Kate—' There's a warning note in Will's voice, but she holds up a hand and he falls silent.

'Let me get this straight. You ruin my sister's life. You leave her to die.' Her eyes burn into me. 'You carry on living your life, while she has to leave everything behind. Travel to the other end of the country.' Her voice rises. 'Endure months of agony, procedure after procedure that doesn't work.'

I want to say something, but she's relentless.

'She started having seizures, did you know that?' I shake my head, but she doesn't want an answer. 'Then it was a stroke, then another. After that, she couldn't walk, couldn't feed herself. Couldn't even go to the loo on her own.'

I can't take in what I'm hearing. Could that really have been Amy? Beautiful, golden, untouchable Amy?

'I had to do everything for her. Everything. I gave up my whole life. Dropped out of university. And you stopped writing to her *because she didn't write back?*'

Her eyes glitter and I can tell she's holding on by a thread. I'm terrified to speak in case whatever I say causes it to snap. But I can't stay silent either, can't let her think I don't care.

'I'm so sorry,' I whisper.

'I don't want your apologies.' She gets up and backs away, like she can't bear to be near me any longer. 'I saw that article in the paper. I read it out to her. I thought she'd realise you were making money out of her misery. "All great art comes from suffering", isn't that what you said?'

I regretted that stupid quote at the time, the pretentiousness of it. I regret it more now.

'I told her I'd make you pay for what you did. Do you know what she said?'

I shake my head, and even now I want to know what Amy thought. I'm still looking for her approval.

'She said she was happy for you.'

I try to absorb that, but there are too many thoughts tangled in my head.

'She believed you, you see. She was the only one who did. She made me promise I wouldn't hurt you.'

My breath hitches.

'I told her she was wrong. I told her there was no way it could have taken you three hours to get help, no matter how lost you'd got. But I promised. I promised if she was right, I'd leave you alone.'

I don't like the sound of this. I try to keep my voice steady. 'Then why am I here?'

'Haven't you understood yet? I thought if nothing else you were cleverer than that.'

I can't bear her mocking tone. I look towards Will. 'What's going on?'

'It was a test, Laura,' he says.

'A test?'

'To see what you'd do if someone else asked for your help.'

Gradually, the pieces start to come together. 'So the two of you set this whole thing up.'

Will won't meet my eyes.

'I needed someone to be my kidnapper. Marina's kidnapper. Will obliged.' Kate sounds pleased with herself.

My mind is whirring. 'But the video in the bookshop... the house in Flyte Gardens...'

'I had to play fair, for Amy's sake. So I gave you clues. A trail to follow.'

'And you did,' Will interjects. But Kate doesn't seem to be listening.

'Did you like the book?'

I'm struggling to follow what she's saying. 'The book?'

'*The Caves of Agoroth.*' She sounds calm now, but I can hear it: the fury just below the surface. 'I saw the cover and it reminded me of here. Did you read the endings? I thought one of those might ring a bell.'

'Choose your own destiny,' I whisper.

'Very good.'

'And Sam?' I ask her. 'Where does he fit in?'

She looks at me curiously. 'Who's Sam?'

*Oh God, I've been so wrong about everything.*

'She's passed though, hasn't she?' Will says hesitantly. 'She found you, so we can let her go.'

Kate rounds on him. 'Don't be so stupid.'

Something cold turns over in my stomach.

'Come on, Kate.' Will's trying to sound calm, but I can hear the fear in his voice. 'You said if she passed the test, we'd let her go.'

'She didn't pass! You saw what she did! She was trying to run away. She would have left me – Marina – here. She didn't care what happened to her.'

She reaches behind her, and I see her arm move upward then still, as if she's holding something out of sight.

'I was coming back,' I stammer. 'I told you that, didn't I? I had to leave, or he'd have found us both. I couldn't have helped you then.'

I'm still talking as if this was real. Even now, part of me believes it was.

'Please, Kate.' Will moves towards her, and she backs away. 'You said you'd stop if she came. You said it would show she'd risk her safety for someone else. And she did, didn't she? Amy was right.'

Kate takes the thing from behind her back and holds it in front of her. It gleams in the half light and the breath catches in my throat. It's a knife.

Will holds out his hands, takes a step back.

'I have to do this,' she says. 'She can't get away with it.'

'Kate, please. This isn't what we talked about. You said if she came—'

'But she was going to run away! Can't you understand that changes everything!'

Will takes a step to the side, moving between Kate and me.

'Will, get out of the way.'

She comes forward and he takes a step back, keeping the distance between them. 'Please, Kate. Let's just talk this through.'

'I'm so tired of talking.' Her voice is weary, but she takes another step forward. Will's no more than a foot in front of me now; he has nowhere left to go. 'I'm so tired of everything.'

'I know,' he says. 'I miss her too.' And then he reaches for her, turning his body in a way that's strangely awkward. In that moment, I feel something hit my lap. I look down and back up again quickly. Will has Kate in his arms, her head buried in his shoulder. She's crying, rasping sobs filled with loneliness and loss. And there's a key inches from my fingertips.

Every second counts. I bend my arm and the chain digs into the inside of my elbow. It bites into the skin, but I keep moving, breathing through the pain. The key is millimetres away now. I stretch my fingers as far as I can, grit my teeth and pull against the chain.

I touch metal. I press down and drag the key towards me, hook it into the palm of my hand. I feel a moment of triumph, but my problems are far from over. I have the key. But I can't even see the padlock.

Kate's sobs are subsiding. She pushes Will away. 'Enough now,' she says.

He nods. 'Let's go. We can leave her here. Call someone when we're far away.'

She smiles. 'You're kind, aren't you, Will? I can see why Amy liked you.'

And then she stabs him in the stomach.

*

*It didn't feel the same, killing Will. Of course, I knew it wouldn't. Amy wanted to die. Holding that pillow over her face was a kindness for us both – but I did it for her. I did everything for her.*

*Will didn't have a life either, not really. He was nothing without Amy, he just didn't realise it. And he had to pay for what he did. Betraying her, sleeping with that little tramp. And then telling Amy, trying to salve his conscience. She was devastated. She'd never have been drinking that day if she hadn't been so upset. Would never have lost her balance.*

*But Laura's different. Sad, desperate little Laura, who somehow persuaded the world to forget what she is. She's the worst by far. That's why I'm going to let myself enjoy what comes next.*

# FORTY-FOUR

The world stops spinning. Will lies on the floor, a red stain spreading around him. It reminds me of the day Amy fell. *Blossoming like a flower*, I think.

Kate is crouched next to him. There's a low murmur and for a moment I think this was all some kind of terrible mistake. She didn't mean to stab him. But then I tune in, and the murmurs become words.

'You didn't think I'd let you live, did you?' she says to him. 'Not after what you did.'

I twist from side to side, desperately trying to spot the padlock. I can't see it, but I feel something heavy against my hip. Is that it?

There's a groan from the floor. 'Does it hurt?' Kate asks Will. 'I hope it does.'

I wriggle in the chains, feel something knock my hip again.

'Don't struggle, Laura.' Kate looks back at me. 'I'll be with you in a minute.'

Her eyes are blank. The way she says it, she could be a receptionist in a doctor's surgery.

'Help us!' I scream. 'Somebody help us!'

She's bending over Will and she doesn't react. I don't want to know what she's doing.

I flex my arms, pull wildly, strike out with my hands. But I'm no match for a metal chain. I try to get to my feet, to take the chair with me and run. It rocks, tips to the side, and suddenly there's a crash and I'm on the floor, wood splintering beneath me.

Hot pain streaks up my arm and instinctively I try to grab the wound. To my shock, the chain gives, allows the movement. It must have been wrapped around the chair. I've barely processed that realisation when a shadow falls over me, and my arm explodes in a burst of fire.

Kate lifts her foot and stamps down again hard. I hear an animal howl and realise the sound has come from me. 'That's good,' she says. 'Do it again.'

She brings down her foot a third time, and the world briefly turns black. 'Amy,' I whisper. 'Amy wouldn't want this.'

'Don't,' she snarls. 'Don't say her name.'

She's moving away, and I grope along the floor with my good hand, the movement jolting my other arm, sending streaks of flame through my body. But then I hear the scrape of metal and I freeze. Kate's back, standing over me. The knife she's holding is dark with Will's blood.

My hand closes around something long and narrow. I inch it closer to my body as Kate lowers herself to her knees.

'It's time,' she says.

She wraps both hands around the handle of the knife, raises it above my chest.

'No, please.'

'Kate.'

The voice is faint, but she pauses, turns. And that's when I swing my good arm as hard as I can.

The fragment of chair arm connects with the side of her head with a dull thump. She turns to me, lips parted in an expression of surprise. I haven't hit her hard enough. At any moment, she's going to raise that knife again, and this will all be over.

I try to summon the strength to hit her again, but my arm is screaming in pain. She raises her hand, touches the place where I struck her. Her fingertips come away red. She looks at me as if about to say something, then she crumples and falls forward. I try to roll away, but there's no time. Her head strikes mine and everything fades away.

---

Voices. Movement. Bright light, then darkness. A bite in my hand. Nothing.

I wake. I try to move, but everything is heavy. I should be afraid, I think, but I don't know why. I don't feel afraid. I don't feel...

'Laura.' Someone is holding my hand. 'You're all right, sweetheart.'

My mother's voice. My mother's hand. I squeeze her fingers, but I don't want to talk to her. All I want to do is sleep.

I wake and I remember. Amy is dead. Will is dead. Kate...?

It was instant, I am told. She would not have suffered.

I know this isn't true.

'I didn't hit her hard,' I told them, not adding that I would have hit her harder if I could. But it didn't matter. There was a nail in the chair arm, and it pierced the pterion, a word I have never heard of and will later look up on Wikipedia. It is the weak point in the skull, I discover. It is easy to pierce the brain through the pterion.

Will, after all, is not dead. I am happy, but my happiness is morphine-edged. It's hard to tell where it begins and ends.

The knife struck his lower abdomen, avoiding major organs. He is in the same hospital, but on a different ward. I am told I cannot see him, although it is not clear why. Some things don't change.

Sam visits. I tell him I'm sorry about taking his flatmate's car. I don't remember her name, but he doesn't seem to notice. I don't tell him I thought he was conspiring against me.

'You've been so brave,' he says.

I thank him for everything, and it sounds like goodbye. 'Guy will give you your job back,' he tells me. 'He understands what you've been through.'

I pretend I'll consider it, but I'm not going back there. I have a message from Oliver Frampton on my voicemail. My story has been in the news and I am irresistible. Hot property. He doesn't say that. He says my work has 'extraordinary depth' and he would be 'honoured to bring it to a new audience'. I plan to graciously accept.

DC Hollis – Nadia, as I call her now – arrives with flowers. She looks tired. I have not been good for her, I suspect. There will have been questions.

She apologises, and I tell her it's okay. She was right, after all. There never was a Marina. In a strange way, I miss her, this woman who never existed. I miss the idea that she chose me, that she needed me.

'You were right that it was connected to Gramwell too,' I tell her. 'It just wasn't in the way you thought.'

She tells me she's sorry she didn't answer her phone. She was on another call apparently, but the way she says it hints at assumptions made. I forgive her: if she hadn't called the cavalry when she eventually picked up my message, Will could have bled to death.

'You shouldn't have lied about having a gun, though,' she says. 'It could have ended very differently.'

I raise an eyebrow, and she has the grace to look embarrassed.


I have surgery on my arm and am discharged with it in a cast. It hurts and everything is difficult, so I go to stay with my parents to be difficult in company. My mother's Nightingale spirit dissipates rapidly in the face of my peevishness, but my brush with mortality gives her bragging rights with her friends. Every cloud.

Two weeks later, I am watching daytime television in my pyjamas when she informs me I have a visitor. It can only be Sam, and I try to tell her I'm in no state to see anyone – but she's already waving him in.

It's not Sam.

'Laura,' he says, and the world tips on its axis, because the man on the train has gone, his beard shaved, and it's Will, my Will. I can see the curve of his lips, the ones that seemed always on the edge of a smile. I remember how it felt to kiss them, the taste of mint chewing gum. This is the boy who called me Laura Fraser. Who lent me books no one else wanted to read.

Except it isn't. I look again and his lips are thin and pinched. There's a hollowness to his cheeks, a weariness in his eyes. Kate hurt him badly, of course. He lost a lot of blood. But I can see he's lost more than that.

I point to an armchair and he takes a seat. 'How are you?' he says.

'I told them you didn't know what Kate was planning. You don't have to worry.' My voice sounds strange. I think I might cry.

I want to believe he's here because he cares, but in my heart, I know the real reason. I hold his life in my hands.

I've told the police the truth: how Kate blamed me for Amy's accident, how she was determined to get revenge. They searched her house and found a diary, photos of me on her phone. She'd been watching me for months, apparently. I told them that Will tried to stop her, that he was trying to protect me, and she turned on him. They couldn't argue with a stab wound.

But DC Hollis isn't a stupid woman. She suspects he was in on it, tried to get me to tell her he was the man on the train. I wouldn't do it. I said the sunglasses and hood made it impossible to tell. I could change my story, though, remember a telling detail. I could make things very difficult for him if I wanted to.

'I'll protect you, Will,' I say, because I want him to understand I know all this.

He bows his head. 'Thank you. But that's not why I'm here.' My stupid heart lifts. 'I wanted to apologise. And to explain.'

I think about telling him he doesn't need to apologise. That I know there had to be a reason for what he did. But the truth is, I want to hear he's sorry. I want to know he cares that I could have died in that room. I motion for him to continue, and he pulls the chair closer, fixes his eyes on the floor, as if he's too embarrassed to look at me.

'Kate rang me about four months ago,' he says. 'She told me Amy had died. I said I'd come down for the funeral and she offered to put me up.'

He was surprised, he says, but didn't want to offend her. He stayed at the house she'd lived in with Amy: 21 Flyte Gardens.

'The next day, I was due to go home. She told me she needed my help. I said, "Anything".' He shakes his head. 'I had no idea.'

She already had the plan, he says. 'At first I tried to dissuade her. But she kept saying she owed it to Amy to find out the truth. That I owed it to her too.'

I'm about to ask him what she meant, but I already know. I remember Kate leaning over his body: *You didn't think I'd let you live? Not after what you did.*

'She knew about us. About the night of Chloe's party.'

He nods miserably. 'I told Amy...' *That I'd thrown myself at him.* 'That we'd had sex.'

Is that how he thought of it? To someone on the outside it might have looked tawdry – a quick fumble in the alley that ran behind Amy's street – but it wasn't like that. Not for me. For me, we made love.

'Why?' I ask him. 'Why did you say anything?'

'I couldn't keep it from her. And I thought... I thought you might tell her.'

Once again, I surrender the hope of something better, the idea that he'd been going to break up with her, that he'd realised we were meant to be together. I turn away, pretend to examine a loose thread on my cuff.

'Amy must have told Kate,' he says.

'What did you say? About how it happened?'

'That I'd seen you after I'd walked her home. That we were drunk.'

'We weren't drunk.'

'That we didn't know what we were doing.'

'We did.'

'I told her it didn't mean anything.'

I look at him and I can't speak.

'This is hard for me to admit, Laura,' he says, 'but I want to be honest. You deserve that.'

I wait for it to come.

'The truth is, I always wondered too. About what happened that day.'

I stare at him. I thought I couldn't be hurt anymore, but I

was wrong. 'You thought I left her deliberately. You thought I left Amy to die.'

He looks at me, shakes his head. 'I'm so sorry. It's just, people were talking...' He tails off. 'There's no excuse. I know how badly I treated you then.'

He tells me what the last nine years were like. 'There's nothing in Gramwell, you know that. And it was hard. I'd led you on, that's what they all thought, made you think I'd be with you if Amy was out of the way. I hoped the gossip would stop in time, but it never really did. I suppose I resented you for that.'

He has no idea how it feels to hear that. But I tell myself he's sorry now. That's why he's here. That's what's important.

He tells me Kate was renting another flat, intending to sell Flyte Gardens, and she let him stay with her. 'I got a job in a bookshop,' he says, and another piece of the puzzle falls into place.

'I'd come back from work and we'd talk about it, how to do it. She said we'd make it like a treasure hunt. It was a game, really. I didn't think it would ever happen.'

It was Kate who came up with the idea of the imaginary kidnapping, he says, Kate who found *The Caves of Agoroth* and wanted to find a way to make it a clue. 'She kept saying it was what you were doing. You were going to choose your destiny.'

I can't speak. I gesture to him to continue.

'I told her about the camera in the shop. Suggested she use the receipt to write that note on. She came in and ordered the book. I took that day off work to make sure I wouldn't be in the footage.'

I find my voice. 'You told Tabitha Marina's husband had been back to collect the book.'

He nods unhappily. 'We never thought you'd go to the police.'

I stare at him, but I understand. 'Because you thought I was the same kid who was always in trouble.'

He doesn't try to deny it. 'Tabitha kept talking about what you'd said. I was worried you'd persuade her to go to the police too. So we had to make her think everything was okay.'

I can't believe Will is capable of this. But I'm starting to understand. 'You told Tabitha it was Marina's husband because you knew I wouldn't buy it. That I'd keep looking for her.'

He nods. 'And I told her he'd said the book was for their niece, not their nephew like Marina – Kate – told her before. I knew you'd remember, that you'd know it wasn't real.'

'You gave me too much credit. I didn't pick up on that.'

He stares at me like he doesn't believe it. But then he shakes his head and carries on.

'I had to disable the cameras. I knew you'd want to see the husband, and we couldn't have Tabitha smelling a rat. But I didn't want you to give up. It wouldn't have been fair. You had to have the chance to pass the test.'

*Fair?* Something bubbles up in my chest, and I want to scream at him. What's been fair about any of this? But I force myself to keep silent, push the thought back down deep. Because however crazy all this was, he was trying to help me. And I see how this could have made sense to him, to Kate too. It's sick, twisted. But it has its own kind of logic.

'We were going to leave that Thorstone tabard at Kate's old house,' he says. 'Park her car there and put it somewhere obvious so you'd see it. But by then you'd been to the police.'

'How did you know I'd done that?'

'Kate,' he says, like it should be obvious. 'She was following you.'

The madness of it all takes my breath away. 'And you really thought it was all a game? You really thought she wasn't going to follow through?'

He looks at me and I see tears in his eyes. 'I know. God help me, I know. I was so stupid.'

I hate seeing him like this. I have to believe it was Kate.

That he would never have done any of this if she hadn't got inside his head. 'And what about Flyte Gardens? Was it you who put that stuff in the house?'

He nods miserably, and even though I shouldn't be surprised, I still feel a pang. 'You set it all up, expecting me to phone the police. What would you have done if I hadn't left before they got there? How would you have got rid of it all?'

His eyes are fixed to the floor. 'I'd have made you leave.'

I'm about to ask how, but I find I don't want to know. He'd have put in an appearance, no doubt. Looked menacing and expected me to turn tail and flee. And that's exactly what I'd have done.

'How did you get rid of it so quickly?'

'She made me practise.' I suppress the thought that Kate couldn't have made him do anything; you don't have to be physically stronger to control someone. She was guilt-tripping him, probably. Telling him he had to go along with everything because he owed it to Amy. Because he'd betrayed her.

'The camera was the hardest part, but I got quicker at taking it down.' He sees the next question on my face. 'I waited upstairs and I saw you on the video when you came in. There were these big cupboards up there, in the eaves. When you left, I shoved all that stuff inside. Then I squeezed myself in there too and hid. Waited until you'd both left.'

'I thought I was crazy,' I tell him. 'I thought I was losing my mind.'

He looks broken. 'I'm so sorry. I tried to point you in the right direction. I even broke into your flat, left the message in that book. So you'd know everything was real. So you wouldn't give up.'

'You broke into my flat to *help me*?'

His eyes widen. 'I thought you knew that? You did see the message?'

The words are imprinted on my brain: *You know what*

*really happened.* 'I thought it was a threat. I thought it was someone telling me they knew what happened in Gramwell. Why else did you write it there? Next to the bit where the character falls onto the rocks?'

He looks at me blankly. 'I didn't. I mean, you'd left the book open, face down. I just wrote it next to the bit you'd been reading. I made you a bookmark so you wouldn't crack the spine.'

I could almost laugh. I've been struggling to connect this man to the Will I knew when we were kids. Everything he's done, everything he's put me through. Yet here he is: the Will who broke into my flat left me a bookmark.

Something else occurs to me. 'And after I went back to Flyte Gardens, it was you who made that call, the one telling me to stay away. You disguised your voice so I wouldn't know it was you.'

The look on his face is all the answer I need. 'I didn't know if you'd notice the tabard, so I wanted to give you another clue. That's why I called from the quarry. So you'd hear the drill.'

'But the sound kept cutting out. I thought you were pressing the "mute" button.'

He nods as if this should all make perfect sense. 'I didn't want to make it too obvious. You might have thought it was a set-up.'

I gape at him in disbelief. And I'd thought I was the one losing my grip on reality.

'You threatened me.'

I don't know why that should hurt, not after everything else. It does, though.

'Kate said we had to make you believe it was dangerous to come. So it would be a proper test. So we'd know you were prepared to do the right thing, even if it risked your own safety. I told her you'd do it.' He smiles, almost like a proud parent. 'We tracked your phone, so we knew when you were on your way.'

'You broke my pots. You scratched out my face in that photograph.'

He looks aggrieved. 'No. I would never have done something like that.'

I shake my head in disbelief. Everything he's done, but he draws the line at breaking some pottery. That was Kate then. I should have guessed as much. There was real hatred in that act.

We sit there in silence while I mull over what he's told me. The broad outlines are what I expected, I suppose. But listening to it all, the sheer, unhinged craziness makes my head spin.

And yet – there's a part of me that admires it too. That almost feels flattered that they've gone to so much trouble. I was always on the outside with Will and Amy, always trying to force their attention on me. But for Will and Kate, I was all they thought about.

Will looks at me, and those eyes are just as beautiful as they always were. 'Can you ever forgive me?' he asks. 'I promise I'll never forgive myself. And I'll tell the police. I'll tell them everything – if that's what you want.'

We all do terrible things, I remind myself. We all do things we regret. Maybe all this has happened for a reason. To bring us back together. To give us a second chance.

I'll always miss Amy. I'll always be sad things had to end the way they did. But I hope she's at peace now. I hope she'd find it in her heart to be happy for us.

It's time to leave the past behind. 'Come here,' I say, and I offer him my hand.

# FORTY-FIVE

*Then*

Amy had reached the top of the rock pile and was standing at the edge, one leg in front of the other.

'I thought you were my friend,' she said, 'but all you care about is yourself. You're disgusting.'

She gritted her teeth, bent her knees. She was going to make the leap, and fear drove every other thought from my head. 'You're pissed!' I screamed at her. 'Just come down. Let's talk about this.'

For one terrifying second, I thought she was going to jump. But then she straightened her knees, and the tension left her shoulders. She took a step back from the edge.

'Okay, just take your time—'

And that's when her foot slid out from beneath her.

She didn't cry out. There was just the sick sound of flesh striking stone again and again, until she came to rest on the sloping rock just above the water. She didn't move, and for a moment I could only stare at her, watching the red pool blossom from her head.

And then something clicked, and I was diving into the water, swimming as fast as I could to reach her. Her body was draped across the rock, one arm hanging down. I grabbed her by the wrist and shook her. 'Amy!' I called. 'Amy!'

Her lips moved, but no sound came. I reached for her hand, squeezed it. 'I have to leave you,' I told her. 'I need to get someone, but I'll be back as fast as I can.'

She tried again to speak, and this time I just made out what she said: 'Help me.'

'Yes,' I told her. 'That's what I'm going to do.' I let her go, dropped back into the water and swam for the ledge.

The moment I was on dry land I grabbed my phone. I knew already there was never a signal here, but I dialled 999 anyway, stabbing out the numbers one-handed as I dragged on my shoes. But the phone just gave a dull chirrup: *No service.*

I threw a T-shirt over my swimming costume and ran up the slope, back to the track. I was about to turn and take the path to the leisure centre when I heard the noise of the quarry works. The workers were closer, I thought. They'd be able to help.

I expected to reach the works in minutes, but time stretched by, and I saw no sign of them. Then a drill rang out again, and I stopped. It had come from my right, not straight in front of me as I'd expected. I must have got turned around in my panic.

I tried my phone, but the cross at the top of the screen showed it was a waste of time. I set off again, telling myself I'd be there soon and that Amy would be all right. My leg had started to ache, and I looked down to see a bruise darkening on my thigh. I hadn't checked my position before I'd dived into the lake: I must have struck my leg on the dump box. I kept moving, trying to ignore the pain, but with every step it got worse. In my mind's eye, I saw Amy lying on the rock, her skin gradually turning blue. I had to keep going.

I limped on along the stony ground, but the drill had stopped. I wasn't sure if I was going in the right direction. I paused, listened, but there was nothing but the sound of crows chattering in the trees above. Though the day was hot, I was suddenly cold, shivering. *Shock*, I noted, in a detached way, *I must be in shock.*

I set off again, but the trees crowded in on every side – everything looked the same. I caught my toe on a root and stumbled, arrows of pain streaking up my bruised leg. I gasped and bent double, trying to get my breath. When I looked up, I knew it: I was lost.

My knees gave out and I crumpled to the ground. A picture of Amy flashed into my head, that red pool spreading slowly from her head. *She could die*, I thought. *If I don't get up and find help, she'll bleed to death.* I thought of Gramwell without Amy in it, and the rush of emotion was so intense I could hardly breathe.

I'd be free of her.

I'd miss her too, of course. So would Will. But we would comfort each other. Things would go back to the way they were before she came. And he'd realise what he already knew deep down – that we were meant to be together.

*I have to do this*, I told myself, *I have to.*

I'd tell them I'd got lost. It was true after all. I just wouldn't hurry to find my way back. An image flashed into my mind: that red pool spreading on the rock. Perhaps it was already too late.

I looked down at my leg, at the bruise forming there. It wasn't as big as the one I'd had before, and the pain from the fall was already starting to subside.

It didn't take long to find what I was looking for. I sat back down on the ground, positioned my leg so that the bruise faced upwards. Then I bunched the hem of my T-shirt in my mouth and bit down hard. I raised the rock above my shoulder and slammed it onto my leg.

The pain hit like a fireball, but the T-shirt muffled my scream. I looked down and saw that I'd done a good job.

Already the skin was turning a darker shade of purple. No one would doubt I couldn't move fast with my leg like this.

*Poor Amy*, I thought. *I really will miss her.*

And then I checked the time on my phone and sat back to wait.

# A LETTER FROM CLAIRE

Dear reader,

Thank you so much for choosing to read *The Couple on the Train*. If you enjoyed it and want to keep up to date with my latest releases, you can sign up at the following link. Your email address will never be shared, and you can unsubscribe at any time.

*www.bookouture.com/claire-cooper*

I've spent a large chunk of my working life as a commuter, and as a dedicated night owl, I often found my mind wandering, half dreaming, on those early-morning journeys. Staring at the other people in the carriage (careful not to catch their eyes, of course) I've often found myself wondering about their stories. So perhaps it was inevitable that one day I'd let my imagination go to town along with the rest of us. I hope you've enjoyed the results.

Hearing from people who've connected with one of my books is hands down the best part of being an author. If you'd like to drop me a line via Instagram or Twitter (long live the blue bird!), I'd love to hear from you.

And if you enjoyed *The Couple on the Train*, I'd be delighted if you could spare a few moments to leave a review. I'd love to hear your thoughts, and it's a great way to help new readers discover one of my books for the first time.

Thank you again for reading, and warmest wishes,

Claire Cooper

x.com/CJCooper_author

instagram.com/cjcooper_author

# ACKNOWLEDGEMENTS

So many people helped bring this book into the world. I'm grateful to each and every one of them.

Special thanks to my wonderful editor, Ruth Tross, not only for improving it immeasurably with your insightful (and tactful) feedback, but for your compassion and kindness through difficult times. You are a class act.

Thank you too to Noelle Holten, Peta Nightingale, Kim Nash, and all the talented team at Bookouture. Working with you is a joy.

Thank you to everyone at Northbank Talent Management for your professionalism and support, and especially to Elizabeth Counsell and Martin Jensen. It's brilliant having you in my corner.

To my generous beta readers, Lisa Oyler, Melanie Sturtevant, and Vicky Reid: thank you all for your time and thoughtful comments. Double thanks to Kathryn Thomas for explaining all the things the police really *wouldn't* do in real life, while kindly giving me the 'out' that they happen all the time in fiction! I hope the remaining liberties aren't too egregious.

To all the lovely writers who've offered friendship, empathy, humour, and kindness: you are a blessing.

To the friends, family and colleagues who've put up with varying degrees of my uselessness while this book was being written: thank you all for your patience. Special thanks to my husband, Mark, for this, and for so much more. I know how lucky I am.

This book is dedicated to my mum. Some people leave behind a light that never dies. She was one of them.

# PUBLISHING TEAM

Turning a manuscript into a book requires the efforts of many people. The publishing team at Bookouture would like to acknowledge everyone who contributed to this publication.

**Audio**
Alba Proko
Sinead O'Connor
Melissa Tran

**Commercial**
Lauren Morrissette
Hannah Richmond
Imogen Allport

**Contracts**
Peta Nightingale

**Cover design**
Henry Steadman

**Data and analysis**
Mark Alder
Mohamed Bussuri

## Editorial
Ruth Tross
Imogen Allport

## Copyeditor
Janette Currie

## Proofreader
Becca Allen

## Marketing
Alex Crow
Melanie Price
Occy Carr
Ciara Rosney
Martyna Młynarska

## Operations and distribution
Marina Valles
Stephanie Straub

## Production
Hannah Snetsinger
Mandy Kullar
Jen Shannon
Ria Clare

## Publicity
Kim Nash
Noelle Holten
Jess Readett
Sarah Hardy

Printed in Great Britain
by Amazon

46894447R00187